Karin Fossum

Don't Look Back

TRANSLATED FROM THE NORWEGIAN BY
Felicity David

VINTAGE

Even though some place names have been changed, the setting for this story will be recognizable to those who live there. That is why I want to emphasize that none of the characters in this book are based on real people.

Karin Fossum, Valstad, February 1996

Published by Vintage 2003

4 6 8 10 9 7 5

Copyright © Karin Fossum, 2002

English translation copyright © Felicity David 2002

Karin Fossum has asserted her right under the Copyright, Designs and Patents Act 1988 to be identified as the author of this work

Originally published with the title *Se Deg ikke Tilbake!* By J. W. Cappelens Forlag, Oslo

First published in Great Britain in 2002 by The Harvill Press

Vintage
Random House, 20 Vauxhall Bridge Road, London SW1V 2SA

Random House Australia (Pty) Limited
20 Alfred Street, Milsons Point, Sydney,
New South Wales 2061, Australia

Random House New Zealand Limited
18 Poland Road, Glenfield, Auckland 10, New Zealand

Random House (Pty) Limited
Endulini, 5A Jubilee Road, Parktown 2193, South Africa

The Random House Group Limited Reg. No. 954009
www.randomhouse.co.uk

A CIP catalogue record for this book
is available from the British Library

ISBN 0 09 945213 8

Papers used by Random House
are natural, recyclable products made from wood grown in sustainable forests. The manufacturing processes conform to the environmental regulations of the country of origin

Printed and bound in Great Britain by
Cox & Wyman Ltd, Reading, Berkshire

CHAPTER 1

Ragnhild opened the door cautiously and peered out. Up on the road everything was quiet, and a breeze that had been playing amongst the buildings during the night had finally died down. She turned and pulled the doll's pram over the threshold.

"We haven't even eaten yet," Marthe complained. She helped push the pram.

"I have to go home. We're going out shopping," Ragnhild said.

"Shall I come over later?"

"You can if you like. After we've done the shopping."

She was on the gravel now and began to push the pram towards the front gate. It was heavy going, so she turned it around and pulled it instead.

"See you later, Ragnhild."

The door closed behind her – a sharp slam of wood and metal. Ragnhild struggled with the gate, but she mustn't be careless. Marthe's dog might get out. He was watching her intently from beneath the garden table. When she was sure that

1

the gate was properly closed, she started off across the street in the direction of the garages. She could have taken the shortcut between the buildings, but she had discovered that it was too difficult with the pram. Just then a neighbour closed his garage door. He smiled to her and buttoned up his coat, a little awkwardly, with one hand. A big black Volvo stood in the driveway, rumbling pleasantly.

"Well, Ragnhild, you're out early, aren't you? Hasn't Marthe got up yet?"

"I slept over last night," she said. "On a mattress on the floor."

"I see."

He locked the garage door and glanced at his watch; it was 8.06 a.m. A moment later he turned the car into the street and drove off.

Ragnhild pushed the pram with both hands. She had reached the downhill stretch, which was rather steep, and she had to hold on tight so as not to lose her grip. Her doll, who was named Elise – after herself, because her name was Ragnhild Elise – slid down to the front of the pram. That didn't look good, so she let go with one hand and put the doll back in place, patted down the blanket, and continued on her way. She was wearing sneakers: one was red with green laces, the other was green with red laces, and that's how it had to be. She had on a red tracksuit with Simba the Lion across the chest and a green anorak over it. Her hair was extraordinarily thin and blonde, and not very long, but she had managed to pull it into a topknot with an elastic band. Bright plastic fruit dangled from the band, with her sprout of hair sticking up in the middle like a tiny, neglected palm tree. She was six and a half, but small for her age. Not until she spoke would one guess that she was already at school.

She met no one on the hill, but as she approached the intersection she heard a car. So she stopped, squeezed over to the side, and waited as a van with its paint peeling off wobbled over a speed bump. It slowed even more when the girl in the red outfit came into view. Ragnhild wanted to cross the street. There was a pavement on the other side, and her mother had told her always to walk on the pavement. She waited for the van to pass, but it stopped instead, and the driver rolled down his window.

"You go first, I'll wait," he said.

She hesitated a moment, then crossed the street, turning around again to tug the pram up on to the pavement. The van slid forward a bit, then stopped again. The window on the opposite side was rolled down. His eyes are funny, she thought, really big and round as a ball. They were set wide apart and

3

were pale blue, like thin ice. His mouth was small with full lips, and it pointed down like the mouth of a fish. He stared at her.

"Are you going up Skiferbakken with that pram?"

She nodded. "I live in Granittveien."

"It'll be awfully heavy. What have you got in it, then?"

"Elise," she replied, lifting up the doll.

"Excellent," he said with a broad smile. His mouth looked nicer now.

He scratched his head. His hair was dishevelled, and grew in thick clumps straight up from his head like the leaves of a pineapple. Now it looked even worse.

"I can drive you up there," he said. "There's room for your pram in the back."

Ragnhild thought for a moment. She stared up Skiferbakken, which was long and steep. The man pulled on the handbrake and glanced in the back of the van.

"Mama's waiting for me," Ragnhild said.

A bell seemed to ring in the back of her mind, but she couldn't remember what it was for.

"You'll get home sooner if I drive you," he said.

That decided it. Ragnhild was a practical little girl. She wheeled the pram behind the van and the man hopped out. He opened the back door and lifted the pram in with one hand.

4

"You'll have to sit in back and hold on to the pram. Otherwise it'll roll about," he said, and lifted in Ragnhild too.

He shut the back doors, climbed into the driver's seat, and released the brake.

"Do you go up this hill every day?" He looked at her in the mirror.

"Only when I've been at Marthe's house. I stayed over."

She took a flowered overnight bag from under the doll's blanket and opened it, checking that everything was in place: her nightgown with the picture of Nala on it, her toothbrush and hair brush. The van lumbered over another speed bump. The man was still looking at her in the mirror.

"Have you ever seen a toothbrush like this?" Ragnhild said, holding it up for him. It had feet.

"No!" he said. "Where did you get it?"

"Papa bought it for me. You don't have one like it?"

"No, but I'll ask for one for Christmas."

He was finally over the last bump, and he shifted to second gear. It made an awful grinding noise. The little girl sat on the floor of the van steadying the pram. A very sweet little girl, he thought, red and cute in her tracksuit, like a ripe little berry. He whistled a tune and felt on top of the world, enthroned behind the wheel in the big van with the little girl in the back. Really on top of the world.

The village lay in the bottom of a valley, at the end of a fjord, at the foot of a mountain. Like a pool in a river, where the water was much too still. And everyone knows that only running water is fresh. The village was a stepchild of the municipality, and the roads that led there were indescribably bad. Once in a while a bus deigned to stop by the abandoned dairy and pick up people to take them to town. There were no night buses back to the village.

Kollen, the mountain, was a grey, rounded peak, virtually neglected by those who lived there, but eagerly visited by people from far-off places. This was because of the mountain's unusual minerals and its flora, which was exceptionally rare. On calm days a faint tinkling could be heard from the mountaintop; one might almost believe it was haunted. In fact, the sound was from sheep grazing up there. The ridges around the mountain looked blue and airy through the haze, like soft felt with scattered woollen veils of fog.

Konrad Sejer traced the main highway in the road atlas with a fingertip. They were approaching a roundabout. Police Officer Karlsen was at the wheel, keeping an attentive eye on the fields while following the directions.

"Now you have to turn right on to Gneisveien, then up Skiferbakken, then left at Feltspatveien. Granittveien goes off to the right. A cul-de-sac," Sejer said pensively. "Number 5 should be the third house on the left."

He was tense. His voice was even more brusque than usual.

Karlsen manoeuvred the car into the housing estate and over the speed bumps. As in so many places, the new arrivals had taken up residence in clusters, some distance from the rest of the local community. Apart from giving directions, the two policemen didn't talk much. They approached the house, trying to steel themselves, thinking that perhaps the child might even be back home by now. Perhaps she was sitting on her mother's lap, surprised and embarrassed at all the fuss. It was 1 p.m., so the girl had been missing for five hours. Two would have been within a reasonable margin, five was definitely too long. Their unease was growing steadily, like a dead spot in the chest where the blood refused to flow. Both of them had children of their own; Karlsen's daughter was eight, Sejer had a grandson of four. The silence was filled with images, which might turn out to be correct – this was what struck Sejer as they drew up in front of the house.

Number 5 was a low, white house with dark blue

trim. A typical prefab house with no personality, but embellished like a playroom with decorative shutters and scalloped edges on the gables. The yard was well kept. A large veranda with a prettily turned railing ran around the entire building. The house sat almost at the top of the ridge, with a view over the whole village, a small village, quite lovely, surrounded by farms and fields. A patrol car that had come on ahead of them was parked next to the letterbox.

Sejer went first, wiping his shoes carefully on the mat, and ducking his head as he entered the living room. It only took them a second to see what was happening. She was still missing, and the panic was palpable. On the sofa sat the mother, a stocky woman in a gingham dress. Next to her, with a hand on the mother's arm, sat a woman officer. Sejer could almost smell the terror in the room. The mother was using what little strength she had to hold back her tears, or perhaps even a piercing shriek of horror. The slightest effort made her breathe hard, as was evident when she stood up to shake hands with Sejer.

"Mrs Album," he said. "Someone is out searching, is that correct?"

"Some of the neighbours. They have a dog with them."

She sank back on to the sofa.

"We have to help each other."

He sat down in the armchair facing her and leaned forward, keeping his eyes fixed on hers.

"We'll send out a dog patrol. Now, you have to tell me all about Ragnhild. Who she is, what she looks like, what she's wearing."

No reply, just persistent nodding. Her mouth looked stiff and frozen.

"Have you called every possible place where she could be?"

"There aren't many," she murmured. "I've called them all."

"Do you have relatives anywhere else in the village?"

"No, none. We're not from around here."

"Does Ragnhild go to kindergarten or nursery school?"

"There weren't any openings."

"Does she have brothers or sisters?"

"She's our only child."

He tried to breathe without making a sound.

"First of all," he said, "what was she wearing? Be as precise as you can."

"A red tracksuit," she stammered, "with a lion on the front. Green anorak with a hood. One red and one green shoe."

She spoke in fits and starts, her voice threatening to break.

9

"And Ragnhild herself? Describe her for me."

"About four foot tall. Two and a half stone. Very fair hair. We just took her for her sixth-year check-up."

She went to the wall by the TV, where a number of photos were hanging. Most of them were of Ragnhild, one was of Mrs Album in national costume, and one of a man in the field uniform of the Home Guard, presumably the father. She chose one in which the girl was smiling and handed it to him. Her hair was almost white. The mother's was jet-black, but the father was blond. Some of his hair was visible under his service cap.

"What sort of girl is she?"

"Trusting," she gasped. "Talks to everybody." This admission made her shiver.

"That's just the kind of child who gets along best in this world," he said firmly. "We'll have to take the picture with us."

"I realise that."

"Tell me," he said, sitting back down, "where do the children in this village go walking?"

"Down to the fjord. To Prestegårds Strand or to Horgen. Or to the top of Kollen. Some go up to the reservoir, or they go walking in the woods."

He looked out the window and saw the black firs.

"Has anyone at all seen Ragnhild since she left?"

"Marthe's neighbour met her by his garage when

he was leaving for work. I know because I rang his wife."

"Where does Marthe live?"

"In Krystallen, just a few minutes from here."

"She had her doll's pram with her?"

"Yes. A pink Brio."

"What's the neighbour's name?"

"Walther," she said, surprised. "Walther Isaksen."

"Where can I find him?"

"He works at Dyno Industries, in the personnel department."

Sejer stood up, went over to the telephone and called information, then punched in the number, and waited.

"I need to speak with one of your employees immediately. The name is Walther Isaksen."

Mrs Album gave him a worried look from the sofa. Karlsen was studying the view from the window, the blue ridges, the fields, and a white church steeple in the distance.

"Konrad Sejer of the police," Sejer said curtly. "I'm calling from 5 Granittveien, and you probably know why."

"Is Ragnhild still missing?"

"Yes. But I understood that you saw her when she left Marthe's house this morning."

"I was just shutting my garage door."

"Did you notice the time?"

"It was 8.06 a.m. I was running a little late."

"Are you quite sure of the time?"

"I have a digital watch."

Sejer was silent, trying to recall the way they had driven.

"So you left her at 8.06 a.m. by the garage and drove straight to work?"

"Yes."

"Down Gneisveien and out to the main highway?"

"That's correct."

"I would think," Sejer said, "that at that time of day most people are driving towards town and that there's probably little traffic going the other way."

"Yes, that's right. There are no main roads going through the village, and no jobs, either."

"Did you pass any cars on the way that were driving towards the village?"

The man was silent for a moment. Sejer waited. The room was as quiet as a tomb.

"Yes, actually, I did pass one, down by the flats, just before the roundabout. A van, I think, ugly and with peeling paint. Driving quite slowly."

"Who was driving it?"

"A man," he said hesitantly. "One man."

"My name is Raymond." He smiled.

Ragnhild looked up, saw the smiling face in

the mirror, and Kollen Mountain bathed in the morning light.

"Would you like to go for a drive?"

"Mama's waiting for me."

She said it in a stuck-up sort of voice.

"Have you ever been to the top of Kollen?"

"One time, with Papa. We had a picnic."

"It's possible to drive up there," he explained. "From the back side, that is. Shall we drive up to the top?"

"I want to go home," she said, a bit uncertain now.

He shifted down and stopped.

"Just a short ride?" he asked.

His voice was thin. Ragnhild thought he sounded so sad. And she wasn't used to disappointing the wishes of grown-ups. She got up, walked forward to the front seat and leaned over.

"Just a short ride," she repeated. "Up to the top and then back home right away."

He backed into Feldspatveien and drove back downhill.

"What's your name?" he asked.

"Ragnhild Elise."

He rocked a little from side to side and cleared his throat, as if to admonish her.

"Ragnhild Elise. You can't go out shopping so early in the morning. It's only 8.15 a.m. The shops are closed."

13

She didn't answer. Instead she lifted Elise out of the pram, put her on her lap and straightened her dress. Then she pulled the dummy out of the doll's mouth. Instantly the doll began to scream, a thin, metallic baby cry.

"What's that?"

He braked hard and looked in the mirror.

"That's just Elise. She cries when I take out her dummy."

"I don't like that noise! Put it back in!"

He was restless at the wheel now, and the van weaved back and forth.

"Papa is a better driver than you are," she said.

"I had to teach myself," he said sulkily. "Nobody wanted to teach me."

"Why not?"

He didn't reply, just tossed his head. The van was out on the main highway now; he drove in second gear down to the roundabout and passed through the intersection with a hoarse roar.

"Now we're coming to Horgen," she said, delighted.

He didn't reply. Ten minutes later he turned left, up into the wooded mountainside. On the way they passed a couple of farms with red barns and tractors parked here and there. They saw no one. The road grew narrower and peppered with holes. Ragnhild's arms were starting to grow tired from

14

holding on to the pram, so she laid the doll on the floor and put her foot between the wheels as a brake.

"This is where I live," he said suddenly and stopped.

"With your wife?"

"No, with my father. But he's in bed."

"Hasn't he got up?"

"He's always in bed."

She peered curiously out of the window and saw a peculiar house. It had been a hut once, and someone had added on to it, first once, then again. The separate parts were all different colours. Next to it stood a garage of corrugated iron. The courtyard was overgrown. A rusty old trowel was being slowly strangled by stinging nettles and dandelions. But Ragnhild wasn't interested in the house; she had her eye on something else.

"Bunnies!" she said faintly.

"Yes," he said, pleased. "Do you want to look at them?"

He hopped out, opened the back, and lifted her down. He had a peculiar way of walking; his legs were almost unnaturally short and he was severely bowlegged. His feet were small. His wide nose nearly touched his lower lip, which stuck out a bit. Under his nose hung a big, clear drop. Ragnhild thought he wasn't that old, although when he walked he swayed like an old man. But it was funny too. A boy's face on an old body. He wobbled over to the rabbit hutches and opened them. Ragnhild stood spellbound.

"Can I hold one?"

"Yes. Take your pick."

"The little brown one," she said, entranced.

"That's Påsan. He's the nicest."

He opened the hutch and lifted out the rabbit. A chubby, lop-eared rabbit, the colour of coffee with a lot of cream. It kicked its legs vigorously but calmed down as soon as Ragnhild took it in her arms. For a moment she was utterly still. She could feel its heart pounding against her hand, as she stroked one of its ears cautiously. It was like a piece of velvet between her fingers. Its nose shone black and moist like a liquorice drop. Raymond stood next to her and watched. He had a little girl all to himself, and no one had seen them.

"The picture," Sejer said, "along with the description, will be sent to the newspapers. Unless they hear otherwise, they'll print it tonight."

Irene Album fell across the table sobbing. The others stared wordlessly at their hands, and at her shaking back. The woman officer sat ready with a handkerchief. Karlsen scraped his chair a bit and glanced at his watch.

"Is Ragnhild afraid of dogs?" Sejer said.

"Why do you ask?" she said with surprise.

"Sometimes when we're searching for children with the dog patrol, they hide when they hear our German shepherds."

"No, she's not afraid of dogs."

The words reverberated in his head. *She's not afraid of dogs.*

"Have you had any luck getting hold of your husband?"

"He's in Narvik on manoeuvres," she whispered. "On the plateau somewhere."

"Don't they use mobile phones?"

"They're out of range."

"The people who are looking for her now, who are they?"

"Boys from the neighbourhood who are home in the daytime. One of them has a phone with him."

"How long have they been gone?"

She looked up at the clock on the wall. "More than two hours."

Her voice was no longer quavering. Now she sounded doped, almost lethargic, as if she were half asleep. Sejer leaned forward again and spoke to her as softly and clearly as he could.

"What you fear the most has probably *not* happened. Do you realise that? Usually, children disappear for all sorts of trivial reasons. And it's a fact that children get lost all the time, just because they're children. They have no sense of time or responsibility, and they're so maddeningly curious that they follow any impulse that comes into their head. That's what it's like to be a child, and that's why they get lost. But as a rule they turn up just as suddenly as they disappeared. Often they don't have a good explanation for where they've been or what they were doing. But generally" – he took a breath – "they're quite all right."

"I know!" she said, staring at him. "But she's never gone off like this before!"

"She's growing up and getting bigger," he said persuasively. "She's becoming more adventurous."

God help me, he thought, I've got an answer for everything. He got up and dialled another number, repressing an urge to look at his watch again – it would be a reminder that time was passing, and they didn't need that. He reached the Duty Officer, gave him a brief summary of the situation and asked him to contact a volunteer rescue group. He gave him the address in Granittveien and gave a quick description of the girl: dressed in red, almost white hair, pink doll's pram. Asked whether any messages had come in, and was told none had been received. He sat down again.

"Has Ragnhild mentioned or named anyone lately whom you didn't know yourself?"

"No."

"Did she have any money? Could she have been looking for a shop?"

"She had no money."

"This is a small village," he went on. "Has she ever been out walking and been given a ride by one of the neighbours?"

"Yes, that happens sometimes. There are about a hundred houses on this ridge, and she knows almost everyone, and she knows their cars. Sometimes she and Marthe have walked down to the church with their prams, and they've been given a ride home with one of the neighbours."

"Is there any special reason why they go to the church?"

"There's a little boy they knew buried there. They pick flowers for his grave, and then they come back up here. I think it seems exciting to them."

"You've searched at the church?"

"I rang for Ragnhild at ten o'clock. When they told me she had left at eight, I jumped in the car. I left the front door unlocked in case she came back while I was out searching. I drove to the church and down to the Fina petrol station, I looked in the auto workshop and behind the dairy, and then I drove over to the school to look in the schoolyard,

19

because they have jungle gyms and things there. And then I checked the kindergarten. She was so keen on starting school, she . . ."

Another bout of sobbing took hold. As she wept, the others sat still and waited. Her eyes were puffy now, and she was crumpling her skirt in her fingers in despair. After a while her sobs died away and the lethargy returned – a shield to keep the terrible possibilities at bay.

The phone rang. A sudden ominous jangle. She gave a start and got up to answer it, but caught sight of Sejer's hand held up to stop her. He lifted the receiver.

"Hello? Is Irene there?"

It sounded like a boy. "Who's calling?"

"Thorbjørn Haugen. We're looking for Ragnhild."

"You're speaking with the police. Do you have any news?"

"We've been to all the houses on the whole ridge. Every single one. A lot of people weren't home, though we did meet a lady in Feltspatveien. A lorry had backed into her farmyard and turned around, she lives in number 1. A kind of van, she thought. And inside the van she saw a girl with a green jacket and white hair pulled into a topknot on her head. Ragnhild often wears her hair in a topknot."

"Go on."

"It turned halfway up the hill and drove back down. Disappeared around the curve."

"Do you know what time it was?"

"It was 8.15 a.m."

"Can you come over to Granittveien?"

"We'll be right there, we're at the roundabout now."

He hung up. Irene Album was still standing.

"What was it?" she whispered. "What did they say?"

"Someone saw her," he said slowly. "She got into a van."

Irene Album's scream finally came. It was as if the sound penetrated through the tight forest and created a faint movement in Ragnhild's mind.

"I'm hungry," she said suddenly. "I have to go home."

Raymond looked up. Påsan was shuffling about on the kitchen table and licking up the seeds they had scattered over it. They had forgotten both time and place. They had fed all the rabbits, Raymond had shown her his pictures, cut out of magazines and carefully pasted into a big album. Ragnhild kept roaring with laughter at his funny face. Now she realised that it was getting late.

"You can have a slice of bread."

"I have to go home. We're going shopping."

"We'll go up to Kollen first, then I'll drive you home afterwards."

"Now!" she said firmly. "I want to go home now."

Raymond thought desperately for a way to stall her.

"All right. But first I have to go out and buy some milk for Papa, down at Horgen's Shop. You can wait here, then it won't take as long."

He stood up and looked at her. At her bright face with the little, heart-shaped mouth that made him think of heart-shaped cinnamon sweets. Her eyes were clear and blue and her eyebrows were dark, surprising beneath her white fringe. He sighed heavily, walked over to the back door and opened it.

Ragnhild really wanted to leave, but she didn't know the way home so she would have to wait. She padded into the little living room with the rabbit in her arms and curled up in a corner of the sofa. They hadn't slept much last night, she and Marthe, and with the warm animal in the hollow of her throat she quickly grew sleepy. Soon her eyes closed.

It was a while before he came back. For a long time he sat and looked at her, amazed at how quietly she slept. Not a movement, not a single little sigh. He thought she had expanded a bit, become larger and warmer, like a loaf in the oven. After a while he grew uneasy and didn't know what to do with his hands, so he put them in his pockets and rocked a little in his chair. Started kneading the fabric of his trousers between his hands as he rocked and rocked, faster and faster. He looked anxiously out the windows and down the hall to his father's bedroom. His hands worked and worked. The whole time he stared at her hair, which was shiny as silk, almost like rabbit fur. Then he gave a low moan and stopped himself. Stood up and poked her lightly on the shoulder.

"We can go now. Give me Påsan."

For a moment Ragnhild was completely bewildered. She got up slowly and stared at Raymond, then followed him out to the kitchen and pulled on her anorak, and padded out of the house as the little brown ball of fur vanished back into its cage. The pram was still in the back of the van. Raymond looked sad, but he helped her climb in, then got into the driver's seat and turned the key. Nothing happened.

"It won't start," he said, annoyed. "I don't understand it. It was running a minute ago. This piece of junk!"

"I have to go home!" Ragnhild said loudly, as if it would help the situation. He kept trying the ignition and stepping on the accelerator; he could hear the starter motor turning, but it kept up a complaining whine and refused to catch.

"We'll have to walk."

"It's much too far!" she whined.

"No, not from here. We're on the back side of Kollen now, we're almost at the top, and from there you can look straight down on your house. I'll pull your pram for you."

He put on a jacket that lay on the front seat, got out and opened the door for her. Ragnhild carried her doll and he pulled the pram behind him. It bumped a little on the pot-holed road. Ragnhild could see Kollen looming farther ahead, ringed by dark woods. For a moment they had to pull off to the side of the road as a car passed them noisily at high speed. The dust hung like a thick fog behind it. Raymond knew the way, and he wasn't very fit, so it was no problem for Ragnhild to keep up. After a while the road grew steeper, ending in a turning space, and the path, which went round to the right of Kollen, was soft and dusty. The sheep had widened the path, and their droppings lay as thick as hail. Ragnhild amused herself by treading on them, they were dry and powdery. After a few minutes there was a lovely glistening visible through the trees.

"Serpent Tarn," Raymond said.

She stopped next to him, stared out across the

lake and saw the water-lilies, and a little boat that lay upside down on the shore.

"Don't go down to the water," said Raymond. "It's dangerous. You can't swim here, you'd just sink into the sand and disappear. Quicksand," he added, with a serious expression. Ragnhild shuddered. She followed the bank of the tarn with her eyes, a wavy yellow line of rushes, except for one place where what might be called a beach broke the line like a dark indentation. That's what they were staring at. Raymond let go of the pram, and Ragnhild stuck a finger in her mouth.

Thorbjørn stood fiddling with the mobile phone. He was about 16, and had dark, shoulder-length hair with a hint of dandruff, held in place with a patterned bandanna. The ends stuck out of the knots at his temples like two red feathers, making him look like a pale Indian. He avoided looking at Ragnhild's mother, staring hard at Sejer instead, licking his lips constantly.

"What you have discovered is important," Sejer said. "Please write down her address. Do you remember the name?"

"Helga Moen, in number 1. A grey house with a kennel outside." He almost spoke in a whisper as he printed the words in big letters on the pad that Sejer gave him.

"You boys have been over most of the area?" Sejer asked.

"We were up on Kollen first, then we went down to Serpent Tarn and went over the paths there. We went to the high tarn, Horgen's Store, and Prestegårds Strand. And the church. Last, we looked at a couple of farms, at Bjerkerud and at the Equestrian Sports Centre. Ragnhild was, uh, I mean *is*, very interested in animals."

The slip of the tongue made him blush. Sejer patted him lightly on the shoulder.

"Sit down, Thorbjørn."

He nodded to the sofa where there was room next to Mrs Album. She had graduated to another phase, and was now contemplating the dizzying possibility that Ragnhild might never come home again, and that she might have to live the rest of her life without her little girl and her big blue eyes. This realisation came in small stabs of pain. Her whole body was rigid, as if she had a steel rod running up her spine. The woman officer, who had hardly said a word the whole time they had been there, stood up slowly. For the first time she ventured to make a suggestion.

"Mrs Album," she asked quietly, "why don't we make everyone some coffee?"

The woman nodded weakly, got up and followed the officer out to the kitchen. A tap was turned on and there was the sound of cups clattering. Sejer motioned Karlsen over towards the hallway. They stood there muttering to one another. Thorbjørn could just see Sejer's head and the tip of Karlsen's shoe, which was shiny and black. In the dim light, they could check their watches without being observed. They did so and then nodded in agreement. Ragnhild's disappearance had become a serious matter, and all the department's resources would have to be utilised. Sejer scratched his elbow through his shirt.

"I can't face the thought of finding her in a ditch."

He opened the door to get some fresh air. And there she stood. In her red jogging suit, on the bottom step with a tiny white hand on the railing.

"Ragnhild?" he said in astonishment.

A happy half-hour later, as their car sped down Skiferbakken, Sejer ran his fingers through his hair with satisfaction. Karlsen thought his hair looked like a steel brush now that it was cut shorter than ever. The kind of brush used to clean off old paint. Sejer's lined face looked peaceful, not closed and serious as it usually did. Halfway down the hill they passed the grey house. They saw the kennel and a face at the window. If Helga Moen was hoping for a visit from the police, she would be disappointed. Ragnhild was sitting safely on her mother's lap with two thick slices of bread in her hand.

The moment when the little girl stepped into the living room was etched into the minds of both officers. The mother, hearing her thin little voice, rushed in from the kitchen and threw herself at Ragnhild, lightning fast, like a beast of prey grasping its victim and never ever wanting to let it go. Ragnhild's thin limbs and the white sprout of hair stuck out through her mother's powerful arms. And there they stood. Not a sound was heard, not a single cry from either of them. Thorbjørn was practically crushing the phone in his hand, the woman officer was making a clatter with the cups, and Karlsen kept twisting his moustache with a blissful grin on his face. The room brightened up as though the sun had suddenly shot a beam through the window. And then, finally, with a sobbing laugh:

"YOU TERRIBLE CHILD!"

"I've been thinking," Sejer cleared his throat, "about taking a week's holiday. I have some time off due to me."

Karlsen crossed a speed bump.

"What will you do with it? Go skydiving in Florida?"

"I thought I'd air out my cabin."

"Near Brevik, isn't that where it is?"

"Sand Island."

They turned on to the main road and picked up speed.

"I have to go to Legoland this year," Karlsen muttered. "Can't avoid it any longer. My daughter is pestering me."

"You make it sound like a punishment," Sejer said. "Legoland is beautiful. When you leave I guarantee you'll be weighed down with boxes of Lego and you'll be bitten by the bug. Do go, you won't regret it."

"So, you've been there, have you?"

"I went there with Matteus. Do you know that they've built a statue of Sitting Bull out of nothing but pieces of Lego? One point four million pieces with special colouring. It's unbelievable."

He fell silent as he caught sight of the church off to the left, a little white wooden church a bit off the road between green and yellow fields, surrounded by lush trees. A beautiful little church, he thought; he should have buried his wife in a spot like that, even though it would have been a long way to come. Of course, it was too late now. She had been dead more than eight years and her grave was in the cemetery in the middle of town, right by the busy high street surrounded by exhaust fumes and traffic noise.

"Do you think the girl was all right?"

"She seemed to be. I've asked the mother to ring

us when things calm down a bit. She'll probably want to talk about it eventually. Six hours," he said thoughtfully, "that's quite a while. Must have been a charming lone wolf."

"He evidently had a driver's licence, at least. So he isn't a total hermit."

"We don't know that, do we? That he has a driver's licence?"

"No, damn it, you're right," Karlsen said. He braked abruptly and turned into the petrol station in what they called "downtown", with a post office, bank, hairdresser and the Fina station. A poster bearing the words "Sale on Medicine" was displayed in the window of the low-price Kiwi grocery, and the hairdresser had a tempting advertisement for a new tanning bed.

"I need something to eat. Are you coming?"

They went in and Sejer bought a newspaper and some chocolate. He peered out the window and down to the fjord.

"Excuse me," said the girl behind the counter, staring nervously at Karlsen's uniform. "Nothing has happened to Ragnhild, has it?"

"Do you know her?" Sejer put some coins on the counter.

"No, I don't know her, but I know who they are. Her mother was here this morning looking for her."

"Ragnhild is all right. She's back at home."

She smiled with relief and gave him his change.

"Are you from around here?" Sejer asked. "Do you know most people?"

"I certainly do. There aren't many of us."

"If I ask you whether you know a man, maybe a little odd, who drives a van, an old, ugly van with its paint peeling off, does that ring a bell?"

"That sounds like Raymond," she said, nodding. "Raymond Låke."

"What do you know about him?"

"He works at the Employment Centre. Lives in a cabin on the far side of Kollen with his father. Raymond has Down's syndrome. About 30, and very nice. His father used to run this station, by the way, before he retired."

"Does Raymond have a driver's licence?"

"No, but he drives anyway. It's his father's van. He's an invalid, so he probably doesn't have much control over what Raymond does. The sheriff knows about it and pulls him over now and then, but it doesn't do much good. He never drives above second gear. Did he pick up Ragnhild?"

"Yes."

"Then she couldn't have been safer," she smiled. "Raymond would stop to let a ladybird cross the road."

They both grinned and went back outside. Karlsen bit into his chocolate and looked around.

"Nice town," he said, chewing.

Sejer, who had bought an old-fashioned marzipan loaf, followed his gaze. "That fjord is deep, more than 300 metres. Never gets above 17 degrees Celsius."

"Do you know anyone here?"

"I don't, but my daughter Ingrid does. She's been here on a folklore walk, the kind of thing they organise in the autumn. 'Know your district.' She loves stuff like that."

He rolled the candy wrapper into a thin strip and stuck it into his shirt pocket. "Do you think someone with Down's syndrome can be a good driver?"

"No idea," Karlsen said. "But there's nothing wrong with them except for having one chromosome too many. I think their biggest problem is that they take longer to learn something than other people do. They also have bad hearts. They don't live to be very old. And there's something about their hands."

"What's that?"

"They're missing a line on their palm or something."

Sejer gave him a surprised look. "Anyway, Ragnhild certainly let herself be charmed."

"I think the rabbits helped."

Karlsen found a handkerchief in his inside

pocket and wiped the chocolate from the corners of his mouth. "I grew up with a Down's syndrome child. We called him 'Crazy Gunnar'. Now that I think of it, we actually seemed to believe that he came from another planet. He's dead now – only lived to be 35."

They got into the car and drove on. Sejer prepared a simple little speech that he would serve up to the department chief when they were back at headquarters. A few days off to go up to his cabin seemed tremendously important all of a sudden. The timing was right, the long-term prospects were promising, and the girl showing up safe and sound at home had put him in a good mood. He stared over fields and meadows, registered that they had slowed down, and saw the tractor in front of them. A green John Deere with butter-yellow wheel rims was crawling at a snail's pace. They had no chance to overtake it; each time they came to a straight stretch, it proved to be too short. The farmer, who was wearing a gardener's cap and earmuffs, sat like a tree stump, as though he was growing straight up out of the seat. Karlsen changed gears and sighed.

"He's carrying Brussels sprouts. Can't you reach out and grab a box? We could cook them in the kitchen at the canteen."

"Now we're going as fast as Raymond does,"

muttered Sejer. "Life in second gear. That really would be something, don't you think?"

He settled his grey head against the head-rest and closed his eyes.

CHAPTER 2

After the quiet of the countryside the city seemed like a filthy, teeming chaos of people and cars. The main route for traffic was still through the town centre; the city council was fighting tooth and nail for a tunnel which they had ready on the drawing-board, but new groups kept popping up to protest against it with one or another weighty argument: the eyesore that the ventilation towers would create in the landscape by the river; the noise and pollution of the construction work; and, last but not least, the cost.

Sejer stared down at the street from the chief's office. He had put in his request, and now he was waiting for the reply. It was a formality: Holthemann would never dream of turning down Konrad Sejer. But the chief did like everything done by the book.

"You've checked the duty rosters? Talked to the rest of the team?"

Sejer nodded. "Soot will take two shifts with Siven; I expect she'll keep him in line."

"Then I don't see any reason to—"

The telephone rang. Two short peeps, as if from a hungry bird. Sejer wasn't religious, but he said a prayer anyway – possibly to Providence – that his holiday wouldn't be snatched from under his nose.

"You want to know if Konrad is in my office?" Holthemann said. "Yes, he's here. Put the call through."

He pulled on the cord and handed Sejer the receiver. He took it, thinking it might be his daughter Ingrid wanting him for something. He hoped it wasn't bad news. It was Mrs Album.

"Is everything all right with Ragnhild?" he asked.

"Yes, she's fine. Perfectly fine. But she told me something very odd when we were finally alone. I had to ring you, I thought it sounded so peculiar, and she doesn't usually make things up, so to be on the safe side I thought I'd better let you know. In any case, I will have told someone."

"What is it about?"

"This man she was with, he showed her the way home. His name is Raymond, by the way, she remembered it afterwards. They drove up the far side of Kollen and past Serpent Tarn, and there they stopped for a while."

"Yes?"

"Ragnhild says there's a woman lying up there."

36

He blinked in surprise. "What did you say?"

"That there's a woman lying up at the lake. Quite still and with no clothes on." Her voice was anxious and embarrassed at the same time.

"Do you believe her?"

"Yes, I do. Would a child think up something like that? But I don't dare go up there alone, and I don't want to take her with me."

"I'll have it looked into. Don't mention this to anyone. We'll be in touch."

He hung up and in his mind he closed up his cabin. The scent of sea spray and fresh-caught cod sprats vanished abruptly. He smiled at Holthemann.

"You know, there's something I have to take care of first."

Karlsen was out on patrol in the only squad car they could spare that day, and it had to cover the entire city centre. So he took Skarre with him instead, a young curly-haired officer about half his age. Skarre was a cheerful little man, mild-mannered and optimistic, with traces of the rhythmic Southland dialect in his speech. They parked again by the letterbox in Granittveien and had a brief talk with Irene Album. Ragnhild clung like a burr to her mother's dress. A number of admonitions had undoubtedly been impressed on the tow-headed child. Her mother pointed and explained, saying they had to follow a sign-posted path from the edge of the woods facing the house, uphill to the left past Kollen. For active men like them it would probably take 20 minutes, she said.

The tree trunks were marked with blue arrows, indicating the way. They eyed the sheep shit balefully, stepping out into the heather now and again, but persevered upwards. The path grew steeper and steeper. Skarre was panting a little, while Sejer walked easily. He stopped once, turning to stare down towards the housing estate. They could see only the roofs, brownish-pink and black in the distance. Then they set off again, no longer talking, partly because they needed their breath for the climb, partly because of what they were afraid of finding. The forest was so thick that they were walking in semi-darkness. Instinctively, Sejer kept his eyes on the path, not because he was afraid of tripping, but if something had indeed happened up here, it was crucial to take note of everything. They had been walking for exactly 17 minutes when the forest opened up and the sunlight shone through. Now they could see the water. A mirror-like tarn, no bigger than a large pond, lying among the spruce trees like a secret space. For a moment they scanned the terrain, following the yellow line of the reeds with their gaze, and caught sight of something that looked like a beach a little farther away. They set out towards it at a good distance from the water; the belt of rushes was fairly wide, and they had only their street shoes.

It could hardly be called a beach, but was more like a muddy patch with four or five large stones, just enough to keep the reeds out, and probably the only place that allowed access to the water. A woman lay in the mud and dirt. She was on her side with her back to them, a dark anorak covering her upper body. Otherwise she was naked. Blue and white clothes lay in a heap next to her. Sejer stopped short and automatically reached for the mobile phone on his belt. Then he changed his mind. He approached carefully, hearing the gurgling in his shoes.

"Don't move," he said in a low voice.

Skarre obeyed. Sejer was at the water's edge. He balanced himself on a rock a little way out in the tarn so he could see the woman from the front. He didn't want to touch anything, not yet. Her eyes had sunk in a little. They were half-open and fixed on a point out in the lake. The eye membrane was dull and wrinkled. Her pupils were large and no longer quite round. Her mouth stood open; above it and extending up over her nose was a yellowish bit of foam, as if she had vomited. He bent down and blew on it; it didn't move. Her face was only a few centimetres from the water. He placed two fingers over her carotid artery. The skin had lost all elasticity, and felt as cold as he had expected.

"Gone," he said.

On her earlobes and on the side of her neck he found some faint reddish-purple marks. The skin on her legs was goosebumped but undamaged. He went back the same way. Skarre stood waiting with his hands in his pockets looking a little puzzled. He was terrified of making a mistake.

"Totally naked under her jacket. No visible external injuries. I should say about 18 to 20 years old."

Then he telephoned Headquarters and requested an ambulance, forensics, photographer and technicians. Explained the route that went up from the back side of Kollen and was accessible by car. He asked them to park some way off so as not to disturb any tyre tracks. When he'd finished he looked round for something to sit on, choosing the flattest stone. Skarre sank down next to him. They stared silently at her white legs and blonde hair, which was straight and shoulder-length. She lay almost in a foetal position. Her arms were folded over her breasts, her knees drawn up. The windbreaker lay loosely over her torso and reached to mid-thigh. It was clean and dry. The rest of her clothes were piled in a heap behind her and were wet and soiled. A pair of dungarees with belt, a blue-and-white checked blouse, brassière, dark blue high-school pullover. Reebok trainers.

"What's that above her mouth?" muttered Skarre.

"Foam."

"But . . . foam? What would that come from?"

"I suspect we'll find out soon enough." Sejer shook his head. "Looks like she lay down to go to sleep. With her back to the world."

"People don't undress to commit suicide, do they?"

Sejer didn't reply. He looked at her again, at the white body by the black water, surrounded by dark spruce trees. The scene had nothing of violence in it; in fact, it looked peaceful. They settled in to wait.

Six men came tramping out of the woods. Their voices died out except for a few faint coughs when they caught sight of the men by the water. A second later they saw the dead woman. Sejer stood up and gestured.

"Stay on that side!" he shouted.

They did as he ordered. They all recognised his grey shock of hair. One of them measured the terrain with a practised eye, trod a bit on the ground, which

41

was relatively solid where he stood, and muttered something about a lack of rain. The photographer went first. He didn't spend much time by the body, but instead looked at the sky, as if he wanted to check the light conditions.

"Take pictures from both sides," Sejer said, "and get the vegetation in the shot. I'm afraid you'll have to go out in the water after that, because I need pictures from the front without moving her. When you've used up half the roll, we'll take off her jacket."

"Mountain lakes like this are usually bottomless," he said sceptically.

"You can swim, can't you?"

There was a pause.

"There's a rowboat over there. We can use that."

"A dinghy? It looks rotten."

"We'll soon know," Sejer said, brusquely.

While the photographer was working, the others stood still and waited. One of the technicians was already working further up the shore, searching through the area, which proved to be quite free of litter. This was an idyllic spot, and in such places there was usually bottle caps, used condoms, cigarette butts, and sweet wrappers. Here they found nothing.

"Unbelievable," he said. "Not so much as a burnt match."

"He probably cleaned up after himself," Sejer said.

"It looks like a suicide, don't you think?"

"She's stark naked," he replied.

"Yes, but she must have done that herself. Those clothes were not pulled off by force, that's one thing for certain."

"They're dirty."

"Maybe that's why she took them off," he smiled. "Besides, she threw up. Must have eaten something she couldn't digest."

Sejer bit back a reply and looked at her. He could understand how the technician had come to that conclusion. It really did look as if she had lain down herself; her clothes were piled carefully next to her, not thrown about. They were muddy but seemed undamaged. Only the jacket that covered her torso was dry and clean. He stared at the mud and dirt and caught sight of something that looked like a shoe print. "Look at that," he said to the technician. The man squatted down in his coveralls and measured all the prints several times.

"This is hopeless. They're filled with water."

"Can't you use any of them?"

"Probably not."

They squinted into the water-filled ovals.

"Take pictures anyway. I think they look small. Maybe a person with small feet."

"Roughly 27 centimetres. Not a big foot. Could be hers." The photographer took several shots of the footprints, then got into the old rowboat and sloshed around. They had found no oars, so he had to keep paddling into position with his hands. Every time he moved, the boat tilted alarmingly.

"It's leaking!" he shouted anxiously.

"Relax, we've got a whole rescue team here!" Sejer said.

When the photographer was done, he had taken more than 50 photos. Sejer went down to the water, took off his shoes and socks and placed them on a rock, rolled up his trousers and waded out. He stood a metre from her head. She had a pendant around her neck. He fished it out carefully with a pen he took from his inside pocket. "A medallion," he said in a low voice. "Probably silver. There's something on it. An H and an M. Get a bag ready."

He bent over and loosened the chain, then he removed the jacket.

"The back of her neck is red," he said. "Unusually pale skin all over, but extremely red on the back of her neck. An ugly blotch, as big as a hand."

Snorrason, the medical examiner, waded out in his gumboots and inspected in turn the eyeballs, the teeth, the nails. Noticed the flawless skin and the light red marks – there were several of them –

scattered seemingly at random across her neck and chest. He noticed every detail: the long legs, the lack of birthmarks, which was uncommon, and found nothing more than a few small spots on her right shoulder. He cautiously touched the foam above her mouth with a wooden spatula. It seemed solid and dense, almost like a mousse.

Sejer nodded to her mouth. "What's that?"

"Right off I would think it's a fluid from the lungs, containing protein."

"Which means?"

"Drowning. But it could mean other things."

He scraped away some of the foam, and soon new foam began oozing out.

"The lungs are collapsed," he said.

Sejer pressed his lips tight as he watched. The photographer took more pictures of her, now without the jacket.

"Time to break the seal," Snorrason said, rolling her carefully on to her stomach. "A slight incipient rigor mortis, especially in the neck. A big, well-built woman in healthy condition. Broad shoulders. Good musculature in upper arms and thighs and calves. Probably played sports."

"Do you see any sign of violence?" Sejer asked.

Snorrason inspected her back and the backs of her legs. "Apart from the reddening of the neck, no. Someone may have grabbed her hard by the back of the neck and pushed her to the ground. Obviously while she was still clothed. Then she was pulled up again, carefully undressed, laid in place, and covered with the jacket."

"Any sign of sexual assault?"

"Don't know yet."

He proceeded to take her temperature, quite unperturbed, in the presence of everyone, and then squinted at the result.

"It's 30 degrees Celsius. Together with the blood spots under the skin and only a slight rigor mortis in the neck, I would estimate the time of death as being within the past ten to twelve hours."

"No," Sejer said. "Not if this isn't where she died."

"Are you doing my job for me?"

He shook his head. "There was a search made here this morning. A group of boys with dogs searched along this tarn for a little girl who was reported missing. They must have been here sometime between midday and 2 p.m. The body wasn't here then – they would have seen it. The little girl turned up by the way, in good shape," he said.

He looked about him, staring down at the mud with his eyes narrowed. Something tiny and pale-coloured caught his attention. He picked it up carefully between two fingers. "What's this?"

Snorrason peered into his hand. "A pill, or a tablet of some kind."

"Do you think you might find more in her stomach?"

"Quite possibly. But I don't see a pill bottle here."

"She could have carried them loose in her pocket."

"In that case we'll find powder in her dungarees. Bag it up."

"Do you recognise it?"

"It could be almost anything. But the smallest tablets are often the strongest. The lab will figure it out."

Sejer nodded to the men with the stretcher and stood watching them with his arms crossed. For the first time in a long while he raised his eyes and looked up. The sky was pale, and the pointed firs stood around the tarn like raised spears. Of course they would figure it out. He made himself a promise. They'd figure everything out.

Jacob Skarre, born and raised in Søgne in the mild Southland, had just turned 25. He had seen naked women plenty of times, but never as naked as the one by the tarn. It struck him just now, as he sat with Sejer in the car, that this one had made more of an impression than all the other corpses he had seen before. Maybe it was because she lay as if trying to conceal her nakedness, with her back to the path, head tucked down and knees drawn up. But they had found her anyway, and they had seen her nakedness. Turned her and rolled her over, pulled back her lips to look at her teeth, raised her eyelids. Took her temperature, as she lay on her stomach with her legs spread. As if she were a mare at auction.

"She was quite pretty, wasn't she?" he said, shaken.

Sejer didn't answer. But he was glad of the comment. He had found other young women, had heard other comments. They drove for a while in silence, staring at the road in front of them, but further in the distance they kept on seeing her naked body – the ripple of her backbone, the soles of her feet with a slightly redder skin, the calves with blonde hair on them – hovering above the asphalt like a mirage. Sejer had an odd feeling. This resembled nothing he had ever seen.

"You're on the night shift?"

Skarre cleared his throat. "Just till midnight. I'm doing a few hours for Ringstad. By the way, I heard you were thinking of taking a week's holiday – is that off now?"

"Looks that way."

He had forgotten all about it.

The missing persons list lay before him on the table. Four names, two men, and two women, both born before 1960 and therefore not the woman they had found by Serpent Tarn. One was missing from the Central Hospital psychiatric ward, the other from a retirement home in the next town. "Height 155 centimetres, weight 45 kilos. Snow-white hair."

It was 6 p.m., and it might be hours before some anxious soul reported her missing. They would have to wait for the photos and the autopsy report, so there wasn't much that could be done until they had the woman's identity. He grabbed his leather jacket from the back of the chair and took the lift down to the first floor. Bowed gallantly to Mrs Brenningen at the front desk, recalling at the same moment that she was a widow and perhaps lived much the same life as he did. She was pretty too, blonde like his wife Elise, but plumper.

He headed for his own car in the car park, an elderly ice-blue Peugeot 604. In his mind he could see the face of the corpse, healthy and round, without make-up. Her clothes were neat and sensible. The straight, blonde hair was well cut, the trainers expensive. On her wrist she wore an expensive Seiko sports watch. This was a woman with a decent background, from a home with order and structure. He had found other women for whom a quite different lifestyle spoke its unequivocal language. Still, he had been surprised before. They didn't know yet whether she was drunk or drugged or full of some other misery. Anything was possible, and things were not always what they seemed.

He drove slowly through the town, past the market square and the fire station. Skarre had promised to call as soon as the woman was reported missing. On the medallion were the letters H.M. Helene, he thought, or maybe Hilde. He didn't think it would be long before someone contacted them. This was an orderly girl who kept appointments.

As he fumbled with the key in the lock he heard the thump as the dog jumped down from the forbidden spot on the armchair. Sejer lived in a block of flats, the only one in town that was 13 storeys high, so it looked out of place in the landscape. Like an outsized Viking monument it loomed in the sky above the surrounding buildings. When he'd moved in 20 years ago with Elise, it was because the flat had an excellent floor plan and a spectacular view. He could see the entire town, and compared with it the other possible flats seemed too closed in. Inside, it was easy to forget what sort of building it was; inside, the flat was cosy and warm with wood-panelling. The furniture, old and of solid sand-blasted oak, had belonged to his parents. For the most part, the walls were covered with books, and in the little remaining space he had hung a few favourite pictures. One of Elise, several of his grandson and Ingrid. A charcoal drawing by Käthe Kollwitz, *Death with Girl on His Lap*, taken from a catalogue and framed in black lacquer. A photograph of himself in freefall above the airport. His parents, solemnly posing in their Sunday best. Each time he looked at the picture of his father, his own old age seemed to advance uncomfortably upon him. He could see how his cheeks would sink in, while his ears and eyebrows would continue to grow, giving him the same bushy appearance.

The rules in this apartment society, in which the families were stacked on top of one another as in Vigeland's monolith, were extremely strict. It was forbidden to shake rugs from the balcony, so they sent them out to be cleaned every spring. It was nearly time to do that again. The dog, Kollberg, shed hair like crazy. This had been discussed at the building's board meeting but had somehow slipped through, probably because he was a detective inspector and his neighbours felt secure having him there. He didn't feel trapped, because he lived on the top floor. The apartment was clean and tidy and reflected what was inside him: order and simplicity. The dog had a corner in the kitchen where dried food was always scattered about with spilt water; this corner indicated Sejer's one weak point: his attachment to his dog was an emotional one. The bathroom was the only room that displeased him, but he would get around to that eventually. Right now he had this woman to deal with, and possibly a dangerous man on the loose. He didn't like it. It was like standing at a bend in the road and not being able to see beyond it.

He braced his legs to receive the dog's welcome, which was overwhelming. He took him out for a quick walk behind the building, gave him fresh water, and was halfway through the newspaper when the phone rang. He turned down the stereo and felt a slight tension as he picked up the receiver. Someone might have called in already; maybe they had a name to give him.

"Hi, Grandpa!" said a voice.

"Matteus?"

"I have to go to bed now. It's nighttime."

"Did you brush your teeth?" he asked, sitting down on the telephone bench.

He could see before him the little mocha-coloured face and pearl-white teeth.

"Mama did it for me."

"And you took your fluoride pill?"

"Uh-huh."

"And said your prayers?"

"Mama says I don't have to."

He chatted to his grandson for a long time, with the receiver pressed to his ear so he could hear all the little sighs and lilts in the lively voice. It was as pliant and soft as a willow flute in the spring. Finally he exchanged a few words with his daughter. He heard her resigned sigh when he told her about the body they had found, as if she disapproved of the way he had chosen to spend his life. She sighed in exactly the same way as Elise had done. He didn't mention her involvement in Somalia, wracked by civil war. He looked at the clock instead and thought that somewhere someone was sitting and doing exactly the same thing. Somewhere else someone was waiting, staring at the window and the telephone, someone who would wait in vain.

Headquarters was a 24-hour institution that served a district of five communities, inhabited by 115,000 citizens, some good, some bad. More than 200 people were employed in the entire courthouse and prison offices, and 150 of them worked at Police Headquarters. Of these, 30 were investigators, but since some staff members were always on leave or attending courses and seminars by order of the Minister of Justice, in practice there were never more than 20 people at work each day. That was too few. According to Holthemann the public was no longer in focus – they were more or less outside the field of vision.

Minor cases were solved by single investigators, while more difficult cases were assigned to larger teams. Between 14,000 and 15,000 cases poured in annually. In the daytime the work might consist of dealing with applications from people who wanted to set up stands to sell things like silk flowers or figures made out of dough at the market, or who wanted to demonstrate against something, such as the new tunnel. The automated traffic cameras had to be reviewed. People would come in, simmering with indignation, to be confronted by undeniable images of themselves in the act of crossing double lines or running red lights. They would sit snorting in the waiting room, 30 or 40 per day, with their wallets quaking in their jackets. Pelle Police Car, the community public relations vehicle, had to be manned, and it had to be admitted that the officers weren't exactly fighting over this important duty. Detainees had to be taken to hearings. The Head-quarters staff came in with applications of their own, requests for leave that had to be dealt with, and the days were packed with meetings. On the fourth floor was the Legal and Prosecution Section, where five lawyers worked in close co-operation with the police. On the fifth and sixth floors was the county jail. On the roof was a yard where the prisoners could get a glimpse of the sky.

The duty officer was the Headquarters representative to the outside world, and the job placed great demands on the flexibility and patience of that officer. Citizens were on the phone 24 hours a day, an almost endless barrage of complaints: bicycles stolen, dogs lost, break-ins, claims of harassment. Excitable parents from the better residential areas would ring to complain about joy-riding in the neighbourhood. Occasionally only a gasping voice was heard, a pitiful attempt to report abuse or rape that expired in despair, leaving nothing but a dead dial tone on the line. Less frequent were calls reporting murder or missing persons. In the midst of this barrage Skarre sat, waiting. He knew that it would come, he could feel the tension mounting as the clock ticked and the hours rolled into evening and then night.

It was almost midnight when Sejer's phone rang for the second time. He was dozing in his armchair with the newspaper on his lap. His blood was flowing gently in his veins, thinned by a shot of whisky. He rang for a cab, and 20 minutes later he was in his office.

"They arrived in an old Toyota," Skarre said. "I was waiting for them outside. Her parents."

"What did you say to them?"

"Probably not the right things. I was a little stressed. They called first, and half an hour later they drove up. They've already gone."

"To the morgue?"

"Yes."

"They were quite certain?"

"They brought along a photo. The mother knew exactly what she was wearing. Everything matched up, from the belt buckle to the underwear. She was wearing a special kind of bra, a sports bra. She exercised a lot. But the anorak wasn't hers."

"Are you kidding?"

"Incredible, isn't it?"

Skarre couldn't help himself – he could feel his eyes light up.

"He left us a clue, free of charge. In the pockets there was a packet of sugar and a reflector shaped like an owl. Nothing else."

"To leave his jacket behind, I can't believe it. Who is she, by the way?"

He looked at his notes. "Annie Sofie Holland."

"Annie Holland? What about the medallion?"

"Belonged to her boyfriend. His name is Halvor."

"Where is she from?"

"Lundeby. They live at 20 Krystallen. It's actually the same street where Ragnhild Album stayed overnight, just a little further up the block. An odd coincidence."

"And her parents? What were they like?"

"Scared to death," he said in a low voice. "Nice, decent people. She talked non-stop, he was practically mute. They left with Siven. As you can probably imagine," he added, "I'm a little shaken."

Sejer put a Fisherman's Friend lozenge in his mouth.

"She was only 15," Skarre continued. "A high-school student."

"That can't be right!" He shook his head. "I thought she was older. Are the pictures ready?" He ran his hand through his hair and sat down.

Skarre handed him a folder from the file. The pictures had been blown up to 20 × 25 cm, except for two that were even larger.

"Have you ever dealt with a sex murder?" Sejer asked.

Skarre shook his head.

"This doesn't look like a sex crime. This is different."

He leafed through the stack. "She's laid out too nicely, looks too good. As if she'd been put to bed with the covers pulled up. No bruises or scratches, no sign of resistance. Even her hair looks as if it's been arranged. Sex offenders don't do things like that, they show off their power. They cast their victims aside."

"But she's naked."

"Yes, I know."

"So what do you think the pictures are telling us? At first glance."

"I'm not really sure. That jacket is arranged so protectively over her shoulders."

"Almost tenderly?"

"Well, look at the pictures. Don't you think so?"

"Yes, I agree. But what are we saying then? Some kind of mercy killing?"

"Well, at least that there were emotions at play. I mean, in between all the rest, he had feelings for her. Positive feelings. In which case he may have known her. As a rule, they do."

"How long do you think we have to wait for the report?"

"I'll breathe down Snorrason's neck as effectively as I can. Too bad it was so damn free of rubbish up there. A few unusable footprints and one pill. But otherwise not even a cigarette butt, not so much as an ice-cream stick."

He crunched the lozenge with his teeth, went over to the sink and filled a paper cup with water.

"Tomorrow we'll go back to Granittveien. We have to talk to the boys who were looking for Ragnhild. Thorbjørn, for one. We have to know exactly when they were at Serpent Tarn."

"What about Raymond Låke?"

"Him too. And Ragnhild. Kids pick up on a lot of

strange things, believe me. I speak from experience," he added. "What about the Hollands? Do they have any other children?"

"Another daughter. Older."

"Thank God for that."

"Is that supposed to be some kind of consolation?" Skarre said.

"For us it is," Seyer said gloomily.

The younger man patted his pocket. "Is it all right if I smoke?"

"Go ahead."

"There are two ways to reach Serpent Tarn," he said, exhaling. "By the marked path that we took, or the road on the far side, which was the way that Ragnhild and Raymond went. If anyone lives along that road, don't you think we should pay them a visit tomorrow?"

"It's called Kolleveien. I don't think there are many houses, I checked on the map at home. Just a few farms. But of course if she was taken to the lake by car, they must have come that way."

"I feel sorry for her boyfriend."

"I guess we'll find out what kind of guy he is."

"If a man takes a girl's life," Skarre said, "by holding her head underwater until she's dead, but then he pulls her out and proceeds to lay out her body, this suggests something along these lines: 'I didn't really mean to kill you, it was something I was forced to do.' It makes me think it was a way of asking for forgiveness, don't you agree?"

Sejer downed the water and crushed the paper cup flat. "I'll talk to Holthemann in the morning. I want you on this case."

"He's assigned me to the Savings Bank case," he stammered, surprised. "Along with Gøran."

"But you're interested?"

"Interested in a murder case? It's like a Christmas present. I mean, it's a big challenge. Of course I'm interested."

He blushed and took the phone that was ringing furiously, listened, nodded, and put down the receiver.

"That was Siven. They've identified her. Annie Sofie Holland, born March 3, 1980. But she says they can't be interviewed until tomorrow."

"Is Ringstad on duty?"

"Just came in."

"Then you should be getting home. It's going to be a rough day tomorrow. I'll take the photos home," he added.

"Are you going to study her in bed?"

"I was thinking of it." He smiled sadly. "I prefer pictures I can put away in a drawer afterwards."

Like Granittveien, Krystallen was a cul-de-sac. It ended in a dense, overgrown thicket where a few citizens had furtively dumped their rubbish under cover of night. The houses stood close together, 21 in total. From a distance, they looked like terrace-houses, but as Sejer and Skarre walked down the street, they discovered narrow passageways between each building, just space enough for a man to pass through. The houses were three storeys high, tall with pitched roofs, and identical. This reminds me of the wharf area in Bergen, Sejer thought. The colours complemented each other: deep red, dark green, brown, grey. One stood out; it was the colour of an orange.

No doubt many of the residents had seen the police car near the garage, and Skarre who was in uniform. Before long the bomb was going to explode. The silence was palpable.

Ada and Eddie Holland lived in number 20. Sejer could almost feel the neighbours' eyes on the back of his neck as he stood at the front door. Something has happened at number 20, they were thinking now; at the Hollands' house, with the two girls. He tried to calm his breathing, which was faster than normal because of the threshold he was about to cross. This sort of thing was such an ordeal for him that many years ago he had fashioned a series of set phrases which now, after much practice, he could utter with confidence.

Annie's parents obviously hadn't done a thing since

coming home the night before – not even slept. The shock at the morgue had been like a shrill cymbal that was still reverberating in their heads. The mother was sitting in a corner of the sofa, the father was perched on the armrest. He looked numb. The woman hadn't yet taken in the catastrophe; she gave Sejer an uncomprehending look, as if she couldn't understand what two police officers were doing in her living room. This was a nightmare, and soon she would wake up. Sejer had to take her hand from her lap.

"I can't bring Annie back," he said in a low voice. "But I hope that I can find out why she died."

"We're not thinking about why!" shrieked the mother. "We're thinking about who did it! You have to find out who it was, and lock him up! He's sick."

Her husband patted her arm awkwardly.

"We don't yet know," Sejer said, "whether the person in question is really sick or not. Not every killer is sick."

"You can't tell me that normal people kill young girls!"

She was breathing hard, gasping for air. Her husband had wrapped himself up in a stony knot.

"Nevertheless," Sejer said, "there's always a reason, even if it's not necessarily one we can understand. But first we have to ascertain that someone really did take her life."

"If you think she took her own life, you'd better think again," the mother said. "That's impossible. Not Annie."

They all say that, Sejer thought.

"I need to ask you about a few things. Answer as best you can. Then, if you want to put your answer another way or think you forgot something, give me a ring. Or if you think of something else. Anytime, day or night."

Ada Holland shifted her eyes past Skarre and Sejer, as if she were listening to the reverberating cymbal, and she wondered where the sound was coming from.

"I need to know what kind of girl she was. Tell me whatever you can." And, at the same time, he thought, what kind of question is that? What are they supposed to say to that? The very best, of course, the sweetest, the nicest. Someone totally special. The very dearest thing they had. *Only Annie was Annie.*

They both began to sob. The mother from deep in her throat, a painfully plaintive wail; the father soundlessly, without tears. Sejer could see the resemblance to his daughter. A wide face with a high forehead. He wasn't particularly tall, but strong and sturdy. Skarre clutched his pen in his hand, his eyes fixed rigidly on his notebook.

"Let's start again," Sejer said. "I'm sorry I have to

distress you, but time is of the essence for us. What time exactly did she leave home?"

The mother answered, staring at her lap, "At 12.30 p.m."

"Where was she going?"

"To Anette's house. A schoolfriend. Three of them were doing a project. They'd been given time off from school to work on it together."

"And she never got there?"

"We rang them at 11 p.m. last night, since it was getting awfully late. Anette was in bed. Only the other girl had turned up. I couldn't believe it . . ."

She hid her face in her hands. The whole day had passed and they hadn't known.

"Why didn't the girls ring you to talk to Annie?"

"They assumed she didn't feel like coming over," she said, stifling her sobs. "Thought she'd just changed her mind. They don't know Annie very well if that's what they thought. She never neglected her homework. Never neglected anything."

"Was she going to walk over there?"

"Yes. It's four kilometres and she usually rides her bike, but it needs repairing. There isn't a bus connection."

"Where does Anette live?"

"Near Horgen. They have a farm and a general store."

Sejer nodded, hearing Skarre's pen scratching across the page.

"She had a boyfriend?"

"Halvor Muntz."

"Had it been going on for long?"

"About two years. He's older. It's been on again, off again, but it's been going fine lately, as far as I know."

Ada Holland didn't seem to know what to do with her hands; they fumbled over each other, opening and clenching. She was almost as tall as her husband, rather stout and angular, with a ruddy complexion.

"Do you know whether it was a sexual relationship?" he asked lightly.

The mother stared at him, outraged. "She's 15 years old!"

"You have to remember that I didn't know her," he said.

"There was nothing like that," she said.

"I don't think that's something we would know," the husband ventured at last. "Halvor is 18. Not a child any more."

"Of course I would know," she interrupted him.

"I don't think she tells you everything."

"I would have known!"

"But you're not much good at talking about things like that!"

The mood was tense. Sejer made his own assumption and saw from Skarre's notebook that he had too.

"If she was going to work on a school project, she must have taken a bag along."

"A brown leather bag. Where is it?"

"We haven't found it."

So we'll have to send out the divers, he thought.

"Was she taking any kind of medication?"

"Nothing. She was never ill."

"What kind of girl was she? Open? Talkative?"

"Used to be," the husband said.

"What do you mean?"

"It was just her age," the mother said. "She was at a difficult age."

"Do you mean she had changed?" Sejer turned again to the father in order to cut the mother off. It didn't work.

"All girls change at that age. They're about to grow up. Sølvi was the same way. Sølvi is her sister," she added.

The husband didn't reply; he still looked numb.

"So she was *not* an open and talkative girl?"

"She was quiet and modest," the mother said. "Meticulous and fair-minded. Had her life under control."

"But she used to be more lively?"

"They make more of a fuss when they're young."

"What I need to know," Sejer said, "is approximately when she changed?"

"At the normal time. When she was about 14. Puberty," she said, as if to explain.

He nodded, staring again at the father.

"There was no other reason for the change?"

"What would that be?" the mother said quickly.

"I don't know." He sighed a little and leaned back. "But I'm trying to find out why she died."

The mother began shaking so violently that they almost couldn't understand what she said. "*Why* she died? But it must be some . . ."

She didn't dare say the word.

"We don't know."

"But was she . . ." Another pause.

"We don't know, Mrs Holland. Not yet. These things take time. But the people who are tending to Annie know what they're doing."

He looked around the room, which was neat and clean, blue and white like Annie's clothing had been. Wreaths of dried flowers above the doors, lace curtains. Photographs. Crocheted doilies. Harmonious, tidy and proper. He stood up and went over to a large photograph on the wall.

"That was taken last winter."

The mother came over to him. He lifted the picture down carefully and stared at it. He was amazed every time he saw a face again that he had seen only devoid of life or lustre. The same person and yet not the same. Annie had a wide face with a large mouth and big grey eyes. Thick, dark eyebrows. She had a shy smile. At the bottom edge of the picture he saw the collar of her shirt and a glimpse of her boyfriend's medallion. Pretty, he thought.

"Was she involved in sports?"

"Used to be," the father said in a low voice.

"She played handball," the mother said sadly. "But she gave it up. Now she runs a lot. More than 20 miles a week."

"Why did she stop playing handball?"

"She's had so much homework lately. That's the way kids are, you know, they try out something and then they give it up. She tried playing in the school band too, the cornet. But she quit."

"Was she good? At handball?"

He hung the picture back on the wall.

"Very good," said the father softly. "She was the goalkeeper. She shouldn't have stopped."

"I think she thought it was boring to stand at the net," the mother said. "I think that's why."

"That may not be the reason," replied her husband. "She never told us why."

Sejer sat down again.

"So you both reacted to her decision in the same way? Thought it was . . . strange?"

"Yes."

"Did she do well at school?"

"Better than most. I'm not boasting, it's just a fact," he said.

"This project that the girls were working on, what was it about?"

"Sigrid Undset. It was due at Midsummer."

"Could I see her room?"

The mother got up and led the way, taking short, shuffling steps. Her husband stayed seated on the armrest, motionless.

The room was tiny, but it had been her own little hideaway. Just enough space for a bed, desk and chair. He looked out the window and stared straight across the street at the neighbour's porch. The orange house. The remains of a sheaf of oats set out for the birds bristled below the window. He searched the walls for teen idols, but found none. On the other hand, the room was full of trophies, certificates and medals; and there were a few pictures of Annie. One picture of her in her goalie's uniform with the rest of the team, and another of her standing on a windsurfing board, looking in fine form. On the wall over the bed she had several photos of little children, one of her pushing a pram, and one of a young man. Sejer pointed.

"Her boyfriend?"

The mother nodded.

"Did she work with children?"

He pointed to a picture of Annie holding a blond toddler on her lap. In the picture she looked proud and happy. She was holding the boy up to the camera, almost like a trophy.

"She babysat for all the children on the street, one after the other."

"So she liked children?"

She nodded again.

"Did she keep a diary, Mrs Holland?"

"I don't think so. I looked for one," she admitted. "I looked all night."

"You didn't find anything?"

She shook her head. From the living room they could hear a low murmur.

"We need a list of names," he said after a moment. "Of people we can talk to."

He looked at the photos on the wall again and studied Annie's uniform, black with a green emblem on the chest.

"That looks like a dragon or something."

"It's a sea serpent," she explained quietly.

"Why a sea serpent?"

"There's supposed to be a sea serpent in the fjord here. It's a legend, a story from the old days. If you're out rowing and hear a splashing sound behind your boat, that's the sea serpent rising up from the depths. You should never look back, just be careful to keep on rowing. If you pretend to ignore it and leave it in peace, everything will be fine, but if you look back into its eyes, it will pull you down into the great darkness. According to legend, it has red eyes."

They went back to the living room. Skarre was still taking notes. The husband was still perched on the armrest. He looked as if he was about to collapse.

"What about your other daughter?"

"She's flying home this morning. She's in Trondheim visiting my sister."

Mrs Holland sank on to the sofa and leaned against her husband. Sejer went to the window and found himself staring right into a face in the kitchen window next door.

"You live close to your neighbours here," he said. "Does that mean you know each other well?"

"Quite well. Everyone talks to each other."

"And everyone knew Annie?"

She nodded wordlessly.

"We'll have to go door to door. Don't let that bother you."

"We have nothing to be ashamed of."

"Could you lend us a few pictures?"

The father got up and went over to the shelf

under the TV. "We have a video," he said. "From last summer. We were at a cabin in Kragerø."

"They don't need a video," the mother said. "Just a picture of her."

"I'd be glad to have it." Sejer took it from the father and thanked them.

"She ran 20 miles a week?" he said. "Did she go alone?"

"No one could keep up with her," the father said.

"So she made time to run 20 miles a week in spite of her school work. Maybe it wasn't her homework that made her give up handball after all?"

"She could run whenever she liked," said the mother. "Sometimes she'd go out before breakfast. But if there was a game, she had to show up, and she couldn't make her own plans. I don't think she liked being tied down. She was very independent, our Annie."

"Where did she go running?"

"Everywhere. In all kinds of weather. Along the highway, in the woods."

"And to Serpent Tarn?"

"Yes."

"Was she restless?"

"She was quiet and calm," the mother said softly.

Sejer went back over to the window and caught

sight of a woman hurrying across the street, a toddler with a dummy clutched in the crook of her arm. "Any other interests? Aside from running?"

"Film and music and books and things like that. And little children," the father said. "Especially when she was younger."

Sejer asked them to make a list of everyone who knew Annie. Friends, neighbours, teachers, family members. Boyfriends, if there were others. When they were done, the list had 42 names with addresses that were at least partially complete.

"Are you going to talk to everyone on the list?" the mother asked.

"Yes, we are. And this is just the beginning. We'll keep you informed of our progress," he said.

"We have to see Thorbjørn Haugen. He was searching for Ragnhild yesterday. He can give us a time frame."

The car moved past the garages. Skarre was reading through his notes.

"I asked the father about the handball business," he said. "While the two of you were in the girl's room."

"And?"

"He said that Annie was very promising. The team had a terrific season, they were in Finland and made it to the finals. He couldn't understand why

73

she gave it up. It made him wonder if something had happened."

"We should find the coach, whoever he or she is. Maybe that would give us a lead."

"It's a man," Skarre said. "He'd been calling for weeks, trying to persuade her to come back. The team had big problems after she left. No one could replace Annie."

"We'll call from Headquarters and get his name."

"His name is Knut Jensvoll, and he lives at 8 Gneisveien, down the hill from here."

"Thanks," Sejer said, raising an eyebrow. "I'm sitting here thinking about something," he continued. "The fact that Annie might have been killed at exactly the time when we were on Granittveien, a few minutes away, worrying about Ragnhild. Call Pilestredet, and ask for Snorrason. See if he can hurry things along. We need the forensic report as soon as possible."

Skarre reached for his mobile phone, dialled the number, asked for Snorrason, waited again, then started mumbling.

"What did he say?"

"That the morgue cold storage is full. That every death is tragic, regardless of the cause, and that a whole list of people are waiting to bury their loved ones, but he understands the urgency, and you can come over in three days to get a preliminary verbal report if you like. You'll have to wait longer for the written one."

"Oh well," Sejer said. "That's not bad for Snorrason."

CHAPTER 3

Raymond spread butter on a piece of thin flatbread. He was concentrating hard so that it wouldn't break, with his big tongue sticking out of his mouth. He had four pieces of flatbread stacked on top of each other with butter and sugar in between; his record was six.

The kitchen was small and cosy, but now it was messy after his efforts with the food. He had a slice of bread prepared for his father too, white bread with the crust cut off, spread with bacon fat from the frying pan. After they had eaten he would wash the dishes, and then sweep the kitchen floor. He had already emptied his father's urine bottle and filled his water mug. Today there was no sun to be seen; it was overcast grey, and the landscape outside was dreary and flat. The coffee had boiled three times, the way it was supposed to. He placed a fifth piece of flatbread on top and felt quite pleased with himself. He was about to pour coffee into his father's mug when he heard a car pull up by the front door. To his terror he saw it was a police car. He stiffened, backed away from the window, and ran into a corner of the living room. Maybe they were coming to put him in prison. Then who would take care of Papa?

Car doors slammed in the courtyard, and he heard voices, mumbling. He wasn't sure whether he had done something wrong. It wasn't always that easy to know. For safety's sake he didn't budge when they knocked on the door, but it was clear that they weren't intending to give up; they knocked and knocked and called his name. Maybe his father would hear them. He started coughing loudly to drown out the sound. After a while it grew quiet. He was still in the corner of the living room, beside the fireplace, when he caught sight of a face at the window. A tall, grey-haired man was waving at him. It was probably just to lure him out, Raymond thought, and shook his head vigorously. He held on to the fireguard and nestled further into the corner. The man outside looked friendly enough, but that was no guarantee of his being nice. Raymond had found out these things long ago, and he wasn't stupid either. After a while he couldn't bear standing there any longer, so he ran to the kitchen instead, but there was a face there too. Fair, curly hair and a dark uniform. Raymond felt like a kitten in a sack, with cold water pouring over him. He hadn't been out with the van today; it still wouldn't start, so it couldn't have anything to do with that. It must be about the matter up by the tarn, he thought desperately. He stood there, rocking a little. After a while he went out to the hall and looked anxiously at the key in the lock.

"Raymond!" one of them called. "We just want to talk. We won't hurt you."

"I wasn't mean to Ragnhild!" he shouted.

"We know that. That's not why we're here. We just need a little help from you."

Still he hesitated, before finally opening the door.

"May we come in?" the taller one said. "We have to ask you a few questions."

"All right. I wasn't sure what you wanted. I can't open the door to just anyone."

"No, you certainly can't," Sejer said, looking around him. "But it's good if you open the door when it's the police."

"We'll sit in the living room then."

Raymond walked ahead of them and pointed to the sofa, which looked oddly handmade. An old tartan blanket lay on the seat. They sat down and studied the room, rather small and square with the sofa, table and two chairs. On the walls were paintings of animals and a photograph of an elderly woman with a boy on her lap. Perhaps his mother.

The child had the features Sejer associated with Down's syndrome, and the woman's age might have been the reason for Raymond's fate. From where they were sitting, no television set was visible, nor a telephone. Sejer couldn't remember having seen a living room without a TV in years.

"Is your father home?" he began, looking at Raymond's T-shirt. It was white and bore the words: I'M THE ONE WHO DECIDES.

"He's in bed. He doesn't get up any more, he can't walk."

"So you take care of him?"

"I make the food and clean the house, just so you know!"

"Your father's pretty lucky to have you."

Raymond gave a big smile, in that uncommonly charming manner characteristic of people with Down's syndrome. An uncorrupted child in a robust body. He had powerful, broad hands with unusually short fingers and big bulky shoulders.

"You were so nice to Ragnhild yesterday, and you took her home," Sejer said, "so she didn't have to walk alone. That was a kind thing to do."

"She's not so big, you know!" he said, trying to sound grown-up.

"No, she isn't. So it was good she had you with her. And you helped her with her doll's pram. But when she came home, she had a story to tell, and we thought we'd ask you about it, Raymond. I'm talking about what the two of you saw at Serpent Tarn."

Raymond stared at him anxiously and stuck out his lower lip.

"You saw a girl, didn't you?"

"I didn't do it!" he blurted out.

"We don't think you did. That's not why we're here. Let me ask you about something else instead. I see you have a watch."

"Yes, I have a watch." He showed it to them. "It's Papa's old one."

"Do you look at it often?"

"Oh no, almost never."

"Why not?"

"When I'm at work the boss keeps track of the time. And here at home Papa keeps track."

"Why aren't you at work today?"

"I have a week off and then I work a week."

"I see. Can you tell me what time it is now?"

Raymond looked at his watch. "It's just after 11.10 a.m."

"That's right. But you don't look at your watch very often, you said?"

"Only when I have to."

Sejer nodded and glanced over at Skarre, who was assiduously taking notes.

"Did you look at it when you took Ragnhild

80

home? Or, for instance, when you were standing by Serpent Tarn?"

"No."

"Can you guess what time it might have been?"

"Now you're asking me hard questions," he said, already tired from thinking so much.

"It's not easy to remember everything, you're right about that. I'm almost finished. Did you see anything else up by the lake – I mean, did you see any people up there? Besides the girl?"

"No. Is she sick?" he said suspiciously.

"She's dead, Raymond."

"Too soon, I think."

"That's what we think. Did you see a car or anything driving by the house here in the daytime? Going up or down? Or people walking past? While Ragnhild was here, for example?"

"A lot of tourists come this way. But not yesterday. Only the ones who live here. The road ends at Kollen."

"So you saw no one?"

He thought for a long time. "Well, yes, one car. Just as we were leaving. It zoomed past, like a regular racing car."

"As you were leaving?"

"Yes."

"Going up or down?"

"Down."

Zoomed past here, Sejer thought. But what does that mean to someone who never drives above second gear?

"Did you recognise the car? Was it someone who lives up here?"

"No, they don't drive that fast."

Sejer did some mental calculations.

"Ragnhild was home a little before two, so it might have been around 1.30 p.m., right? It didn't take you very long to go up to the lake, did it?"

"No."

"The car was going fast, you said?"

"It kicked up a cloud of dust. But it's been quite dry lately."

"What kind of car was it?"

Then he held his breath. A car sighting would be something to go on. A car in the vicinity of the crime scene, driving at high speed at a specific time.

"Just an ordinary car," Raymond said, pleased.

"An ordinary car?" Sejer said. "What do you mean, exactly?"

"Not a truck, or a van or anything. A normal car."

"I see. A normal passenger car. Are you good at recognising makes?"

"Not really."

"What kind of car does your father have?"

"A Hiace," he said proudly.

"Do you see the police car outside? Can you see what kind it is?"

"That one? You just told me. It's a police car."

Raymond squirmed in his chair and suddenly looked uncomfortable.

"What about the colour, Raymond? Did you notice the colour?"

He tried hard to remember but gave up, shaking his head.

"It was so dusty. Impossible to see the colour," he muttered.

"But could you tell us whether it was dark or light?"

Sejer refused to give in. Skarre kept on writing. He was impressed by the mild tone of voice his boss was using. Normally he was more brusque.

"In between. Maybe brown or grey or green. A dirty colour. It was so dusty. You could ask Ragnhild, she saw it too."

"We've already asked her. She also says the car was grey, or maybe green. But she couldn't tell us whether it was old or new."

"Not old and junky," he said firmly. "In between."

"Fine. I understand."

"There was something on the roof," he said suddenly.

"Is that right? What was it?"

"A long box. Flat and black."

"A ski-box maybe?" Skarre suggested.

Raymond hesitated. "Yes, maybe a ski-box."

Skarre smiled and made a note of it, delighted at Raymond's eagerness.

"Good observation, Raymond. Did you get that, Skarre? So your father is in bed?"

"He's waiting for his food now, I think."

"We didn't mean to hold you up. Could we peek in and say hello before we go?"

"Sure, I'll show you the way."

He walked through the living room, and the two men followed. At the end of the hall he stopped and opened a door very gently, almost with reverence. In the bed lay an old man, snoring. His teeth were in a glass on the bedside table.

"We won't disturb him," Sejer said, withdrawing from the room. They thanked Raymond and went out to the courtyard. He trotted after them.

"We might come back again. You've got nice rabbits," Skarre said.

"That's what Ragnhild said. You can hold one if you want."

"Another time."

They waved and then jolted off along the bumpy road. Sejer drummed on the steering wheel in annoyance.

"That car is important. And the only thing we've got to go on is something 'in between'. But a ski-box on the roof, Skarre! Ragnhild didn't say anything about that."

"Everyone under the sun has a ski-box on their car."

"I don't. Stop at that farm."

They drove up to the house and parked next to a red Mazda. A woman wearing a cap and gumboots caught sight of them from the barn and came walking across the yard.

"Police," Sejer said politely, nodding towards the red car. "Do you have any other cars on the farm?"

"Two others," she said, surprised. "My husband has a station-wagon, and my son has a Golf. Why?"

"What colour are they?" he asked.

She stared at him in astonishment. "The Mercedes is white and the Golf is red."

"What about the farm next door, what kind of vehicles do they have?"

"A Blazer," she said. "A dark-blue Blazer. Has something happened?"

"Yes, it has. We'll come back to that. Were you home yesterday in the middle of the day?"

"I was in the fields."

"Did you see a car coming down the hill at high speed? A grey or green car with a ski-box on the roof?"

She shrugged. "Not that I recall. But I don't hear much when I'm driving the tractor."

"Did you see anyone around that time of day?"

"Hikers. A group of boys with a dog," she said. "No one else."

Thorbjørn and his group, he thought.

"Thanks for your help. Are your neighbours home?"

He nodded towards the farm further down the road as he looked at her. Her face was one of someone who worked outdoors often, healthy-looking and attractive.

"The owner of the farm is away, there's only a caretaker there. He left this morning and I haven't seen him come back."

She shaded her face with her hand and stared in that direction. "The car's not there."

"Do you know him?"

"No. He's not the talkative sort."

Sejer thanked her, and they got back into the car.

"He had to drive up there first," Skarre said.

"He wasn't a murderer then. He might been driving very slowly, and that's why no one noticed him."

They drove in second gear down to the highway. Shortly afterwards they saw a small country shop on the left-hand side of the road. They parked and went in. A tiny bell rang above their heads, and a man wearing a blue-green nylon smock appeared from the back room. For several seconds he simply stood and stared at them with a look of horror. "Is it about Annie?"

Sejer nodded.

"Anette feels so terrible," he said, sounding shocked. "She rang up Annie today. All she heard was a scream on the other end of the line."

A teenage girl appeared and stood motionless in the doorway. Her father put his arm around her shoulders.

"We're letting her stay home today."

"Do you live next to the store?"

Sejer went over and shook hands.

"Five hundred metres from here, down by the shore. We can't believe it."

"Did you see anyone unusual in the area yesterday?"

He thought for a moment. "A group of boys came in and each bought a coke. Otherwise only Raymond. He came in around midday and bought milk and flatbread. Raymond Låke. He lives with his father up near Kollen. We don't have many customers, we're going to have to shut down soon."

He kept on patting his daughter on the back as he talked.

"How long did it take for Låke to buy his bread and milk?"

"I don't know, a few minutes. A motorcycle

stopped here too, by the way. Must have been between 12.30 and 1 p.m. Stopped for a minute and then left. A big bike with large saddlebags. Might have been a tourist. No one else."

"A motorcycle? Can you describe it?"

"Oh, what can I say? Dark, I think. Shiny and impressive. He was sitting with his back to me, wearing a helmet. Sat and read something that he held in front of him on his bike."

"Did you see the number plates?"

"No, sorry."

"Do you remember seeing a grey or green car with a ski-box on the roof?"

"No."

"What about you, Anette?" Sejer said, turning to the daughter. "Is there anything you can think of that might be important?"

"I should have called her," she said.

"You can't blame yourself for this, you couldn't have done anything to prevent it. Someone probably picked her up on the road."

"Annie didn't like people to get upset. I was afraid she'd get mad if we tried to pressure her."

"Did you know Annie well?"

"Pretty well."

"And you can't think of anyone she might have met along her route? Had she mentioned any new acquaintances?"

"Oh, no. She had Halvor, you know."

"I see. Well, please call if you think of anything. We'd be happy to come over again."

They thanked them and went out, while shop-keeper Horgen disappeared into the back room. Sejer caught a glimpse of the stooped figure in the window next to the entrance.

"When he's sitting in his office he can see the road."

A motorcycle that stops and then takes off again, between 12.30 p.m. and 1 p.m. That's something we need to make note of, he thought. All right.

He slammed the door of the car. "Thorbjørn thought they went past Serpent Tarn about 12.45 p.m. when they were searching for Ragnhild. At that time, the body wasn't there. Raymond and Ragnhild saw the body at approximately 1.30 p.m. That gives us a window of 45 minutes. That almost never happens. A car drove past them at high speed just before they left. An ordinary car, sort of in between. A dirty colour, not light, not dark, not old, not new."

He slammed his hand against the dashboard.

"Not everybody is a car expert," Skarre said with a smile.

"We'll ask him to come forward. Whoever it was that drove past Raymond's house between 1 p.m.

and 1.30 p.m. yesterday, at high speed. Possibly with a ski-box on the roof. We'll also put out an APB on the motorcycle. If no one comes forward, I'm going to have to put pressure on those kids about that car."

"How are you going to do that?"

"Don't know yet. Maybe they can draw. Kids are always drawing things."

Afterwards they ate in the cafeteria at the court-house.

"This omelette is dry," Skarre said. "It was in the frying pan too long."

"That right?"

"The point is for the egg to solidify after it's on your plate. You have to take it out of the pan while it's still soft."

Sejer wasn't going to dispute this; he couldn't cook at all.

"And besides, they put milk in it. Which ruins the colour."

"Did you go to cooking school?"

"Just one course."

"Jesus, the things we don't know."

He mopped up the last scraps on his plate with a piece of bread, then carefully wiped his mouth with his napkin.

"We'll start with Krystallen. We'll take one side

each, ten houses apiece. But we'll wait until after five, when people are home from work."

"What should I be looking for?" Skarre said, checking his watch. Smoking was permitted after 2 p.m.

"Irregularities. Anything at all out of the ordinary. Ask about Annie in the past too, about whether they think she had changed. Turn on the charm, whatever you've got of it, and make them open up. In short: Get them to talk."

"We'd better talk to Eddie Holland by himself."

"I thought of that. I'll ask him to come out here after a few days. But you should remember that the mother is in shock. She'll calm down after a while."

"They made very different observations about Annie, don't you think?"

"That's how it goes. You don't have kids, Skarre?"

"No."

He lit a cigarette and blew the smoke away from his boss.

"Her sister must be home by now, from Trondheim. We need to talk to her too."

When they had finished, they went over to the forensics institute, but no one could tell them anything significant about the blue anorak that had covered the body.

"Imported, from China. Sold by all the discount

chains. The importer said they'd brought in two thousand jackets. A packet of butterscotch in the right pocket, a reflector and a few light-coloured hairs, possibly dog hairs. And don't ask me what breed. Otherwise nothing."

"The size?"

"Extra large. But the sleeves must have been too long, the cuffs were folded back."

"In the old days people had name tags sewn into their jackets," Skarre said.

"Oh sure, that must have been back in the Middle Ages."

"What about the pill?"

"Not very exciting, I'm afraid. It's nothing more than a menthol lozenge, the kind that are popular right now. Very tiny and incredibly strong."

Sejer was disappointed. A menthol lozenge told them nothing. Everyone had that sort of thing in their pockets; even he always carried a packet of Fisherman's Friends.

They drove back. There was more traffic on Krystallen now. It was teeming with children, on various vehicles: tricycles, tractors, some with doll's prams, and one homemade go-cart with a mangy flag flapping in the wind. When the police car pulled up next to the letterboxes, the colourful tableau froze like ice. Skarre couldn't resist checking the brakes on one of the toy vehicles, and he was positive that the owner of a blue and pink Massey Ferguson wet his pants from sheer fright when he told him that the rear light was out.

Almost everyone realised that something had happened, but they didn't know what. No one had dared to call the Hollands to enquire.

They presented their questions at every house, one on each side of the street. Time after time they had to watch disbelief and shock flood the frightened faces. Many of the women started to cry, the men turned pale and fell silent. They would wait a proper amount of time and then ask their questions. Everyone knew Annie well. Some of the women had seen her leave. The Hollands lived at the end of the cul-de-sac; she had to pass all the houses on her way out. For years she had baby-sat their children, up until last year, when she started getting too old for it. Almost everyone mentioned her handball career and their surprise when she had left the team. Annie had been such a good player that her name was often in the local paper. One elderly couple remembered that she had been livelier and much more outgoing in the past, but they ascribed the change to her getting older. She had changed tremendously, they said. She'd been quite short and thin; then all of a sudden she'd shot up so tall.

Skarre didn't take the houses in order; he went

first to the orange one. It belonged to a bachelor named Fritzner, who was in his late 40s. In the middle of the living room was a little boat with full sails. In the bottom of the boat lay a mattress and lots of cushions, and a bottle holder was fastened to the gunwale. Skarre stared at it, intrigued. The boat was bright red, its sails were white. An image of his own apartment and its lack of any unorthodox furnishings flitted through his mind.

Fritzner didn't know Annie well, but occasionally he had offered her a lift into town. If the weather was bad she accepted, but if it was fine, she would wave him on. He liked Annie. A damn good handball goalie, he said.

Sejer moved on down the street, coming to a Turkish family at number 6. The Irmak family were just about to eat when he rang the bell. They were sitting at the table, and steam was rising from a large pot in the middle of it. The man of the house, a stately figure wearing an embroidered shirt, stretched out a brown hand. Sejer told them that Annie Holland was dead, and that it seemed that someone had murdered her.

"No!" they said, horrified. "It can't be true. Not that pretty girl in number 20, not Eddie's daughter!" The Hollands were the only family that had welcomed them warmly when they moved in. They had lived other places, and they hadn't been equally welcome everywhere. It couldn't be true! The man grabbed Sejer's arm and pulled him towards the sofa.

Sejer sat down. Irmak did not have the meek, submissive air that he had so often seen in immigrants; instead, he was bursting with dignity and self-confidence. It was refreshing.

His wife had seen Annie leave. She thought it must have been around 12.30 p.m. She was walking calmly past the houses with a backpack on. They hadn't known Annie when she was younger, they had lived there only four months.

"Nice girl," she said, straightening the shawl draped over her head. "Big! Lots of muscles." She lowered her eyes.

"Did she ever baby-sit for your daughter?"

Sejer nodded towards the table where a young girl was waiting patiently. A silent, unusually pretty girl with thick lashes. Her gaze was as deep and penetrating as a mine-shaft.

"We were going to ask her," the husband said swiftly, "but the neighbours said she was too old for that now. So we didn't want to bother her. And my wife is at home all day, so we get by. I'm only gone in the morning. We have a Lada. The neighbours say it's not a proper car, but it's fine for us. Every day, without fail, it takes me to Poppels Gaten, where I have a spice shop. You could get rid of that rash you have on your forehead with spices. Not spices from the Rimi shop. Real spices, from Irmak's."

"Really? Is that possible?"

"They cleanse the system. Drive the sweat out faster."

Sejer nodded. "So you've never had anything to do with Annie?"

"Not really. A few times, when she ran past, I stopped her and shook my finger. I told her: You're running away from your own soul. That made her laugh. I told her: I will teach you to meditate instead. Running along the streets is a clumsy way to find peace. That made her laugh even more, and then she'd set off round the corner."

"Has she ever been to your house?"

"Yes. She came from Eddie on the day we moved in, with a flower in a pot. As a welcome from them. Nihmet cried," he said, and glanced at his wife. That's what she was doing now too. She pulled her shawl over her face and turned her back to them.

When Sejer left, they thanked him for his visit and said he was welcome to come again. They stood in the little hall and watched him. The girl clung to her mother's dress; she reminded him of Matteus, with her dark eyes and black curls. On the street he paused for a moment and stared straight across at

Skarre, who was just coming out of number 9. They nodded to each other and went on their separate ways.

"Did you find many locked doors?" Skarre asked.

"Only two. Johnas in number 4 and Rud in number 8."

"I got notes from all of mine."

"Any immediate thoughts?"

"Nothing except that she knew everybody and had been in and out of their houses for years. And that she was well-liked by everyone."

They rang the Hollands' bell. A girl opened the door. She was obviously Annie's sister; they were alike, and yet they were different. Her hair was just as blonde as Annie's, but it was darker at the roots. Her eyes were outlined with mascara. Her eyes were trapped inside, very pale blue and uncertain. She wasn't big and tall like Annie, or sporty and muscular. She was wearing lavender stretch pants with stitched seams and a white blouse that was unbuttoned halfway down.

"Sølvi?" Sejer said.

She nodded and offered him a limp hand, then led the way inside and at once sought refuge next to her mother. Mrs Holland was sitting in the same corner of the sofa as before. Her face had changed somewhat over the course of a few hours; her expression was no longer so painfully desperate, but she looked sombre and strained and a good deal older. The father was not in evidence. Sejer tried to study Sølvi without staring. Her features and figure differed from her sister's; she didn't have Annie's wide cheekbones or firm chin or big grey eyes. Weaker and a little plump, he thought.

After half an hour of conversation it became clear that the two sisters hadn't been especially close. Each had led her own life. Sølvi had a cleaning job at a beauty parlour, had never been interested in other people's children, and had never played sports. Sejer thought that in all likelihood she had been preoccupied with herself, and with her appearance. Even now, as she sat on the sofa with her mother, in the aftermath of her sister's death, she had arranged her body in an attractive pose, out of habit. One knee was drawn up, her head was tilted slightly, her hands were clasped around her leg. Several gaudy rings glittered on her fingers. Her nails were long and red. A soft body without edges, without defini-tion, as if she lacked a skeleton or muscles and was merely skin stretched over a lump of modelling clay, pink in colour. Sølvi was a good deal older than Annie, but her face had a naïve look to it. Her mother had assumed a protective posture and patted Sølvi's arm steadily, as if she had to be comforted, or maybe admonished, Sejer couldn't decide which. The sisters were in fact very different. Annie's face in the photo was more mature. She peered at the camera with a wary expression, as if she didn't like being photographed but had nevertheless conceded to authority, perhaps simply out of good manners. Sølvi was posing more or less all of the time. She looks more like her mother, he thought, while Annie takes after her father.

"Do you know whether Annie had made any new friends recently? Met any new people? Did she talk about anything like that?"

"She wasn't interested in meeting people." Sølvi smoothed out her blouse.

"Do you know whether she kept a diary?"

"Oh no, not Annie. She wasn't like that. She was different from other girls, more like a boy. Didn't even use any make-up. Hated getting dressed up. She wore Halvor's medallion, but only because he pestered her about it. In fact, it got in the way when she went running."

Her voice was bright and sweet, as if she were a little girl and not six years older than Annie. Please be nice to me, her voice pleaded gently, you can see how small and fragile I am.

"Do you know her friends?"

"They're younger than me, but I know who they are."

She played with her rings and hesitated for a moment, as if she was trying to make sense of this new situation she had found herself in.

"Who do you think knew her best?"

"She spent time with Anette, but only when they had something specific to do. Not just to talk, I don't think."

"You live a little out of the way here," he said. "Do you think she would ever hitchhike?"

"Never. Neither would I," she said. "But we often can catch a ride when we walk along the road. We know just about everybody."

Just about, he thought.

"Do you think she seemed unhappy about anything?"

"Not unhappy. But she wasn't exactly jumping with joy either. She wasn't interested in much. I mean, girls' things. Just school and running."

"And Halvor, perhaps?"

"I'm not really sure. She seemed a little indifferent about Halvor too. Couldn't ever make up her mind."

Sejer saw an image in his mind's eye of a girl turned slightly away with a sceptical look on her face, a girl who did as she pleased, who went her own way, and who had kept all of them at a distance. Why?

"Your mother says she used to be livelier," he said. "Do you agree?"

"Oh yes, she used to be more talkative."

Sejer cleared his throat. "This change," he said, "did it happen suddenly, do you think? Or did it happen gradually, over a long period of time?"

"No," the two of them glanced at each other. "We're not quite sure. She just became different."

"Can you say anything about when it happened, Sølvi?"

She shrugged. "Last year sometime. She broke up with Halvor and right after that she stopped playing handball. Plus she was growing so tall. She grew out of all her clothes and got so quiet."

"Do you mean angry or sullen?"

"No. Just quiet. Disappointed, in a way."

Disappointed.

Sejer nodded. He looked at Sølvi. Her stretch pants were dazzling, the colour of lilacs from his childhood.

"Do you know whether Annie and Halvor had a sexual relationship?"

She turned bright red. "I'm not sure. You'll have to ask Halvor."

"I will."

"The sister," Sejer said, when they were back in the car, "is the kind of girl who often ends up a victim. Of a man with bad intentions, I mean. She's so preoccupied with herself and her appearance that

101

she wouldn't notice the danger signals. Sølvi. Not Annie. Annie was reserved and sporty. Didn't care about making an impression on anyone. She didn't hitchhike and wasn't interested in meeting new people. If she got into someone's car, it would have been somebody she knew."

Skarre looked at him. 'That's what we keep saying."

"I know."

"You have a daughter who's been through puberty," he said inquisitively. "So what was it like?"

"Oh," Sejer said, looking out the window. "It was mostly Elise who handled that type of thing. But I do remember it. Puberty is a really rough time. She was a sunbeam until she turned 13, then she began to snarl. She snarled until she was 14, then she began to bark. And then it wore off."

It wore off, and he remembered when she turned 15 and became a young woman, and he didn't know how to talk to her. It must have been like that for Holland too. When your child is no longer a child, and you have to find a new language. Difficult.

"So it took a year or two? Before it was over?"

"Yes," he said thoughtfully, "I suppose it did."

"You seem to be focusing on this change in her."

"Something must have happened. I have to find

out what it was. Who she was, who killed her and why. It's time we paid a visit to Halvor Muntz. No doubt he's been waiting for us. How do you think he feels?"

"No idea. Can I smoke in the car?"

"No. By the way, your hair is looking a little shaggy, don't you think?"

"I guess so, now that you mention it. Here, have a mint."

They each stared out at the road. Skarre fiddled with a lock of hair at the back of his neck and stretched it out full-length. When he let go, it curled up as swiftly as a worm on a hotplate.

CHAPTER 4

She thought there was something familiar about him. That's why she'd scooted her chair closer and stuck her wrinkled face all the way up to the television. The light of the screen fell on her so that he could see the whiskers on her chin which were still growing. They should have been shaved off, he thought, but he wasn't sure how to mention it to her.

"It's Johann Olav Koss!" she shrieked. "He's drinking milk."

"Hmm."

"Good heavens, how handsome that boy is. I wonder if he knows it? He's just like a sculpture, he really is. A living sculpture!"

Koss wiped off his milk moustache and smiled with white teeth.

"Oh, just look at the teeth that boy has! Teeth as white as chalk! It's because he drinks milk. You should too, you should drink more milk. But he probably had a school dentist. We didn't."

She tucked the tartan blanket around her lap.

"We couldn't afford to have our teeth fixed, just had to get them pulled out as they rotted away, one by one, but today all of you have school dentists and milk and vitamins and healthy diets and toothpaste and fluoride, and all manner of things."

She sighed heavily. "Let me tell you, I sat and cried in class, yes I did. Not because I didn't know my lessons, but because I was so hungry. Of course you're handsome, all of you young people today. I envy you! Do you hear what I'm saying, Halvor? I envy you!"

"Yes, Grandmother."

His hands shook as he pulled photos out of a yellow Kodak envelope. A slender young man with narrow shoulders, he didn't look much like the skater in the TV commercial. He had a small mouth, like a girl, and one corner was stretched taut – when he smiled, which happened rarely, it refused to turn upwards. Close up, it was possible to see the scar from the stitches; it extended from the right side of his mouth to his temple. His hair was brown, cut soft and short, and his sideburns were sparse. From a distance he was often taken for a 15-year-old, and for a long time he'd had to show his ID at the cinema. He never made a fuss about it though, he was no troublemaker.

Slowly he shuffled through the pictures, which

he had looked at countless times before. But now they had acquired a new dimension. Now he was searching them for signs of what was to happen later on, things that he hadn't known when he'd taken them. Annie with a wooden mallet, pounding in a tent peg with great force. Annie on the end of the diving board, erect as a pillar in her black bathing suit. Annie asleep in the green sleeping bag. Annie on her bike, her face hidden by her blonde hair. A picture of him as he struggled with the Primus stove. One of both of them, taken by the people in the next tent. He had to nag her to get her to agree. She couldn't stand being photographed.

"Halvor!" cried his grandmother from the window. "There's a police car outside!"

"Yes," he said in a low voice.

"Why are they coming here?" She looked at him, suddenly anxious. "What do they want?"

"It's because of Annie."

"What's wrong with Annie?"

"She's dead."

"What did you say?"

Frightened, she stumbled back to her chair and leaned on the armrest.

"She's dead. They're coming here to interrogate me. I knew they would come. I've been waiting for them."

"Why are you saying that Annie's dead?"

"Because she *is* dead!" he shouted. "She died yesterday! Her father called me."

"Yes, but why?"

"How should I know! I don't know why, all I know is that she's dead!"

He hid his face in his hands. His grandmother collapsed like a sack of flour into her chair, looking even paler than usual. Things had been so peaceful for such a long time. But it couldn't last, of course it couldn't.

Someone knocked loudly on the door. Halvor gave a start, shoved the photos under the table-cloth, and went to open the door. There were two of them. They stood on the porch for a moment and looked at him. It wasn't hard to guess what they were thinking.

"Are you Halvor Muntz?"

"Yes."

"We've come to ask you some questions. Do you know why?"

"Her father called last night." Halvor nodded over and over. Sejer caught sight of the old woman in the chair and said hello to her.

"Is she a relative of yours?"

"Yes."

"Is there somewhere we can talk in private?"

"My room's the only place."

"Well, if it's all right with you . . ."

Halvor led the way out of the living room, through a cramped little kitchen, and into his bedroom. This must be an old house, Sejer thought, they don't make houses with this floor plan any more. The two men cleared a place to sit on a sagging sofa, Muntz sat down on his bed. An old-fashioned room with green-painted panelling and wide windowsills.

"Is she your grandmother? The woman in the living room?"

"Yes, my father's mother."

"And your parents?"

"They're divorced."

"Is that why you live here?"

"I was allowed to choose where I wanted to live."

The words sounded terse and clacking, like pebbles falling.

Sejer looked around, searching for pictures of Annie, and found a small one in a gold frame on the bedside table. Next to it stood an alarm clock and a statue of the Madonna and child, perhaps a souvenir from the Mediterranean. A single poster hung on the wall, presumably a rock singer, with the words "Meat Loaf" printed across the picture. A stereo and CD player. A wardrobe, a pair of trainers, not as fancy as Annie's. A motorcycle helmet hung from the doorknob of the wardrobe.

The bed had not been made. Beside the window stood a narrow desk with a good computer. Next to it was a box containing diskettes. Sejer could see the one on top: Chess for Beginners. From the window he looked out on the courtyard, and he could see their Volvo parked in front of the shed, an empty doghouse, and a motorcycle covered with plastic.

"You ride a motorcycle?" he began.

"When it's running. It doesn't always start. I have to get it fixed, but I don't have the money right now."

He fidgeted with the collar of his shirt.

"Do you have a job?"

"At the ice cream factory. Been there two years."

The ice cream factory, Sejer thought. For two years. So he must have left at the end of middle school and gone to work. Might not be such a bad idea after all; he was getting work experience. It was clear that he wasn't athletic – a little too thin, a little too pale. Annie was much fitter in comparison, training diligently and working hard at school, while this young man packed ice cream and lived with his grandmother. Sejer didn't think it added up. But this was an arrogant thought, and he pushed it aside.

"I'm going to have to ask you about various things. Is that all right with you?"

"Yes."

"Let's start with this: When did you last see Annie?"

"On Friday. We went to the movies, the 7 p.m. show."

"What did you see?"

"*Philadelphia*. Annie cried."

"Why?"

"It's a sad movie."

"I see, of course. And then?"

"We ate at the Kino Pub and took the bus back to her house. Sat in her room and listened to music. I took the bus home at 11 p.m. She walked me to the bus stop on Meieriet."

"And you didn't see her again?"

He shook his head. The tight pull of his mouth gave him a sullen look. Actually that's unfair, thought Sejer, because otherwise he had quite a nice face, with green eyes and regular features. The compressed lips made it look as if he wanted to hide bad teeth or something. Later Sejer would discover that they were more than perfect. Four up and two down were made of porcelain.

"And you didn't talk to her on the phone or anything?"

"Oh yes," he said at once. "She called me the next evening."

"What did she want?"

"Nothing."

"She was a very quiet girl, wasn't she?"

"Yes, but she liked to talk on the phone."

"So she didn't want anything, but she called you all the same. What did you talk about?"

"If you really must know, well ... we talked about all sorts of things."

Sejer smiled. Halvor stared out of the window the whole time, as if he wanted to avoid eye contact. Perhaps he felt guilty, or maybe he was just shy. They felt a sad empathy for him. His girlfriend was dead, and probably he had no one to talk to except his grandmother who was waiting in the living room. And maybe, Sejer thought, he's our killer.

"And yesterday you were at your job, as usual? At the ice cream factory?"

He hesitated for a moment. "No, I was at home."

"You were home? Why?"

"I wasn't feeling too good."

"Do you often call in sick?"

"No, I don't often call in sick."

His voice was raised. For the first time they caught a glimpse of anger.

"Your grandmother can confirm all this, of course?"

"Yes."

"And you didn't go out at all during the day?"

"Just for a short while."

"Even though you were sick?"

"We have to eat! It's not easy for Grandmother to get to the shops. She can only manage to walk on her good days, and there aren't many of those. She has arthritis," he said.

"OK, I understand. Can you tell us a little about what was wrong with you?"

"Only if I have to."

"You don't have to right now, but you may have to later on."

"Well, OK. There are some nights when I can't sleep."

"Is that right? So then you stay home?"

"I can't tend to the machines if my mind's not sharp."

"That sounds reasonable. Why do you have these sleepless nights?"

"Oh, it's just some stuff from my childhood. Isn't that what people say?" He gave them a bitter smile; and suddenly there was something strangely adult about his young face.

"Approximately when did you go out?"

"Around 11 a.m., I guess."

"On foot?"

"On my motorcycle."

"Which store did you go to?"

"The Kiwi shop in town."

"So your bike started OK yesterday?"

"Actually, it always starts if I keep at it long enough."

"How long were you out?"

"Don't know. How could I know that someone would be demanding an explanation?"

Sejer nodded. Skarre was moving his pen like crazy to keep up.

"But approximately?

"Maybe an hour."

"And your grandmother can confirm that?"

"Probably not. She doesn't pay much attention."

"Do you have a licence to drive a car?"

"No."

"How long were you together, you and Annie?"

"A long time. A couple of years." He wiped his nose and kept on staring out at the courtyard.

"Do you think it was a good relationship?"

"We split up a few times."

"Was she the one who wanted to break up?"

"Yes."

"Did she say why?"

"Not really. But she wasn't always enthusiastic. Wanted to keep things on a friendship basis."

"And you didn't?"

He blushed and looked down at his hands.

"Was it a sexual relationship?"

He coloured even more and shifted his glance back to the courtyard.

"Not really."

"Not really?"

"Like I said. She wasn't very enthusiastic."

"But the two of you gave it a try? Is that right?"

"Yes, sort of. A couple of times."

"So it wasn't especially successful?"

Sejer sounded extremely kind as he asked the question.

"I don't know what you'd call successful."

His face was now so strained that it had lost all expression.

"Do you know whether she'd had sex with anyone else?"

"I have no idea, but it's hard for me to imagine that she did."

"So you and Annie were together for two years, meaning ever since she was 13. She broke up with you several times, she wasn't particularly interested in having sex with you – and yet you continued the relationship? You aren't exactly a child, Halvor. Are you really so patient?"

"I guess I am."

His voice was low and matter-of-fact, as if he were constantly wary of showing any emotion.

"Do you think you knew her well?"

"Better than a lot of people."

"Did she seem unhappy about anything?"

"Not exactly unhappy. More . . . I don't know. Maybe more sad."

"Is that something different? Being sad?"

"Yes," he said, looking up. "When someone is unhappy, he still hopes for something better. But when he gives up, sadness takes over."

Sejer listened with surprise to this explanation.

"When I met Annie two years ago, she was different," he said suddenly. "Joking and laughing with everybody. The opposite of me," he added.

"And then she changed?"

"All of a sudden she grew so tall. And then she became quieter. Not as playful any more. I waited, thinking that it might pass, that she'd be her old self again. Now there's nothing left to wait for."

He clasped his hands and stared at the floor; then he made an effort and met Sejer's gaze. His eyes were as shiny as wet stones. "I don't know what you're thinking, but I didn't do anything to hurt Annie."

"We're not thinking anything. We're talking to everyone. You understand?"

"Yes."

"Did Annie drink or take drugs?"

Skarre shook his pen to get the ink down to the tip.

"Don't make me laugh! You're way off the mark."

"Well," Sejer said, "I didn't know her."

"I'm sorry, but it just sounded so ridiculous."

"What about you?"

"It would never occur to me."

Good heavens, Sejer thought. A sober, hard-working young man with a steady job. This certainly looks promising.

"Do you know any of Annie's friends? Anette Horgen, for instance?"

"A little. But we were mostly alone. Annie sort of wanted us to keep to ourselves."

"Why was that?"

"Don't know. But she's the one who decided."

"And you did what she wanted?"

"It wasn't difficult. I don't care much for crowds myself."

Sejer nodded sympathetically. Maybe they were compatible after all.

"Do you know whether Annie kept a diary?"

Halvor hesitated for a moment, stopped an impulse at the last moment, and shook his head. "You mean one of those pink, heart-shaped books with a padlock?"

"Not necessarily. It might not have been that sort of thing."

"I don't think so," he muttered.

"But you're not sure?"

"Well, fairly sure. She never mentioned one." Now his voice was barely audible.

"Do you have anyone to talk to?"

"I have my grandmother."

"You're close to her?"

"She's OK. It's quiet and peaceful here."

"Do you own a blue anorak, Halvor?"

"No."

"What do you wear when you go outdoors?"

"A denim jacket. Or a padded jacket if it's cold."

"Will you call me if there's anything you want to talk about?"

"Why should I do that?" He looked up in surprise.

"Let me rephrase that. Will you call the station if you happen to think of anything, anything at all, that you think might explain Annie's death?"

"Yes."

Sejer looked around the room to memorise it. His eyes rested on the Madonna. It looked nicer than it had at first glance.

"That's a beautiful statue. Did you buy it in the south?"

"It was a gift from Father Martin. I'm Catholic," he said.

Sejer looked at him more intently. There was something remote and tense about him, as if he were guarding something they weren't allowed to see. They might have to force him to open up, put him in boiling water like a clam. The thought fascinated him.

"So, you're a Catholic?"

"Yes."

"Forgive my curiosity – but what attracted you to that particular faith?"

"It's obvious. Absolution of sins. Forgiveness."

Sejer nodded. "But aren't you rather young?" He stood up and smiled. "Surely you haven't managed to commit many sins, have you?"

The question hung in the air.

"I've had a few evil thoughts."

Sejer did a quick survey of his own thoughts. "What you've told us will be verified, of course. We do that with everyone. And we'll be in touch."

He gave the boy a firm handshake. Tried to give him good thoughts. They went back through the kitchen, which smelled faintly of boiled vegetables. In the living room the old woman was sitting in a rocking chair, wrapped up warmly in a blanket. She gave them a frightened look as they passed. Outside stood the motorcycle covered with plastic. A black Suzuki.

"Are you thinking the same thing I am?" Skarre asked as they drove off.

"Probably. He didn't ask us a single question. Someone has murdered his girlfriend, and he didn't seem the least bit curious. But that might not mean anything."

"It's still strange."

"Maybe it didn't really sink in until right now, as we drove away."

"Or maybe he knows what happened to her. That's why it didn't occur to him."

"The anorak we found, it would be too big for Halvor, don't you think?"

"The sleeves were turned up."

It was late afternoon, and they needed a break. They drove back, putting the village behind them and leaving its residents to their shock and their own thoughts. In Krystallen people were dashing across the street, doors were opening and closing, phones were ringing. People were rummaging through drawers for old pictures. Annie's name was on everyone's lips. The first tiny rumours were being conceived in the glow of candles, and then spreading like weeds from house to house. Drinks appeared on the tables. A state of emergency existed on the short street.

Raymond, meanwhile, was preoccupied with other things. He was sitting at the kitchen table, gluing pictures into a book about Tommy and Tiger, and Pip and Sylvester. The ceiling light was on, his father was taking an afternoon nap, the radio was playing requests. "And now here's one for Glenn Kåre, with a happy birthday from his grandmother." Raymond listened and sniffed at the glue stick, enjoying the delicious scent of

119

essence of almonds. He didn't notice the man staring at him intently through the window.

Halvor closed the door to the kitchen and switched on his computer. He logged on to the hard drive and stared pensively at the rows of files: games, tax forms, budgets, address lists, a database of his CD collection, and other trivial items. But there was one other thing. A file labelled "Annie", the contents of which were unknown to him. He sat there, staring at it while he pondered for a while. By double-clicking the mouse the files would open, one after the other, and a second later their contents would appear on the screen. But there were exceptions. He had a file marked "Personal". To open it he had to enter a password. The same was true of Annie's file. He had taught her how to protect it from anyone else, quite a simple procedure. He had no idea what password she had chosen or what the file might contain. She had insisted on keeping it secret, giving a little laugh when she saw his disappointment. So he'd shown her how to do it, and then he'd left and sat in the living room while she entered her password. He double-clicked anyway and immediately received the message: "Access denied. Password required."

Now he was going to open it. This was all he had

left of her. What if there was something about him in there, something that might be dangerous? Maybe it was some kind of diary. It's an impossible job, of course, he thought, staring in bewilderment at the keyboard where ten numbers, 29 letters, and a whole series of various symbols offered more possible combinations than he could even imagine. He tried to relax, and suddenly he realised that for his own password he had chosen a name. The name of a legendary woman who was burned at the stake and later declared a saint. It was the perfect choice, and not even Annie would have thought of it. Maybe she had chosen a date. It was very common to choose a birth-date, maybe of a close friend. He sat for a moment and stared at the file: just a modest little grey square with her name on it. She hadn't intended for him to open it, she had put a lock on it to keep it secret. But now she was gone, so the same rules no longer applied. Perhaps it contained something that would explain why she was the way she was. So damned inscrutable.

All his reservations crumbled and settled like dust in the corners. He was alone now, with an endless amount of time and nothing with which to fill it. As he sat there in the dimly lit room, staring at the glowing screen, he felt very close to Annie. He decided to begin with numbers –

birth-dates, social security numbers. He had a few of them memorised: Annie's, his own, his grandmother's. The others he could get. It was somewhere to begin. Of course she might have chosen a word. Or several words, maybe a saying or a familiar quote, or maybe even a name. It was going to be a tedious job. He didn't know if he would ever find it, but he had plenty of time and lots of patience.

He started with her birthday, which of course she hadn't chosen: March 3, 1980, zero three zero three one nine eight zero. Then the same numbers backwards.

"Access denied," flashed up on the screen. Suddenly his grandmother was standing in the doorway.

"What did they say?" she asked, leaning against the doorframe.

He gave a start and straightened up.

"Nothing much. They just asked me a few questions."

"Yes, but it's all so terrible, Halvor! Why is she dead?"

He stared at her mutely. "Eddie said they found her in the woods. Up by Serpent Tarn."

"But why is she dead?"

"They didn't say," he whispered. "I forgot to ask."

*

Sejer and Skarre had taken over the lecture room in the courthouse. They closed the curtains and shut out most of the light. The video had been rewound to the beginning. Skarre was ready with the remote control.

The soundproofing in this hastily erected annexe was far from satisfactory. They could hear phones ringing and doors slamming, voices, laughter, cars roaring past in the street and a drunk bellowing from the courtyard outside. But at least the sounds were muted, marked by the waning hours of the day.

"What in the world is that?"

Skarre leaned forward. "Someone running. It looks like Grete Waitz. Could be the New York Marathon."

"Maybe he gave us the wrong tape."

"I don't think so. Stop there. I saw some islands and skerries."

The picture hopped and jumped for a moment before it settled and focused on two women in bikinis, lying on rocks.

"Sølvi and her mother," Sejer said.

Sølvi was lying on her back with one knee bent. Her sunglasses were pushed up on her head, perhaps to avoid getting white circles around her eyes. Her mother was partially covered by a newspaper, the *Aftenposten*, judging by its size.

Next to her lay magazines and suntan lotion and thermos bottles, along with several large towels and a portable radio.

The camera had been aimed long enough on the two sun worshippers. Now the lens turned towards the shoreline further away, and a tall, blonde girl came walking along from the right. She was carrying a windsurfer on her head and was facing away from the camera. Her gait was not in the least provocative, her sole aim was to keep going, and she didn't slow down even when the water reached her knees. They could hear the roar of the waves, quite loud, suddenly pierced by the sound of her father's voice.

"Smile, Annie!"

She waded on, further and further into the water, ignoring his request. Then she finally turned around, though it took some effort under the weight of the board. For several seconds she stared straight at Sejer and Skarre. Her blonde hair was caught by the wind and fluttered around her ears, a quick smile flitted across her lips. Skarre looked into her grey eyes and felt the goosebumps rise on his arms as he watched the long-legged girl striding into the waves. She was wearing a black bathing suit, the kind that swimmers wear, with the straps crossed over her shoulder-blades, and a blue life-vest.

"That board isn't for beginners," he said.

Sejer didn't reply. Annie was still walking out into the water. Then she stopped, got on to the board, grabbed the sail with strong hands, and found her balance. The board made a 180° turn and picked up speed. The men were silent as Annie sailed out. She swept through the waves like a pro. Her father followed her with the camera. They became the father's eyes now, watching his own daughter through the lens. He tried hard to hold it still, mustn't shake too much, had to grant the windsurfer the greatest possible respect. Through the images they could feel his pride, what he must have felt for her. She was in her element. She wasn't the least bit afraid of falling and ending up in the water.

And then she vanished, and they were staring at a table that had been set with a flowered tablecloth, plates and glasses, polished silverware, wildflowers in a vase. Pork chops, hot dogs, bacon on a platter. The barbecue glowing nearby. Sunlight glinting on bottles of coke and Farris. Sølvi and her mother again, chattering in the background, the tinkling of ice-cubes, and there was Annie pouring a coke. Once more she turned around slowly, with a bottle in her hand, and asked the camera: "Coke, Papa?"

She had a surprisingly deep voice. In the next

instant they were inside the cabin. Mrs Holland was standing at the kitchen counter, slicing a cake.

Coke, Papa. Her voice was terse and yet gentle. Annie had loved her father, they could hear that in the two little words; they heard warmth and respect – as apparent as the difference between juice and red wine in a glass. Her voice had depth and vibrancy. Annie was her daddy's girl.

The rest of the video flickered past. Annie and her mother playing badminton, out of breath in a wind that was much too strong, great for windsurfing but merciless to a shuttlecock. The family gathered around the table indoors, playing Trivial Pursuit. A close-up of the board clearly showed who was winning, but it wasn't Annie. She didn't say much; Sølvi and her mother talked all the time, Sølvi in a sweet, fragile voice, her mother's voice deeper and hoarser. Skarre blew his cigarette smoke down towards his knees and felt older than he had done for a long time. The tape flickered a little and then a ruddy face appeared with a gaping mouth. An impressive tenor voice filled the room.

"No man shall sleep," Sejer said in English and stood up with some effort.

"What did you say?"

"Luciano Pavarotti. He's singing Puccini. Put the tape in the file," he added.

"She was good at windsurfing," Skarre said with awe.

The phone rang before Sejer could reply. Skarre picked it up, grabbing a notepad and pencil at the same time. It was an automatic response. He believed in three things in this world: thoroughness, zeal and good humour. Sejer read along as he wrote: Henning Johnas, 4 Krystallen. 12.45 p.m. Horgen's Shop. Motorcycle.

"Can you come down to the station?" Skarre said. "No? Then we'll come to you. This is very important information. Thanks for calling. That's fine."

He hung up.

"One of the neighbours. Henning Johnas. He lives at number 4. Just got home and heard about Annie. He picked her up at the roundabout yesterday and let her out near Horgen's Shop. He says there was a motorcycle there. It was waiting for her."

Sejer perched on the edge of the table. "That motorcycle again, the one Horgen saw. And Halvor has a motorcycle," he said. "Why couldn't the man come here?"

"His dog is about to have puppies."

Skarre put the piece of paper in his pocket. "It might be hard for Halvor to verify how long he was out on his motorcycle. I hope he isn't the one who did it. I liked him."

"A killer is a killer," Sejer said. "And sometimes they're quite nice."

"Yes," Skarre said, "but it's easier to lock someone up if we can't stand his ugly face."

Johnas stuck his hand under the dog's stomach and pressed gently. She was breathing hard and her tongue was hanging out of her mouth, a moist pink tongue. She lay very still and let him touch her. It wouldn't be long now. He stared out the window, hoping it would soon be over.

"Good girl, Hera," he said, petting her.

The dog stared past him, unmoved by his praise, so he sank down on to the floor a short distance away. Sat there and watched her. The silent, patient animal had his full attention. There was never any trouble with Hera, she was always obedient and kind as an angel. Never left his side when they went out for a walk, ate the food he gave her, and padded quietly over to her corner when he went upstairs to bed at night. He would have liked to sit there like that, very close, until it was all over, just listening to her breathe. Perhaps nothing would happen until early morning. He wasn't tired. Then the doorbell rang, one brief, shrill ring. He got up and opened the door.

Sejer gave him a firm, dry handshake. The man radiated authority. The younger officer was different, a thin, boyish hand with slender fingers. Johnas invited them in.

"How's it going with your dog?" Sejer asked. A nice-looking Dobermann lay motionless on a black and crimson Oriental rug. Surely nobody would let a pregnant dog lie on a genuine Oriental rug, he thought. The dog was breathing hard, but otherwise she lay without moving, not even aware of the two strangers who had come into the room.

"It's her first time. Three pups, I think. I tried to count them. But it'll go fine. There's never any trouble with Hera."

He looked at them and shook his head. "I'm so upset about what happened that I can't concentrate on anything."

Johnas glanced at the dog as he talked, running a powerful hand over the top of his head, which was bald. A fringe of brown curls ringed his skull, and he had unusually dark eyes. A man of average build, but with a powerful torso and a few extra kilos around his waist, possibly in his late thirties. As a younger man he might have looked like a darker version of Skarre. He had handsome features and good colouring, as if he had been in the south lately.

"You don't want to buy a pup, do you?"

He gave them a look of appeal.

"I've got a Leonberger," Sejer said. "And I don't think he'd forgive me if I came home with a puppy in tow. He's very spoiled."

Johnas directed them to the sofa, and pulled the coffee table out so the two men could slip past. "I met Fritzner by the garage this evening, as I was coming back from a trade fair in Oslo. He told me about it. I don't think it's really sunk in yet. I shouldn't have let her out of the car, I shouldn't have done that."

He rubbed his eyes and glanced at the dog again.

"Annie came here often. She baby-sat for us. I know Sølvi too. If it had been her," he said in a low voice, "I could better understand it. Sølvi is more the type that would take off with someone if she got an invitation, even if she didn't know him. Doesn't think about anything but boys. But Annie . . ."

He looked at them. "Annie wasn't all that interested. And she was very cautious. And besides, I believe she had a boyfriend."

"That's right, she did. Do you know him?"

"No, no, not at all. But I've seen them in the street, from a distance. They seemed shy, weren't even holding hands."

He smiled rather sadly at the thought.

"Where were you headed when you picked up Annie?"

"I was going to work. For a while it looked as if Hera was going to have the puppies, but then there was another delay."

"When does your shop open?"

"At 11 a.m."

"That's rather late, isn't it?"

"Yes, well, people need milk and bread in the morning, but Persian carpets come later, after their more basic needs have been satisfied." He gave an ironic smile. "I have a carpet shop," he explained. "Downtown, on Cappelens Gaten."

Sejer nodded. "Annie was going over to Anette Horgen's to work on a school assignment. Did she mention that to you?"

"A school assignment?" he said. "No, she didn't mention it."

"But she had a book bag with her?"

"Yes, she did. But that might have been a cover for something else, how would I know? She was going to Horgen's Shop, that's all I can tell you."

"What did you see?"

"Annie came running down the steep slope at the roundabout, so I pulled over into the bus stop and asked her if she wanted a lift. She was going to Horgen's after all, and that's quite a distance. Not that she was lazy or anything; Annie was very active. She was always out running. I'm sure she was very fit. But she got in anyway and asked me to put her down at the shop. I thought she was going there to buy something, or maybe to meet someone. I let her out and drove off. But I saw the motorcycle. It was parked next to the shop, and the last I saw of her, Annie was heading right towards it. I mean, I don't know for sure that he was waiting for her, and I didn't see who he was. I just saw that she made a beeline for the bike, and she didn't turn around."

"What kind of bike was it?" Sejer asked.

Johnas threw out his hands. "I realise you have to ask, but I don't know much about bikes. I'm in a whole different line of work, to put it mildly. For me it was just chrome and steel."

"What about the colour?"

"Aren't all bikes black?"

"Definitely not," he said.

"It wasn't bright red, at any rate, I would have remembered that."

"Was it a big, powerful bike, or a smaller one?" Skarre said.

"I think it was big."

"And the driver?"

"There wasn't a lot to see. He was wearing a helmet. There was something red on the helmet, that much I remember. And he didn't look like a grown man. He was probably a young guy."

Sejer nodded and leant forward. "You've seen her boyfriend. He has a motorcycle. Could it have been him?"

Now Johnas frowned as if on his guard. "I've seen him walk past in the street, from a distance. But this person was a long way off, wearing a helmet. I can't say whether it was him. I don't even want to suggest that."

"Not that it *was* him." Sejer's eyes narrowed. "Just that it *might* have been him. You say he was young. Was he of slight build?"

"That's not easy to tell when a person's wearing leathers," he said.

"But why did you assume he was young?"

"Oh," he said in confusion, "what can I say? I suppose I made that assumption because Annie's young. Or maybe there was something about the way he was sitting." He looked embarrassed. "I didn't know that it was going to turn out to be so important."

He got up and knelt down by the dog. "You have to try and understand what it's like living in this place," he said, upset. "Rumours spread fast. And besides, I can't believe that her boyfriend would do anything like that. He's just a boy, and they'd been together for a long time."

"Leave the judgements to us," Sejer said. "That motorcycle is important, of course, and another witness saw it too. If he's innocent he won't be convicted."

"Is that right?" Johnas said, doubtfully. "No, but it's bad enough being a suspect, I would think. If I say that he looked like her boyfriend, then I'm sure you're going to put him through hell. And the truth is that I have no idea who it was."

He shook his head sharply. "All I saw was someone wearing a leather outfit and a helmet. It could have been anybody. I have a 17-year-old son; it could have been him. I wouldn't have recognised him in that get-up. See what I mean?"

"Yes, I see," Sejer said. "You've answered my question anyway. It could have been him. And when it comes to that hell you mentioned, he's probably in it already."

Johnas swallowed hard.

"What did you and Annie talk about in the car?"

"She didn't say much. I passed the time talking about Hera and her pups."

"Did she seem anxious or nervous about anything?"

"Not at all. She was the same as always."

Sejer looked around the living room and noticed that it was sparsely furnished, as if he hadn't finished decorating. But there were plenty of carpets, both on the floor and on the walls, big Oriental carpets that looked expensive. Two photographs hung on the wall; one was of a tow-headed boy about two years old, the other was of a teenager.

"Are those your sons?" Sejer pointed, to change the subject.

"Yes," he said. "But not recent photographs."

He went back to petting the dog, stroking her black, silky-soft ears and damp snout.

"I live alone now," he added. "Finally found myself an apartment in town, on Oscarsgaten. This place is too big for me. I haven't seen much of Annie lately. I think she was a little upset when my wife left. And there weren't kids to take care of any more."

"And you sell Oriental carpets?"

"I deal mostly with Turkey and Pakistan. Occasionally Iran, but they tend to hike the prices. I take a trip to southern Europe a couple of times a year and stay for several weeks. Take my time. People there are getting to know me," he said with satisfaction. "I've made some good contacts. That's the important thing, you know, to develop a relationship of trust. They've had rather mixed experiences with the West."

Skarre manoeuvred his way past the coffee table and went over to the far wall which was almost entirely covered by a large carpet, from floor to ceiling.

"That one's a Turkish Smyrna," Johnas said.

"One of the most beautiful ones I own. I really can't afford to have it. Two and a half million knots. Incomprehensible, isn't it?"

Skarre looked at the carpet. "Is it true that they're made by children?" he asked.

"Often, yes, but not mine. It's bad for the reputation of the business. You may not like it, but the fact is that children make the finest carpets. Grown-up fingers are too thick."

They stood gazing at the carpet, at all the geometric shapes, one inside the other, getting smaller and smaller, an almost endless number of nuances in colour.

"Is it true that the children are chained to the looms?" Sejer said.

Johnas shook his head, resigned.

"It sounds appalling when you put it that way. The children with weaving jobs are the lucky ones. A good weaver has food and clothing and warmth. He has a life. If they are chained to the looms, it's at the behest of their parents. Often a young weaver supports a whole family of five or six people. He saves his mother and sisters from prostitution, and his father and brothers from becoming beggars or thieves."

"I've heard it just postpones things," Sejer said. "By the time they grow up and their fingers are too thick, they're often blind or have weak eyes from labouring over a loom. They can't work at all, and so they end up being beggars just the same."

Johnas smiled "You've been watching too much TV. You should go there yourself. The weavers are happy little people, and they enjoy great respect among the populace. It's that simple. But we have to help the rich maintain their moral standards; no one is more sensitive than they are when it comes to things like this. That's why I avoid child labour. If you ever want to buy a carpet, come over to Cappelens Gaten," he said eagerly. "I'll see you get a good deal."

"I doubt it's within my price range."

"Why is it discoloured?" Skarre asked.

Johnas had to smile a bit at such complete ignorance; at the same time he livened up, as if talking about his great passion was like a puff of air on a dying ember. His enthusiasm swelled. "It's a nomad carpet."

That didn't tell Skarre anything at all.

"The nomads are always on the move, right? It might take them a year to make such a large carpet. And they dye the wool using plants, which they have to gather during different seasons, in shifting terrain, in varying conditions. This blue here," he said, pointing at the carpet, "is from the indigo plant. And the red is from the madder plant. But inside the hexagon there's a different red that is made from crushed insects. This orange colour is henna, the yellow is saffron."

He placed his hand on the carpet and stroked downward. "This is a Turkish rug, made with Gordian knots. Every square centimetre has approximately a hundred knots."

"Who designs the patterns?"

"They weave them from patterns that are centuries old, and many have never even been sketched out. The old weavers walk around the workshop, singing the patterns to the younger weavers."

The old blind weavers, Sejer thought.

"Here in the West," Johnas said, "it's taken us a long time to discover this handwork. Traditionally we prefer figurative patterns, something that tells a story. That's why carpets with hunting and gardening patterns were the first to catch our attention, because they include flower and animal motifs. Personally I prefer this type. First the wide outer border that holds everything in place. Then your eye moves further and further in, until at last you come to the treasure, in a sense." He pointed to the medallion in the centre of the rug.

"Forgive me," he said all of sudden. "Here I am, rattling on about me and my interests." He looked embarrassed.

"The helmet," Skarre said, tearing himself away. "Was it a half or a whole helmet?"

"Is there such a thing as a half helmet?" Johnas asked, surprised.

"A whole helmet has a piece that fits over the jaw and cheek. An ordinary helmet covers only the skull."

"I didn't notice."

"What about the leather suit. Was it black?"

"Dark, at any rate. It didn't occur to me to study him. There's something completely normal about watching a pretty girl cross the road and head towards a guy on a motorcycle. It's as though that's the way things should be, don't you think?"

They thanked him and paused a moment at the door. "We'll probably be back; I hope you understand."

"Of course. If the puppies come tonight, I'll be home for a few days."

"Can you leave the shop closed?"

"My customers call me at home if there's something they want."

Hera gave a heavy sigh and whined plaintively, lying there on her Oriental rug. Skarre gave her a long look and then reluctantly followed his boss.

"Maybe we'll get to see them if we come back," he said. "The pups, I mean."

"No doubt," Johnas said.

"Don't come back," Sejer said. He was thinking about his own dog, Kollberg.

"Do you remember Halvor's helmet? The one he had hanging up in his room?"

They were sitting in the car.

"A whole helmet, black with a red stripe," Sejer said. "I guess we can call it a night now. And I have to take the dog for a walk."

"What do you think, Konrad? Do you have as much passion for your job as Johnas does?"

Sejer looked at him. "Of course. But maybe you don't think it shows?"

He fastened his seatbelt and started the engine. "I find it annoying when people gag themselves, in a show of solidarity for someone they don't even know, because they're convinced that he's an honourable person."

He thought about Halvor and felt a little sad. "Up until the day someone kills for the first time, he's not a murderer. He's just an ordinary person. But afterwards, when the neighbours find out that he actually did commit murder, then he's a murderer for the rest of his life, and from then on he's going to kill people right and left, like some kind of killing machine. Then they hug their children close, and nothing feels safe any more."

Skarre gave him a searching look. "So now Halvor is in the spotlight?"

"Of course. He was her boyfriend. But I wonder why Johnas wanted so badly to protect a boy he has only seen from a distance."

CHAPTER 5

Ragnhild Album bent over the paper and started drawing. The notebook was new, and she had opened it reverently to the first untouched page. A car in a cloud of dust might not, in a sense, be worthy of the task that was going to rob the notebook of its chalk-white purity. The box held six different crayons. Sejer had been out shopping: one box for Ragnhild and one for Raymond. Today she had two pigtails on top of her head, pointing straight up like antennae.

"I like the way you've fixed your hair today," he said.

"With this one," said her mother, tugging on one pigtail, "she can get Operation White Wolf in Narvik, and with the other she gets her grandmother, who lives way up north on Svalbard."

He had to laugh.

"She says it was just a cloud of dust," she went on, anxiously.

"She says it was a car," said Sejer. "It's worth a try."

He put his hand on the child's shoulder. "Close your eyes," he said, "and try to picture it. Then draw it as best you can. And not just any old car. You should draw the car that you and Raymond saw."

"I know," she said impatiently.

He ushered Mrs Album out of the kitchen and into the living room so Ragnhild could draw in peace. Mrs Album went over to the window and looked at the blue mountains in the distance. It was a hazy day, and the landscape might have come straight out of an old romantic painting.

"Annie took care of Ragnhild for me lots of times," she said. "And whenever she baby-sat, she did a good job. That was a few years ago now. They would take the bus to town and stay out all day. Ride the train at the market, ride up and down on the escalator and in the lift at the department store, things that Ragnhild liked doing. She had a natural talent with children. She was different. Thoughtful."

Sejer could hear the little girl taking crayons out of the box in the kitchen. "Do you know her sister too? Sølvi?"

"I know who she is. But she's only her half-sister."

"Oh?"

"Didn't you know that?"

"No, I didn't."

"Everyone knows," she said. "It's not a secret or anything. They're very different. For a while they had difficulties with her father. Sølvi's father, I mean. He lost his visitation rights, and apparently he's never got over it."

"Why?"

"The usual trouble. Drunk and violent. That's the mother's version, of course, but Ada Holland is hard to take, so I'm not sure how much is true."

"But Sølvi is over 21 by now, isn't she? And can do what she wants?"

"It's probably too late. I dare say that things have probably gone sour between them. I've been thinking a lot about Ada," she said. "She didn't get her little girl back, the way I did."

"I'm done!" came a shout from the kitchen.

They got up and went in to have a look. Ragnhild was sitting with her head tilted, not looking especially pleased. A grey cloud filled most of the page, and out of the cloud stuck the front end of a car, with headlights and bumper. The bonnet was long, like on a big American car, the bumper was coloured black. It looked as if it had a big grin with no teeth. The headlights were slanted. Chinese eyes, Sejer thought.

"Did it make a lot of noise when it drove past?"

He leaned over the kitchen table and noticed the sweet smell of her chewing gum.

"It was really noisy."

He stared at the drawing. "Could you make me another drawing? If I ask you to draw the headlights on the car? Just the headlights?"

"But they looked just like this!" She pointed to the drawing. "They were slanted."

He nodded, as if to himself. "What about the colour, Ragnhild?"

"Well, it wasn't really grey. But there wasn't much to choose from here," she said precociously, shaking the box of crayons. "It was a colour that doesn't exist."

"What do you mean?"

"Well, I mean a colour that doesn't have a name."

A string of colours swirled through his mind: sienna, petrol, sepia, anthracite.

"Ragnhild," he said, "can you remember if the car had anything on the roof?"

"Antennae?"

"No, something bigger. Raymond thought there was something big on top of the car."

She stared at him, thinking hard. "Yes!" she exclaimed. "A little boat."

"A boat?"

"A little black one."

"I don't know what I would have done without you," Sejer said, smiling, as he flicked his fingers at her antennae.

"Elise," he said, "you have a nice name."

"No one wants to call me that. Everyone calls me Ragnhild."

"But I can call you Elise."

She blushed shyly, put the lid on the box, closed up the notebook, and slid them over to him.

"No, they're yours to keep."

She opened the box at once and went back to drawing.

"One of the rabbits is lying on its side!"

Raymond was standing in the doorway to his father's room, rocking back and forth uneasily.

"Which one?"

"Caesar. The giant Belgian."

"Then you'll have to kill it."

Raymond got so scared that he farted. But the little release didn't make any difference in the stale air of the room.

"But it's breathing so hard!"

"We're not about to feed rabbits that are dying, Raymond. Put it on the chopping block. The axe is behind the door in the garage. Watch your hands!"

Raymond went outdoors and plodded dejectedly across the courtyard towards the rabbit cages. He stared at Caesar for a moment through the netting. It's lying there just like a baby, he thought, rolled up like a soft little ball. Its eyes were closed. It didn't move when he opened the cage and stuck his hand cautiously inside. It was just as warm as always. He took a firm grip of the skin on the scruff of its neck and lifted it out. It kicked half-heartedly, seeming to have little strength.

Afterwards he slumped in his chair at the kitchen table. In front of him lay an album with pictures of the national soccer team and birds and animals. He was looking very depressed when Sejer arrived. He was wearing nothing but tracksuit bottoms and slippers. His hair stood up from his head, his belly was soft and white. His round eyes looked sulky, and his lips were pursed, as if he were sucking hard on something.

"Hello, Raymond." Sejer gave a deep bow to appease him a bit. "Have I come at a bad time?"

"Yes, because I was just working on my collection, and now you're interrupting me."

"That can be awfully annoying. I can't imagine anything worse. But I wouldn't have come if I didn't have to, I hope you realise that."

"Yes, of course, yes."

He relaxed a little and went back to the kitchen. Sejer followed him and put the drawing materials on the table.

"I'd like you to draw something for me," he said.

"Oh no! Not on your life!"

He looked so worried that Sejer put his hand on Raymond's shoulder.

"I can't draw."

"Everybody can draw," Sejer said.

"Well, I can't draw people."

"You don't have to draw any people. Just a car."

"A car?"

Now he looked suspicious. His eyes narrowed and looked like ordinary eyes.

"The car that you and Ragnhild saw. The one that was driving so fast."

"You keep on talking about that car."

"That's true, but it's important. We've put out a bulletin, but no one has contacted us. Maybe he's a bad person, Raymond, and if he is, we have to catch him."

"But I told you it was driving too fast."

"You must have seen something," Sejer said, lowering his voice. "You noticed that it was a car, didn't you? Not a boat or a bike. Or a caravan of camels, for instance."

"Camels?" He laughed heartily, making his white belly quiver. "That would have been funny, seeing a bunch of camels going down the road! There weren't any camels. It was a car. With a ski-box on the roof."

"Draw it," Sejer commanded.

Raymond gave in. He sank on to a chair at the

148

table and stuck his tongue out, like a rudder. It only took a few minutes to realise that he had been right. His drawing looked like a piece of crispbread on wheels.

"Could you colour it too?"

Raymond opened the box, carefully examined all the crayons, and finally selected the red one. Then he concentrated hard, trying not to colour outside the lines.

"Red, Raymond?"

"Yes," he said brusquely, and kept on colouring.

"So the car was red? Are you sure? I thought you said it was grey."

"I said it was red."

Sejer pulled a stool out from under the table, and thought carefully before he spoke. "You said you couldn't remember the colour. But that it might have been grey, like Ragnhild said."

Raymond scratched his stomach, looking offended. "I remember things better after a while, you know. I told him that yesterday, the man who was here, I told him it was red."

"Who was that?"

"Just a man who was out walking and stopped in the courtyard. He wanted to see the rabbits. I talked to him."

Sejer felt a faint prickling on the back of his neck.

"Was it someone you know?"

"No."

"Can you tell me what he looked like?"

Raymond put down the red crayon and stuck out his lower lip. "No," he said.

"Don't you want to tell me?"

"It was just a man. And you won't like what I say, anyway."

"Please tell me. I'll help you. Fat or thin?"

"In between."

"Dark or light hair?"

"Don't know. He was wearing a cap."

"Is that right? A young man?"

"Don't know."

"Older than me?"

Raymond glanced up.

"Oh no, not as old as you. Your hair is all grey."

Thanks a lot, thought Sejer.

"I don't want to draw him."

"You don't have to. Did he come by car?"

"No, he was walking."

"When he left, did he head down the road or up towards Kollen?"

"Don't know. I went in to see to Papa. He was really nice," he said.

"I'm sure he was. What did he say to you, Raymond?"

"That I had great rabbits. And did I want to sell one if they ever had babies."

"Go on, go on."

"Then we talked about the weather. And how dry it's been. He asked me if I'd heard about the girl at the tarn and if I knew her."

"What did you tell him?"

"That I was the one who found her. He thought it was too bad the girl was dead. And I told him about you, that you had been here and asked me about the car. 'The car,' he said, 'that noisy one that's always driving too fast on the roads around here?' Yes, I told him. That's the one I saw. He knew which one it was. Said it was a red Mercedes. I must have been mistaken when you asked me before, because now I remember. The car was red."

"Did he threaten you?"

"No, no, I don't let anyone threaten me. A grown man doesn't let people threaten him. I told him that."

"What about his clothes, Raymond. What was he wearing?"

"Just ordinary clothes."

"Brown clothes? Or blue? Can you remember?"

Raymond gave him a confused look and hid his face in his hands. "Stop bothering me so much!"

Sejer let Raymond sit for a moment and calm down. Then he said, in a very soft voice, "But the car was really grey or green, wasn't it?"

"No, it was red. I told the truth, and there's no

use threatening me. Because the car was red, and that pleased him."

He bent over the paper and scribbled a little over the drawing. His lips were set in a stubborn line.

"Don't wreck it. I'd like to have it."

Sejer picked up the drawing. "How's your father?" he asked.

"He can't walk."

"I know. Let's go and see him."

He stood up and followed Raymond down the hall. They opened the door without knocking. The room was in semi-darkness, but there was more than enough light for Sejer to notice at once the old man standing next to the night table, wearing an old undershirt and underwear that were much too big. His knees were shaking perilously. He was just as gaunt as his son was round and stout.

"Papa!" cried Raymond. "What are you doing?"

"Nothing, nothing."

He fumbled for his false teeth.

"Sit down. You'll break a leg."

He was wearing support stockings, and at the top edge his knees were swollen like two pale bread puddings, with liver spots that resembled raisins.

Raymond helped him get back in bed and handed him his teeth. He avoided Sejer's gaze and stared up at the ceiling. His eyes were colourless, with tiny little pupils framed by long bushy eyebrows. He put his teeth in his mouth. Sejer went over and stood in front of him, looking up at the window, which faced the courtyard and road. The curtains were drawn, letting in only a minimum of light.

"Do you watch what goes on out on the road?" he asked.

"You're from the police?"

"Yes. You have a good view if you open the curtains."

"I never do that. Unless it's overcast."

"Have you noticed any strange cars around here, or motorcycles?"

"Could be. Police cars, for instance."

"Anyone on foot?"

"Hikers. They head up to Kollen, come hell or high water, to collect pebbles. Or they go and stare at that rotten tarn, which, by the way, is full of sheep carcasses. To each his own."

"Did you know Annie Holland?"

"I know her father from my days at the garage. He delivered cars, when there were any."

"You were in charge?"

He pulled up the comforter and nodded. "He had two girls. Blonde hair, pretty."

"Annie Holland is dead."

"I know that. I do read the paper, just like anybody else."

He gestured towards the floor where a thick

stack of papers was stuffed under the bedside table, along with something else, something gaudier, on glossy paper.

"A man was out in the courtyard here yesterday evening, talking to Raymond. Did you see him?"

"I heard them mumbling out there. Raymond may not be so quick-witted," he said sharply, "but he has no idea what malice is. Do you understand? He's so good-natured that you can lead him by a piece of string. But he does what he's told."

Raymond nodded eagerly and scratched his stomach.

Sejer looked into the colourless eyes. "I know that," he said. "So you heard them talking? You weren't tempted to pull the curtain aside a bit?"

"No."

"You aren't very curious, are you, Låke?"

"That's right, I'm not. We keep our eyes to ourselves, not on others."

"What if I told you that there's a tiny chance that the man in the courtyard is mixed up in the murder of the Holland girl – would you then realise how serious this is?"

"Even then. I didn't look outside, I was busy with the newspaper."

Sejer looked around the small room and shuddered. It didn't smell good, his kidneys probably didn't function properly. The room needed to be cleaned, the window should have been opened, and the old man should have a piping hot bath. He went out to get some fresh air, drawing in several deep breaths. Raymond trotted after him and stood with his arms crossed as Sejer got into his car.

"Have you got your car fixed, Raymond?"

"Papa says I need a new battery. But I can't afford it right now. Costs over 400 kroner. I don't drive on the roads," he said quickly. "At least almost never."

"That's good. Go on back inside, you'll catch cold."

"Yes," he said, and shivered. "And I gave my jacket away."

"That wasn't so smart, was it?" Sejer said.

"I felt like I had to," he said sadly. "She was lying there with nothing on."

"What did you say?"

Sejer looked at him in astonishment. The jacket on the body belonged to Raymond!

"Did you spread it over her?"

"She wasn't wearing any clothes at all," he said, kicking at the ground with his slipper.

He had imagined that she was cold and that someone should cover her up. The light-coloured hairs might be rabbit hair. He ate sweets. Sejer stared into his eyes, the eyes of a child, as pure as

155

spring water. But he had muscles, as heavy as Christmas hams. Involuntarily he shook his head.

"That was a kind thought," Sejer said. "Did you talk to each other?"

Raymond looked at him in surprise, and the angelic eyes shifted away a bit, as if he might have caught the scent of a trap.

"You said she was dead!"

Afterwards, when Sejer was gone, Raymond slipped out and peeked into the garage. Caesar was lying in a far corner under an old jumper, and he was still breathing.

Skarre finished going over the reports with a No. 5 Microball pen sticking out of the shoulder-strap on his shirt. He smiled with satisfaction, humming a few verses of "Jesus on the Line". Life was good, and a murder case was more exhilarating than armed robbery. It would soon be summer. And there stood his boss, waving a Krone ice cream bar at him. He put the papers quickly aside and took it.

"The anorak that was spread over the body belongs to Raymond," Sejer said.

Skarre was so startled that his ice cream slid sideways.

"But I believe him when he says that he put it there on his way back, after he took Ragnhild home. He spread it over her nicely because she was naked. I rang up Irene Album, and Ragnhild insists that it wasn't there when they went past the tarn. But . . . it's his jacket. We'll have to keep an eye on him. I told him that unfortunately he couldn't have it back right away, and he was so disappointed that I promised to give him an old one, one that I never wear. Find anything exciting?" he asked.

Skarre tore the rest of the paper wrapper off his ice cream bar. "I've run checks on all of the landlord's neighbours. They seem decent people for the most part, but a lot of speeding tickets have been given on that street."

Sejer licked strawberry ice cream from his upper lip.

"Out of 21 households, eight people have had one or more speeding tickets. That's way above the average."

"They have a long commute to work," Sejer said. "They work in the city, or at Fornebu Airport. There aren't any jobs in Lundeby."

"Precisely. But still. A respectable bunch with lots of speeders on the roads, all the same. But I found something else. Have a look at this." He leafed through the statements and pointed.

"Knut Jensvoll, 8 Gneisveien. Annie's handball coach. He served time for rape. Did 18 months, at Ullersmo."

Sejer bent down to look. "He may have managed

to keep that quiet. Better watch what you say when we're out there."

Skarre nodded and licked his ice cream. "Maybe we should bring in the whole team. Perhaps he's tried something on some of the girls. How did you get on? Did you bring back all the details of the suspicious car?"

Sejer sighed and pulled the drawings from his inside pocket.

"Ragnhild says the ski-box was blue. And Raymond's drawing is pretty funny. But what's more interesting is a hiker who was in Raymond's courtyard yesterday evening and seems to have tried to convince Raymond that the car was red."

He placed the drawing in front of him on the table.

Skarre's eyes grew big. "What? Could he describe . . ."

"Something in between," Sejer said laconically. "Wearing a cap. I didn't dare push him too hard, he gets so upset."

"I call that fast work."

"I call it bold, more than anything else," Sejer said. "But now we're talking about someone who knows who Raymond is. He was seen. He wanted to find out what Raymond saw. So we have to focus on the car. He must be very close to us, for God's sake."

"But to go to Raymond's house, that's pretty reckless. Do you think anyone else might have seen him?"

"I went to every house nearby. No one saw him. But if he came by way of Kollen, then the Låke house is the first one, and there's not much of a view of the courtyard from the farm below."

"What about the old man?"

"He says he heard them outside, and wasn't tempted to look out of his window."

They ate their ice creams in silence.

"Shall we forget about Halvor? And the motorcycle?"

"Absolutely not."

"When do we bring him in?"

"Tonight."

"Why wait?"

"It's quieter at night. You know, I talked to Ragnhild's mother while the girl was scribbling her crystal-clear evidence on the paper. Sølvi isn't Holland's daughter. And the biological father lost his visitation rights, apparently because of drunkenness and violence."

"Sølvi is 21, isn't she?"

"She is now. But evidently there have been years of painful conflicts."

"What are you getting at?"

"In a sense he lost his child. Now his ex-wife,

with whom he has a strained relationship, is going through the same thing. Maybe he wanted revenge. It's just a thought."

Skarre gave a low whistle. "Who is he?"

"That's what you're going to find out as soon as you're done with your ice cream. Then come over to my office. We'll leave the moment you locate him."

He left. Skarre punched in the Hollands' phone number and licked his ice cream as he waited.

"I don't want to talk about Axel," Mrs Holland said. "He just about destroyed us, and after all these years we're finally rid of him. If I hadn't taken him to court, he would have destroyed Sølvi."

"I'm only asking you for his name and address. This is just routine, Mrs Holland, there are thousands of things we have to check up on."

"He's never had anything to do with Annie. Thank God!"

"Please give me his name, Mrs Holland."

Finally she gave in. "Axel Bjørk."

"Do you have any other information?"

"I have it all. I have his social security number and his address. Provided he hasn't moved. I wish he *would* move. He lives too close, only an hour away by car."

She was getting more and more agitated.

Skarre took notes, and thanked her. Then he

switched on his computer and did a search for "Bjørk, Axel", thinking how paper-thin personal privacy had become, nothing but a transparent cloth that it was impossible to hide behind. He found the man with no trouble and began reading.

"God damn it all!" he exclaimed with a swift, apologetic glance up at the ceiling. He clicked on "Please Print" and leaned back in his chair. He picked up the page, read it again, and crossed the corridor to Sejer's office. The chief inspector was standing in front of the mirror with one of his shirt sleeves rolled up. He scratched his elbow and grimaced.

"I've run out of ointment," he said.

"I've got him. He's got a record, of course."

Skarre sat down and put the sheet of paper on the blotting pad.

"Well, let's have look. Bjørk, Axel, born 1948—"

"Police officer," said Skarre quietly.

Sejer didn't react. He read slowly through the report.

"Former officer. All right, but perhaps you'd rather stay here?"

"Of course not. But it *is* a little sensitive."

"We're no better than anyone else, now are we, Skarre? We'll have to hear the man's side of the story. You can count on it being different from Mrs Holland's version. So, we're going to have to take a trip to Oslo. He obviously does shift work, so there's a chance that we'll find him at home."

"Number 4 Sognsveien, that's in the Adamstuen district. The big red apartment building near the trolley stop."

"Do you know Oslo well?" Sejer asked, surprised.

"I drove a taxi there for two years."

"Is there anything you haven't done?"

"I've never done any skydiving."

CHAPTER 6

Skarre demonstrated his knowledge from his cab-driving days by directing Sejer to the shortest route, along Skøyen, left on Halvdan Svartes Gaten, past Vigeland Park, up Kirkeveien, and down Ullevålsveien. They parked illegally outside a beauty salon and found the name Bjørk on the third floor of a block of flats. They rang the bell and waited. No answer. A woman came out of a door further down the hall, clattering a rubbish bin and a long-handled broom.

"He went to the shop," she said. "Or at least he left with some empty bottles in a shopping bag. He shops at Rundingen, right next door."

They thanked her and went back outside. Got into their car and settled down to wait. Rundingen was a little grocery shop with pink-and-yellow sale signs in the windows, making it hard to see inside. People came and went, mostly women. Not until Skarre had smoked a cigarette with the window open and his arm hanging out did a man come out alone, wearing a thick checked lumberjack shirt and trainers. Through the open window they could hear a clinking sound from his bag. He was very tall and muscular, but he lost a good deal of his height by walking with his head bent, his fierce gaze fixed on the pavement. He didn't notice their car.

"Definitely looks like he could be a former colleague. Wait until he goes around the corner, then get out and see if he goes into the building."

Skarre waited, opened the door, and dashed around the corner. Then they waited two or three minutes before going back upstairs.

Bjørk's face in the half-open doorway was a study of muscles, nerves and ticks that made his dark face shift from one expression to another in seconds. First the open, neutral face that wasn't expecting anyone, sparked with curiosity. Then sizing up Skarre's uniform, a swift sweep through his memory to explain this uniformed person at his own door. The recollection of the newspaper story about the body at the tarn – and then the connection and what they must be thinking. The last expression, which stuck, was a bitter smile.

"Well," he said, opening the door wide. "If you hadn't turned up, I wouldn't have a particularly high opinion of modern detective work. Come on in. Is this the master and his apprentice?"

They ignored his remark and followed him

down the short corridor. The smell of alcohol was unmistakable.

Bjørk's apartment was a tidy little place with a spacious living room and sleeping alcove and a small kitchen facing the street. The furniture didn't match, as if it had been collected from several different places. On the wall above an old desk hung a picture of a little girl, about eight years old. Her hair was darker, but her features hadn't changed much over the years. It was Sølvi. Attached to one corner of the frame was a red bow.

They caught sight of a German shepherd, lying perfectly still in a corner, staring at them with watchful eyes. It hadn't moved or barked when they came into the room.

"What have you done with that dog?" Sejer said. "Something I obviously haven't managed to do with mine. He charges at people as soon as they set a foot in the door and carries on so they can hear him all the way down on the ground floor. And I live on the 13th."

"If that's the case, you're too attached to him," he said curtly. "You shouldn't treat a dog as if it's the only thing you have in the world. But maybe it is?"

He studied Sejer with narrowed eyes, aware that the rest of the conversation wasn't going to proceed in as friendly a tone. His hair was cut short, but unwashed and greasy, and he hadn't shaved in a while. A dark shadow covered the lower part of his face.

"So," he said after a moment, "you want to know whether I knew Annie, right?" He wriggled the words out of his mouth like a fishbone.

"She's been here several times, with Sølvi. No reason to hide that. Then Ada found out and put a halt to any kind of visiting. Sølvi actually liked coming here. I don't know what Ada has done to her, but it looks a lot like brainwashing. Now she's not interested any more. She's let Holland take over."

He rubbed his jaw and when they didn't say anything, he continued.

"Maybe you were thinking that I killed Annie to take revenge? Let me assure you I didn't. I have nothing against Eddie Holland, and I wouldn't want even my worst enemy to lose a child. I don't have the energy left to fight, but I admit that the thought did cross my mind, of course, that now she knows what it's like, that prudish old hag, what it's like to lose a child. Now she knows what it feels like, goddammit. But now my chances of contacting Sølvi are even slimmer. Ada will keep close tabs on her. And I would never put myself in that situation."

Sejer sat motionless and listened. Bjørk's voice was angry and sharp as acid.

"Where was I at the time in question? She was found on Monday, wasn't she? Sometime in the middle of the day, if I remember rightly. So here's my answer: in my apartment, no alibi. Most likely I was drunk, I usually am when I'm not at work. Do I get violent? Absolutely not. It's true that I hit Ada, but she was asking for a good smack in the face. That's what she wanted. She knew that if she got me to cross the line, she would have something to take to court. I hit her once, with my fist. It was pure impulse, the only time in my whole life that I've actually hit someone. I was extremely unlucky, I hit her hard and broke her jaw and several teeth, and Sølvi was sitting on the floor and saw it all. Ada had set the whole thing up. She put Sølvi's toys on the floor in the living room so that she would be sitting there, watching us, and she had filled the refrigerator with beer. Then she started arguing, she was very good at that. And she didn't give up until I exploded. I walked right into the trap."

Beneath the bitterness there was a kind of relief, perhaps because someone was finally listening.

"How old was Sølvi when you divorced?"

"She was five. Ada had already taken up with Holland, and she wanted Sølvi to herself."

"That's an awfully long time ago. You haven't been able to put it all behind you?"

"You don't leave your child behind."

Sejer bit his lip. "You were suspended?"

"I started drinking too much. Lost my wife and child, my job and my house, and the respect of nearly everybody. Actually," he said with a bitter smile, "it wouldn't really make much difference, one way or the other, if I turned into a killer. It really wouldn't."

He smiled, a sudden devilish glint in his eye. "But then I would have acted at once, not waited all these years. And to be quite honest, Ada is the one I would have chosen to throttle."

"What did the two of you fight about?" Skarre asked.

"We fought about Sølvi."

He crossed his arms and stared out the window, as if his memories were parading past in the street outside. "Sølvi is a little different, she's always been like that. I'm sure you've met her, so you've seen how she's turned out in life. Ada always wanted to protect her. She's not very independent, may even be a little slow. Abnormally obsessed with boys and her appearance. Ada wants her to find a husband as fast as possible, someone who will take care of her. I've never seen anyone steer a girl so wrongly. I tried to explain that what she needs is exactly the opposite –

she needs self-confidence. I wanted to take her on fishing trips and things like that, teach her to chop wood, play soccer, sleep in a tent. She needs physical exercise, needs to get her hair mussed up without panicking. Right now she slouches around in a beauty salon, looking at herself in the mirror all day. Ada accused me of having some kind of complex. Said I really wanted a son and never could accept the fact that we had a girl. We fought all the time," he sighed. "All the years we were married. And we've kept on fighting ever since."

"How do you make your living now?"

Bjørk stared at Sejer with a gloomy expression. "I'm sure you already know that. I work for a private security company. Run around at night with a dog and a torch. It's okay. Not much action, of course, but I guess I've had my share."

"When was the last time the girls were here?"

He rubbed his forehead, as if he were trying to dredge up the date from the depths of his mind. "Sometime last autumn. Annie's boyfriend was here too."

"So you haven't seen the girls since then?"

"No."

"Did you go out to see her?"

"Several times, and each time Ada called the police, claiming that I was trying to force my way in. That I was standing at the door and making threats. I'd have had problems at work if there was any more trouble, so I had to give up."

"What about Holland?"

"Holland's all right. Actually, I suspect he thinks it's a nasty business, but he's a wimp. Ada has got him by the balls, she really has. He does what he's told, and so they never fight. You've talked to them, I'm sure you've seen the set-up."

He got up suddenly and went over to stand by the window with his back to them, pulling himself up to his full height.

"I don't know what happened to Annie," he said in a low voice. "But I would have understood it better if something had happened to Sølvi. She's so unbelievably gullible."

Sejer wondered why everyone said that. As if the whole thing were a big misunderstanding, and Annie had been killed by mistake.

"Do you own a motorcycle, Bjørk?"

"No, I don't," he said. "I had one when I was younger. Kept it in a friend's garage, but I finally sold it. A Honda 750. I only have the helmet left."

"What kind of helmet?"

"It's hanging in the hallway."

Skarre peered into the hall and caught sight of the helmet, a full helmet, all black, with a smoke-coloured visor.

"A car?"

"I only drive the Peugeot from the security company. I've made an important discovery," he said, looking at them. "I've seen the mother-child phenomenon up close. It's a kind of holy pact that no one can break. It would be more difficult to separate Ada and Sølvi than to pull Siamese twins apart with your bare hands."

The image made Sejer blink.

"I have to be honest with you," he continued. "I hate Ada, and I don't feel like hiding it. And I know what the worst possible thing would be for her. It would be for Sølvi to grow up enough to fully understand what happened, so that sooner or later she would dare to defy Ada and come here. So we could have a father-daughter relationship, what we were always meant to have, and what we're both entitled to. A proper relationship. That would take the wind out of her sails."

He suddenly looked worn out. A tram thundered past outside, its bell clanging, and Sejer stared at the picture of Sølvi again. He tried to imagine his own life taking a different turn. What if Elise had ended up hating him and had moved out, taking Ingrid with her, even winning a court ruling forbidding them from seeing each other? The thought made him dizzy.

"So," he said softly, "Annie Holland was the kind of girl you wish Sølvi had been?"

"Yes, in a way. She's independent and strong. Was," he said, and turned around. "This is god-damned awful. I hope for Eddie's sake that you find the bastard who did it, I really do."

"For Eddie's sake? Not for Ada's?"

"No," he said fervently. "Not for Ada's sake."

"Quite an eloquent man, wasn't he?"

Sejer started the car.

"Do you believe him?" Skarre asked, signalling for him to turn right at Rundingen.

"I don't know. But there was a lot of despair behind that gruff mask of his, and it seemed genuine. I'm sure there are mean and calculating women in the world. And women do have a kind of first claim to their children. It must be bitter to be slapped with something like that, accusations that it won't do any good to deny. Maybe it really does have to be that way," he said as he steered the car away from the tram tracks. "Perhaps it's a bio-logical phenomenon that's supposed to protect the children. A real bond with the mother that is totally unbreakable."

"Jesus!" Skarre listened, shaking his head. "You've got a child – do you really believe what you're saying?"

"No, I'm just thinking out loud. What do you think?"

"I don't have any children!"

"But you have parents, don't you?"

"Yes, I have parents. And I'm afraid that I'm an incurable mama's boy."

"I am too," Sejer said.

Eddie Holland left the accounting offices, said a few words to his secretary, and left. After driving for 20 minutes, he pulled the green Toyota into a large car park. He turned off the engine and sank back against the seat. After a moment, he closed his eyes and stayed like that, quite still, waiting for something that would make him turn around and drive back without completing his mission. Nothing happened.

After a while he opened his eyes and looked around. It was a beautiful place, of course. There was a good-sized building, nestled in the landscape like a large flat rock, surrounded by shimmering, green lawns. He stared at the narrow pathways where the gravestones stood in symmetrical rows. Lush trees with drooping crowns. Solace. Silence. Not a soul, not a sound. He dragged himself reluctantly out of the car, slammed the door hard with the faint hope that someone might hear it and come out of the door to the crematorium to ask him what he wanted. Make it easy for him. But no one came.

He wandered along the paths, reading a few names, but mainly taking note of the dates, as if he were searching for someone who wasn't very old, who might have been only 15, like Annie. He found several. He realised after a while that lots of people had been through this before him, they had merely made it a little further along in the process. They had made a series of decisions, for instance that their son or daughter should be cremated, and what kind of gravestone should be placed over the urn and what kind of plants should be planted. They had brought flowers and music to the funeral and told the minister what their child had been like, so that the sermon would have as personal a ring as possible. His hands were shaking, and he stuffed them in his pockets. He was wearing an old coat with a tattered lining. In his right pocket he felt a button, and it occurred to him that it had been there for years.

The cemetery was quite large and at the far end, down by the road, he caught sight of a man wearing a dark blue nylon coat, walking around among the graves, perhaps someone who worked there. Without thinking, he headed in the man's direction, hoping he was the talkative type. He wasn't feeling very outgoing himself, but maybe the man would stop and say something about the weather. There was always the weather, thought Eddie. He looked up at the sky and saw that it was slightly overcast, mild and with a faint breeze.

"Hello!"

The dark blue coat did stop, after all.

Holland cleared his throat. "Do you work here?"

"Yes." He nodded towards the crematorium. "I'm what you call the superintendent here."

The man gave him a pleasant smile, as if he were not afraid of anything in the world and had seen what there was to see of human inadequacy.

"Been working here for 20 years. It's a beautiful place to spend your days, don't you think?"

He had a casual and friendly manner. Holland nodded.

"Yes, I do. And here I am walking around," he stammered, "thinking about the future and things like that." He laughed nervously. "Sooner or later we all end up in the ground. There's no getting away from it."

He clenched his hands in his pockets, and felt the button.

"You're right about that. Do you have family members here?"

"No, not here. They're buried in the cemetery back home. We don't have a tradition of cremation in my family. I don't really know what it is," he said. "To be cremated, I mean. I suppose there's not much difference when it comes right down to it, but a person has to make up his mind. Not that I'm so old, but I've been thinking that I ought to decide soon whether to be buried or cremated."

The other man wasn't smiling any more. He stared intently at the stout man in the grey coat, and considered what it must have cost him in pride to say what was on his mind. People had all kinds of reasons for wandering around among the graves. He never risked making a blunder.

"It's an important decision, I think. Something to take your time over. Most people ought to think more than they do about their death."

"Yes, don't you think so?" Holland looked relieved. He pulled his hands out of his pockets and waved them around a little. "But a person might be reluctant to dig around in such topics." He gave a start at his choice of words. "He might be afraid of being considered strange, or not altogether sane . . . if he wants to find out something about the cremation process, what goes on."

"Folks have the right to know," the super-intendent said simply, moving off a few steps. "It's just that no one ever asks. Or they don't want to know. But if a few people do want to know, I can fully understand why. We could go inside and I could explain things, if you like?"

Holland nodded gratefully. He felt comfortable in the company of this friendly man. A man of his own age, of lean build, with thinning hair. They strolled up the paths together, the gravel crunching softly under their feet, and the breeze caressing Holland's head like a consoling hand.

"It's all quite simple, actually," the superintendent said. "But first I should tell you, for the sake of good order, that the entire casket containing the deceased is put into the oven. We have special caskets for cremation. Everything is made of wood, including the handles and everything else. Just so you don't think that we lift out the deceased and place him or her in the oven without the casket. But maybe that's not what you thought. Most people have seen enough American movies to know," he said with a smile.

Holland nodded and clenched his fists again.

"The oven is quite large. We have two of them here. They run on electricity, and with the help of gas, they create a powerful furnace. The temperature reaches almost two thousand degrees Celsius."

He looked up and smiled, as if he wanted to catch a few faint rays of sun.

"Everything that the deceased is wearing in the casket ends up in the oven. Also jewellery or things that don't burn but are placed in the urn afterwards. We remove pacemakers and surgical bolts or splints. When it comes to precious metals, you may have heard rumours that they end up elsewhere. But you mustn't believe that," he said firmly. "You really mustn't believe that."

They were approaching the door to the crematorium.

"Bones and teeth are ground up in a mill into a fine, almost sand-like, greyish powder."

The moment the man mentioned the part about the mill, Eddie thought about her fingers. Her delicate, slender fingers with the little silver ring. Horrified, he curled up his own fingers inside his pockets.

"We monitor the whole process, to check on how far along it has progressed. The oven has glass doors. After about two hours everything is swept out of the oven, forming a small heap of fine ash, a lot smaller than people might think."

Monitor the process? Through the glass door? Could they peek inside and look at what was inside — *look at Annie as she burned?*

"I can show you the ovens, if you like."

"No, no!"

He pressed his arms tight to his sides, trying desperately to hold them still.

"The ash is very clean, practically the cleanest thing that exists. Looks like fine sand. In the old days the ash was used for medicinal purposes. Did you know that? Among other things, it was applied to eczema with good results, or even ingested. It contains salts and minerals, but we filter it into an urn. I'll show you one so you can see how they look. You can select your urn, they come in many shapes. We prefer a standard urn, and that's what most people choose. It is closed and sealed and then placed in the grave through a small shaft. We call this ceremony the 'burial of the urn'."

He held open the door for Holland, who stepped into the dimly lit building.

"In reality it's nothing more than a hastening of the natural process. Cleaner, in a way. We are all going to return to ashes, but with a traditional burial it's quite a lengthy process. It takes about 20 years, sometimes 30 or 40, depending on what kind of soil we're talking about. In this area there's a lot of sand and clay, so it takes longer."

"I like that," said Holland softly, "'return to ashes'."

"It's true, isn't it? Some people want to be spread to the winds. Unfortunately, that's illegal in this country; we have very strict laws regarding the matter. According to law, each body must be placed in consecrated ground."

"Not a bad idea," Holland said, clearing his throat. "But it's so strange with all the images that go through your mind. When you try to imagine what it's like. If you're buried in the ground, your

179

body decays. And that doesn't sound very nice. But then there's the idea of burning."

Decay or burning, he thought. What choice should he make for Annie?

He paused for a moment, feeling as though his knees were about to buckle, but then he was able to continue, encouraged by the patience of the other man.

"There's something about burning that makes me think of – well, you know – of Hell. And when I picture my girl . . ."

He stopped abruptly, slowly turning red. The other man stood motionless for a long time, and then finally gave him a pat on the shoulder and said, "You have to make a decision for . . . your daughter? Is that right?"

Holland bowed his head.

"I think you should take this very seriously. It's like having a double responsibility. It's not easy, no, it's not." He shook his lean face from side to side. "And you should take your time. But if you decide on cremation, you'll have to sign a statement that she never uttered a word of objection. Unless she's under 18, that is, then you can make the decision for her."

"She's 15," he said.

The superintendent closed his eyes for a few seconds. Then he started walking again. "Come with me to the chapel," he said. "I'll show you an urn."

He led Holland down some stairs. An invisible hand had been placed over them, shutting out the rest of the world. They leaned towards each other, the superintendent to lend support, Holland to receive warmth. Downstairs the walls were rough and whitewashed. At the bottom stood a red-and-white floral arrangement, and a suffering Christ stared down at them from the cross on the wall. Eddie pulled himself together. He sensed that his cheeks had regained their colour, and he felt more at ease.

The urns stood on shelves along the walls. The superintendent lifted one down and handed it to Holland. "Go ahead and hold it. Nice, isn't it?"

He touched the urn and tried to envision what had been his daughter, that he was holding her in his arms. The urn looked like metal, but he knew that it was a biodegradable material, and it felt warm in his hands.

"So now I've told you what happens. That's all there is to it, I haven't left anything out."

Eddie Holland ran his fingers over the gold-coloured urn. It did feel good in his hand, with a solid weight to it.

"The urn is porous so that air from the earth can get in and speed up the process. The urn will disappear too. There's something mysterious and grand about the fact that everything disappears, don't you think?"

He smiled with reverence. "And we will too. Even this building, and the paved road outside. But all the same," he said, taking a firm grip on Eddie's arm, "I still like to believe that there's something greater in store for us. Something different and exciting. Why shouldn't there be?"

Holland looked at him, almost in surprise.

"On the outside we put a label with her name on it," he said in conclusion.

Holland nodded. Realised that he was still on his feet. Time would go on passing, minute after minute. Now he had felt a small part of the pain, moved a little bit down the path, with Annie. Imagined the flames, and the roar of the oven.

"It should say Annie," he said. "Annie Sofie Holland."

When he came home, Ada was bending over the sink, listlessly washing some muddy red potatoes. Six potatoes. Two each. Not eight, like she was used to. It looked so paltry. Her face was still set in pain, it had set rigid the second she bent over the gurney at the hospital and the doctor drew back the sheet. Afterwards the expression remained like a mask that she couldn't move.

"Where have you been?" she asked tonelessly.

"I've been thinking about it," Holland said. "And I think we should have Annie cremated."

She dropped the potato and stared at him. "Cremated?"

"I've been thinking about it," he said. "The fact that someone . . . assaulted her. And left a mark on her. I want it gone!"

He leaned heavily against the counter and gave her an imploring look. It was rare for him to ask for anything.

"What kind of mark?" she asked as if she hardly cared, picking up the potato again. "We can't have Annie cremated."

"You just need time to get used to the idea," he said, a little louder than before. "It's a beautiful custom."

"We can't have Annie cremated," she repeated, as she continued to scrub. "They called from the prosecutor's office. They said we couldn't have her cremated."

"But why not?" he cried, wringing his hands.

"In case they need to bring her up again. When they find the man who did it."

CHAPTER 7

Bardy Snorrason stuck a hand under the steel handle and pulled Annie out of the wall. The drawer slid almost soundlessly on well-oiled runners. He didn't associate the body of the young girl with his own life or mortality, or the mortality of his daughters. He didn't do that any more. He had a good appetite and he slept well at night. And because he handled the misfortune and deaths of others with the utmost respect, he figured that those who came after him would do the same with his own body when that day arrived. Nothing in his 30 years as a medical examiner had given him cause to think otherwise.

It took him two hours to go through all the points. The picture gradually took on familiar signs as he worked. The lungs were speckled like a bird's egg, and reddish-yellow foam could be pressed out of the incisions. There was plenty of blood in the brain and stripe-shaped haemorrhages in the throat and breast muscles, which indicated that she had gasped violently for air. He read his notes into a

Dictaphone: brief, terse, barely comprehensible observations that could be interpreted only by the initiated, and sometimes not at all. Later his assistant would translate them into precise terminology for the written report.

After he'd been through everything he put the top of the skull back in place, pulled the skin over it, rinsed the body thoroughly, and filled the empty chest cavity with crumpled newspaper. Then he sewed the body back up. He was very hungry. He needed to have some food before he could start on the next one, and he had four open sandwiches with Jubel salami and a thermos of coffee waiting for him in the canteen.

He caught sight of someone through the translucent glass in the door. The person stopped and stood motionless for a moment, as if wanting to turn around. Snorrason pulled off his gloves and smiled. There weren't many people of such a towering height.

Sejer had to duck a little as he came in. He cast an indifferent glance at the trolley, where Annie was now wrapped in a sheet. He had pulled on the mandatory plastic coverings over his shoes, which were baggy and pastel-coloured and looked quite comical.

"I've just finished," Snorrason said. "She's over there."

Now Sejer gave the body on the trolley a look of greater interest.

"So I'm in luck."

"That's questionable."

The doctor began washing his hands and arms from the elbow down, scrubbing his skin and fingernails with a stiff brush for several minutes and finishing by rinsing them for an equal amount of time. Then he dried off, using paper towels from a holder on the wall, pulled out a chair and slid it towards the chief inspector.

"There wasn't much to discover here."

"Don't destroy all my hopes straight away. Surely there must be something?"

Snorrason pushed aside his hunger pangs and sat down.

"It's not my job to determine the value of what we find. But usually we do find something. She seems so untouched."

"Presumably he was a strong, healthy individual. He had the benefit of complete surprise. And he removed her clothing afterwards."

"Presumably. But she wasn't assaulted. She's not a virgin, but she wasn't sexually assaulted, or mistreated in any other way. She drowned, plain and simple. Her clothes were taken off, nice and easy after her death, all the buttons are in place on her shirt, none of the seams are ripped. Maybe he wanted to interfere with her, but was scared off by something. Or maybe he lost his nerve, or his virility; it could have been anything."

"Or maybe he just wanted us to believe that he's a sex offender."

"Why would he want to do that?"

"To hide his real motive. And that could mean there's something behind all this that could be traced, that it wasn't an impulsive act by a disturbed individual. And besides, she must have gone with him willingly. She must have known him, or he must have made an impression on her. And from what I understand, it wasn't easy to make an impression on Annie Holland."

He opened a button in his jacket and leaned over the counter.

"Go ahead. Tell me what you found."

"A 15-year-old girl," Snorrason said, intoning like a minister, "height 174 centimetres, weight 65 kilos, minimum of fat; for the most part the fat had been converted into muscle due to hard exercise. Perhaps too hard for a girl of 15. They should take things a little easy at that age, but that's probably not so simple once they've started. So, a lot of muscle, more than many boys of the same age. Her lung capacity was excellent, which would indicate that it took a long time for her to lose consciousness."

Sejer looked down at the worn linoleum and noticed that the pattern was similar to the one in his bathroom.

"How long does it actually take?" he asked. "How long does it take for an adult to drown?"

"Anywhere from two to ten minutes, depending on the physical condition. If she was in as good a condition as I think, it most likely took closer to ten."

Up to ten minutes, Sejer thought. Multiply that by 60, and that makes 600 seconds. Think of all he could do in ten minutes. Take a shower. Eat a meal.

"Her lungs are enlarged. If she reacted as most people would, she first took a couple of deep breaths as she went under, what we call *'respiration de surprise'*. Then she pressed her lips together until she lost consciousness, and after that a limited amount of water forced its way into her lungs. In the brain and bone marrow I found the presence of diatoms, a type of silica algae; not much, it's true, but that lake wasn't very polluted. The cause of death was drowning.

"She had no scars from any operations, no deformities, no signs of malnutrition, no tattoos, no skin blemishes of any kind. She had her natural hair colour, her fingernails were unpolished and clipped short, there were no particulates of interest except for mud. Very nice teeth. A single ceramic filling in a lower molar.

"No traces of alcohol or other chemicals in her blood. No marks from injections. Ate a good meal that day, bread and milk. No irregularities in the brain. She has never been pregnant. And," he sighed suddenly and fixed his gaze on Sejer, "she never would have been."

"What? Why not?"

"She had a large tumour in her left ovary that had started spreading to her liver. Malignant."

Sejer sat there and stared at him. "Are you saying that she was seriously ill?"

"Yes. Are *you* saying that you didn't know?"

"Her parents didn't know either." He shook his head in disbelief. "Otherwise they would have said something, wouldn't they? Is it possible that she could not have known herself?"

"Well, you'll need to find out if she had a doctor, and whether it was known. But she would have felt pain in her abdomen, at least during menstruation. She trained hard. Perhaps she had so many endorphins circulating in her body that the pain was masked. But the truth is, she was done for. I doubt they could have saved her. Liver cancer is virulent."

He nodded towards the gurney where Annie's head and feet were clearly outlined under the sheet. "She would have been dead in a matter of months."

The news made Sejer completely lose track of why he was there. It took him a minute to collect himself.

"Should I tell them? Her parents?"

"You'll have to make that decision yourself. But they're going to want to know what I have discovered."

"It'll be like losing her all over again."

"Yes, it will."

"They're going to blame themselves for not knowing."

"Probably."

"What about her clothes?"

"Soaked through with muddy water, except for the anorak, which I sent over to you. But she had a belt with a brass buckle."

"Yes?"

"A big buckle shaped like a half-moon with an eye and a mouth. The lab found fingerprints on it. Two different ones. One of them was Annie's."

Sejer narrowed his eyes. "And the other?"

"Unfortunately, it's not complete; it's not much to go on."

"Damn," Sejer said.

"The owner of that print clearly has something to do with all this. But it should be useful in eliminating people. That's something, isn't it?"

"What about the mark on her neck? Can you tell if he was right-handed?"

"No, I can't. But since Annie was in such good shape, he couldn't have been a weakling. There must have been a struggle. Strange that she's so unmarked."

Sejer stood up, "Well, she's not untouched any more."

"Oh yes, she is! You can have a look for yourself. This is an art, and I'm not sloppy about it."

"When can I get this in writing?"

"I'll let you know, and you can send over that young officer with the curls. And what about you? Have you found a lead?"

"No," he said. "Not a thing. I can't see any reason in the world why anyone would kill Annie Holland."

Maybe Annie had chosen the title of a song and made that her password – maybe that flute tune she liked so much, "Annie's Song".

Halvor brooded as he sat in front of the screen. The door to the living room stood open in case his grandmother called. She didn't have much of a voice left, and it took a great effort for her to get up from her armchair when her arthritis was bad. He leaned his chin on his hands and stared at the screen. "Access denied. Password required." He was actually hungry, but like so much else right now, that had to take low priority.

At Headquarters Sejer sat reading a thick stack of pages covered with text and stapled at one corner. The initials BCH, standing for Bjerkeli Children's Home, kept popping up. Halvor's childhood made for depressing reading. His mother spent most of her time in bed, whimpering and fragile, with frayed nerves and an ever-growing armoury of sedatives in reach. She couldn't bear bright lights or loud noises. The children weren't allowed to scream or shout. Halvor had certainly been through the wringer, Sejer thought. Impressive that he could hold down a steady job and take care of his grandmother on top of everything else.

Halvor typed various song titles into the blank field as they occurred to him. "Access denied" kept appearing, rather like a fly that you think you've killed but keeps on buzzing around. He'd been through all the numeric codes he could think of, all the relevant birth-dates and even the serial number on her bicycle which he'd found on the extra key he kept for her in a jar. She had a DBS Intruder bike and insisted that he keep one of the keys at his house. Which reminded him that he should give it back to Eddie, and at the same time he typed "Intruder" on the screen.

His father's alcohol problem and his mother's

delicate nerves had marked the family from the outset. Halvor and his brother bumbled around in the house, getting their own food, when there was any. Their father was usually in town, first drinking up his salary cheque and later his welfare payments. A few kind neighbours helped out as best they could, in secrecy behind their father's back. As the years passed, he became more and more violent. The boys would retreat to their room and lock the door. They grew thinner and quieter.

Annie probably hadn't used a number password, he thought. She was a girl and would have come up with something more imaginative. A combination of words was most likely – two or three words, possibly words with a symbolic meaning. Or a name, of course, but he'd already tried so many, even her mother's name, although he knew that was one she would never have chosen. He had also typed in the name of Sølvi's father, Axel Bjørk, and his dog Achilles. "Access denied".

He had slender hands with thin fingers. Not meant for slamming into the chin of a raging, uncontrollable drunk on the verge of collapse. It must have been a tough job to fight with his father. The two brothers showed up regularly at the emergency room with bruises and abrasions, and the tell-tale doe-eyed look that said: I'll be good. You mustn't hit me. They said they'd been fighting with boys on the street, tumbled down the stairs, or fallen off their bikes, but they were protecting their father. Home was a rough place, but it was a known quantity. The alternative was a children's home or foster parents, and the possibility of being separated from each other. Halvor fainted frequently in school, due to undernourishment and lack of sleep. He was the elder one; his younger brother got most of the food.

Halvor switched to books she'd read and talked about. Titles, characters in the books, things they had said. He had plenty of time. He felt so close to Annie as he worked. Finding the password would be like finding his way back to her. He imagined that she was following his search, that maybe she would give him a sign, if only he stuck at it long enough. The message would come in the form of a memory. Something she had said, something stored away in his mind that would reveal itself if only he dug far enough. He remembered more and more things. It felt as if he were wiping away layer upon layer of delicate cobwebs, and behind each layer he found another one: a camping trip, a bike ride, an evening at the movies, as they'd done so often. And Annie's laugh. A deep, almost masculine laugh. Her strong fist when she pounded him on the back and said: "Give up, Halvor!" in her own special way. Loving and admonishing at the same time. Any other caress was rare.

Every time the child welfare authorities announced a visit, their father would gulp down some Antabuse, wash himself, clean the house, and take the younger boy on his lap. He was very strong and could muster a thoroughly stubborn expression, which made the terrified social workers retreat immediately. Their mother would smile faintly from under the covers. Poor Torkel had so many responsibilities when she was sick, she'd say, surely they could understand that, and the children were at a difficult age. The social workers would leave without proving their case. Everyone deserved a second chance. Halvor spent most of his time with his mother and his younger brother. He never did his homework, but he still got good grades, so he was definitely bright. Gradually their father lost his grip on reality. One night he came bursting into the room where the two boys slept. On that night, as so often, the younger brother was asleep in Halvor's bed. Their father had a knife. Halvor saw it gleaming in his hand. They could hear their mother whimpering, terrified, downstairs. Suddenly he felt the sharp pain of the knife as it struck his temple; he flung himself away and the knife sliced through his cheek, splitting it in half, then down towards his mouth, where it stuck in his molars.

His father's eyes could suddenly see what was real again: the blood on the pillow and the younger brother screaming. He raced down the stairs and into the yard. Hid in the woodshed. The door slammed behind him.

Halvor scratched the corner of his mouth with a sharp fingernail and suddenly remembered Annie's enthusiasm for the book *Sophie's World*. And since her name was Annie Sofie, he typed in the title. He thought it would be a clever password, but she evidently hadn't felt the same way, because nothing happened. He kept on trying. His stomach growled, and a throbbing in his temples signalled a headache.

Sejer and Skarre locked up the office and walked down the hall. The boys had done well at Bjerkeli. Halvor developed an attachment to a Catholic priest who visited the home now and then. This was at the time that he graduated from the ninth grade. The younger brother was put into a foster home, and then Halvor was all alone. After a while he chose to move in with his grandmother. He was used to taking care of someone. When he wasn't doing that, he felt useless.

"Strange that they could turn out all right in spite of everything," said Skarre, shaking his head.

"Maybe we don't really know how Halvor has turned out," said Sejer bluntly. "It remains to be seen."

Skarre nodded with embarrassment, fiddling with his car keys.

Halvor's headache was getting worse. It was finally night-time. His grandmother had been sitting alone for a long time, and his eyes were sore from staring at the flickering screen. He kept at it for a while longer, realising he had no idea what chance he had of ever finding Annie's password, or what he might find if he did. Maybe she had a secret. He *had* to find it, and he had plenty of time, at any rate. Eventually he got up, almost reluctantly, to get something to eat. He left the monitor on and went out to the kitchen. His grandmother was watching a programme about the American Civil War on TV. She was cheering for the ones in blue uniforms because she thought they were more handsome. And besides, she thought the ones wearing grey uniforms spoke with such a disgusting accent.

Skarre drove nice and slowly; he had learned that his boss had an aversion to high speeds, and the road was unbelievably bad – buckled by frost, narrow and meandering across the landscape. It was still chilly, as if someone had waylaid summer, detained it elsewhere with idle conversation. Birds huddled under shrubbery, regretting their return home. People had stopped planting seeds. The ground was completely bare, after all. A dry, hard crust on which no tracks were left.

Halvor poured cornflakes into a bowl and sprinkled them liberally with sugar. He carried the cereal into the dining room and rolled up a woven tablecloth so as not to spill on it. The spoon shook in his hand. His blood sugar was extremely low, and there was a ringing in his ears.

"A black man has started working at the Co-op grocery," his grandmother said out of the blue. "Have you seen him, Halvor?"

"It's called the Kiwi now. The Co-op is gone. Yes, his name is Philip."

"He talks with a Bergen accent," she said. "I don't like it when a fellow looks like that and talks with a Bergen accent."

"But he *is* from Bergen," said Halvor, slurping milk and sugar from his spoon. "He was born and raised there. His parents are from Tanzania."

"It would have been much better if he spoke his own language."

"The Bergen dialect *is* his own language. Besides, you wouldn't understand a word if he spoke Swahili."

"But I get such a fright every time he opens his mouth."

"You'll get used to it."

That's the way they talked to each other. Usually they agreed about things. His grandmother would toss out her latest worry, and Halvor would pick it up, swiftly and easily, as if it were a faulty paper aeroplane that needed to be refolded.

The car approached the driveway. From a distance the house didn't look particularly inviting. An aerial view would have revealed just how isolated it was, as if it wanted to hide from the rest of the neighbourhood, set back from the road, partially concealed by shrubs and trees. Little windows high up on the wall. Faded grey clapboard weatherproofing. The courtyard half-overgrown with weeds.

Through the dining-room window Halvor saw a faint light. He heard the car and some of his milk dribbled down his chin. The headlights flickered through the dim light of the room. Moments later, they were standing in the doorway, looking at him.

"We need to have a little talk," said Sejer. "You'll have to come with us, but you can finish eating first."

He wasn't hungry any more, but then he hadn't thought he was going to get off easily. He went calmly out to the kitchen and carefully rinsed the bowl under the tap. He slipped into his room and turned off the monitor, muttered something into his grandmother's ear, and followed them out. He had to sit by himself in the back seat of the car, and he didn't like that. It reminded him of something else.

*

"I'm trying to put together a picture of Annie," Sejer said. "Who she was and how she lived. I want you to tell me everything about what kind of girl she was. What she did and said when the two of you were together, all the thoughts and fantasies you must have had about why she'd withdrawn from everyone she knew, and about what happened up there at Serpent Tarn. Everything, Halvor."

"I have no idea."

"You must have had some thoughts about it."

"I've thought about a lot of things, but nothing makes any sense."

Silence. Halvor studied Sejer's blotting pad, which was a map of the world, and found the approximate location of where he lived.

"You were an important part of Annie's landscape," Sejer said. "That's actually what I'm getting at. I'm trying to map out the area that was hers."

"So that's what you're doing?" said Halvor dryly. "You're drawing a map?"

"Perhaps you have a better idea?"

"No," he said.

"Your father is dead," Sejer said abruptly. He searched the young face in front of him, and Halvor felt Sejer's looming presence like a tension in the room. It sapped his strength, especially when they had eye contact. So he sat with his head bowed.

"He took his own life. But you said that your parents were separated. Is it hard for you to talk about that?"

"I suppose so."

"Is that why you concealed the truth from me?"

"It's not exactly something to boast about."

"I understand. Can you tell me what you wanted from Annie?" he said. "Since you were waiting for her at Horgen's Shop on the day she was murdered."

His surprise seemed genuine.

"I'm sorry, but you're really on the wrong track!"

"A motorcyclist was observed in the vicinity at a crucial moment. You were out riding around. It could have been you."

"You better check that man's eyesight as soon as possible."

"Is that all you have to say?"

"Yes."

"Then I will. Do you want something to drink?"

"No."

More silence. Halvor listened. Someone was laughing nearby; it all seemed so unreal. Annie was dead, and people were making noise and behaving as if nothing had happened.

"Did you get the impression that Annie wasn't well?"

"What?"

"Did you ever hear her complain of pain, for example?"

"Nobody was as healthy as Annie. Are you saying she was sick?"

"Unfortunately, I'm not allowed to divulge certain information to you, even though the two of you were close. She never mentioned anything of the kind?"

"No."

Sejer's voice was not unkind, but he spoke with deliberate slowness, enunciating carefully, and it lent the grey-haired figure a good deal of authority.

"Tell me about your job. What you do at the factory."

"We move around. One week we do the packing, one week we take care of the machines, and one week we do deliveries."

"Do you like it?"

"You don't have to think," he said.

"You don't have to think?"

"About the job. You can do it on automatic, and think about other things."

"Like what, for instance?"

"Anything at all," he said. His tone was defensive. Maybe he didn't realise it, maybe it was a habit from his childhood, years of reprimands and beatings having forced him to weigh every word.

"How are you spending your time these days?

The time you normally would have spent with Annie?"

"Trying to find out what happened," he blurted out.

"Do you have any leads for us?"

"I'm searching my memory."

"I'm not sure that you're telling me everything you know."

"I didn't do anything to Annie. You think I did it, don't you?"

"To be honest, I don't know. You're going to have to help me, Halvor. It sounds as if Annie had undergone some sort of change in personality. Do you agree?"

"Yes."

"The reason for such an occurrence is partially understood. Several factors can be responsible. For example, people might change drastically if they lose someone close to them; or if they experience serious trauma, or suffer a serious illness. Young people who are known as decent, hard-working, and diligent can become completely indifferent to the world even though they might recover from a physical trauma. Another thing that can lead to a change in personality is drug abuse. Or a brutal assault, such as rape."

"Was Annie raped?"

Sejer chose not to answer this question. "Does any of this sound familiar?"

"I think she had a secret," he said at last.

"You think she had a secret? Go on."

"Something that had upset her whole life. Something she couldn't ignore."

"Are you going to tell me that you don't know what it was?"

"Yes. I have no idea."

"Who, aside from you, knew Annie best?"

"Her father."

"But they didn't really communicate?"

"It's still possible to know someone well."

"I see. So if anyone might understand her silence, it would be Eddie?"

"It's a question of whether you can get him to say anything. It'd be better if you got him to come here without Ada. Then he'll talk more."

Sejer nodded. "Did you ever meet Axel Bjørk?"

"Sølvi's father? Once. I went with the girls to visit him."

"What did you think of him?"

"He was OK. Said we should come back. Looked unhappy when we left. But Ada went totally berserk when she found out, and so Sølvi had to go there in secret. After a while she didn't feel like it any more, so I guess Ada had her way."

"What kind of a girl is Sølvi?"

"There's not much to say about her. You must have seen all there is to see; it doesn't take long."

Sejer hid his face by leaning his head on his hands. "Why don't we have a Coke? The air is so dry in here. Nothing but synthetic materials and fibreglass and misery."

Halvor nodded and relaxed a bit. But then he grew tense again. Maybe this was some kind of tactic, this first small glimpse of sympathy from the grey-haired inspector. He probably had some reason for being friendly. He must have taken courses, studied interrogation techniques and psychology. Knew how to find a crack and then drive in a wedge. The door closed behind him, and Halvor took the opportunity to stretch his legs. He went over to the window and looked out. On the desk stood a PC, an American Compaq model. Maybe that's where they had discovered his background. Maybe they had passwords, just like Annie; information was a sensitive matter, after all. He wondered what kind of passwords they used, and who had thought them up.

Sejer came back and, seeing Halvor looking at the PC, said, "That thing is just a toy. I don't like it much."

"Why not?"

"It's not really on my side."

"Of course not. It can't choose sides at all; that's why you can depend on it."

"You have one, don't you?"

205

"No, I have a Mac. I play games on it. Annie and I used to play games together."

All of a sudden he opened up a tiny bit and smiled that half-smile of his. "What she liked best was the downhill run. It's set up so you can choose the kind of snow – coarse or fine-grained, dry or wet – the temperature, the length and weight of your skis, the wind conditions, everything. Annie always won. She would choose the hardest course, either Deadquin's Peak or Stonies. She would make the run in the middle of the night in a huge storm on wet snow with the longest skis, and I never had a chance."

Sejer gave him a look of incomprehension and shook his head. He poured some Coke into two plastic cups and sat down again.

"Do you know Knut Jensvoll?"

"The coach? I know who he is. I went to handball matches with Annie once in a while."

"Did you like him?"

Halvor shrugged.

"Not such a great guy?"

"I thought he chased after the girls too much."

"Annie too?"

"Don't be funny!"

"I rarely am. I was just asking."

"He didn't dare. She didn't let anyone get too close."

"So she was tough?"

"Yes."

"But I don't understand it, Halvor."

He shoved his plastic cup aside and leaned forward.

"Everyone speaks so well of Annie – about how strong and independent and sporty she was. Didn't care too much about her appearance, seemed almost stand-offish. Didn't let anyone get too close, as you say. And yet she went with someone deep into the woods, to the lake. Apparently of her own free will. And then," he lowered his voice, "she let herself get killed."

Halvor gave him a frightened look, as if the absurdity of the situation finally dawned on him, in all its horror.

"Someone must have had power over her."

"But was there anyone who had power over Annie?"

"Not as far as I know. I didn't, that's for sure."

Sejer drank his Coke. "A damn shame she didn't leave anything behind. A diary, for example."

Halvor bent his head over his cup and took a long gulp.

"But could it be true?" Sejer said. "That someone actually had some kind of hold over her? Someone she didn't dare defy? Could Annie have been mixed up in something dangerous that she needed to keep secret? Could someone have been blackmailing her?"

"Annie was very law-abiding. I don't think she would have done anything wrong."

"A person can do lots of wrong things and still be law-abiding," Sejer said. "One act doesn't describe a whole person."

Halvor noted those words, carefully storing them away.

"Are drugs available in that little village of yours?"

"Jesus, yes. Have been for years. You guys show up at regular intervals and raid the pub in the middle of town. But this can't have anything to do with that. Annie never set foot in there. She scarcely even bought anything at the shop next door."

"Halvor," Sejer said, "Annie was a quiet, reserved girl who liked to be in control of her life. But think carefully: did she also seem scared of something?"

"Not exactly scared. More ... closed down. Sometimes almost angry, sometimes resigned. But I *have* seen Annie really scared. Not that it has anything to do with this, but I remember it clearly."

He was suddenly eager to talk. "Her mother and father and Sølvi were in Trondheim, where her aunt lives. Annie and I were home alone. I was going to stay over. It was last spring. First we took a

208

ride on our bikes, then we stayed up late, listening to music. It was really warm, so we decided to sleep in a tent in the yard. We set everything up and then went inside to brush our teeth. I went back to the tent first. When Annie came, I knelt down and opened the sleeping bag. And there was a snake inside. A big black snake, coiled up inside the sleeping bag. We rushed out of the tent, and I went to get one of the neighbours who lives across the road. He thought it must have crawled into the sleeping bag to get warm. The neighbour managed to kill it. Annie was so scared that she threw up. And from then on I had to shake out her sleeping bag when we went camping."

"A snake in her sleeping bag?" Sejer shivered, remembering his own camping trips in his distant youth.

"Fagerlund ridge is crawling with snakes; it's a rocky slope. We put butter out and catch a lot of them."

"Butter? Why butter?"

"They eat it until they're practically in a stupor. Then all you have to do is pick them up."

"I hear you also have a sea serpent at the bottom of the fjord."

"That's right," Halvor said. "I've seen it myself. It only shows itself once in a while, when the wind is blowing in a certain way. It's actually a rock in the lake, just below the surface of the water, and when the wind changes from an onshore to an offshore, there's a loud roaring, three or four times. Then it's quiet again. It's really odd. Everyone knows what it is, but if you're out there all alone, you don't doubt for a minute that something is rising up from the deep. The first time I rowed away like crazy without turning around even once."

"But you can't think of a single person who knew Annie and might have wanted to harm her?"

"Not one," he said. "I've thought over and over about everything that happened, and I can't make sense of it. It must have been a madman."

Yes, Sejer thought, it could have been a madman. He drove Halvor home, manoeuvring the car right up to the front steps.

"I suppose you have to get up early," he said kindly. "It's late."

"I usually don't have any trouble setting up."

Halvor liked him and didn't like him. It was confusing.

He climbed out, opened the door cautiously, hoping his grandmother was asleep. To make sure, he peeked through a crack in the door and heard her snoring. Then he sat down in front of the monitor again and continued where he had left off. He kept on thinking of new things. Suddenly he remembered that she once had a cat that they found in a snowdrift, as flat as a pizza. He typed in the name Baghera. Nothing happened, but he hadn't really expected it to. He thought of this as a long-term project, and besides, there were other ways. In the back of his mind an idea for a simple solution to the problem was forming. But he hadn't lost hope yet. Besides, that would be cheating. If he managed to find the password on his own, he felt the breach of his promise to Annie would not be as great. He scratched the back of his neck and typed in "Top Secret". Just in case. And then he typed "Annie Holland", both backwards and forwards, because it suddenly occurred to him that he hadn't tried the simplest possibility, the most obvious, which of course she wouldn't have used, and yet might have used after all. "Access denied". He shoved his chair back a little from the desk, stretched, and put his hand on the back of his neck again. It prickled, as if something on his neck was annoying him. There was nothing there, but the feeling continued. Surprised, he turned around and stared out the window. A sudden impulse made him stand up and draw the curtains. He had a strong sense that someone was watching him, and the feeling made the hairs on his head stand on end. Swiftly he turned off the light. Outside he heard retreating footsteps, as though someone were running away. He peered through a crack in the curtains but couldn't see anyone. Nonetheless, he was positive that someone had been standing there, all his senses told him this was so, with an undeniable, physical certainty. He switched off the Mac, tore off his clothes, and climbed under the covers. He lay in bed, quiet as a mouse, and listened. Now there was total silence, he couldn't even hear the swaying of the trees in the wind outside. Then, after several minutes, he heard a car start up.

CHAPTER 8

Knut Jensvoll didn't hear the car because he was working with an electric drill, trying to put up a shelf where he could leave his wet trainers to dry after exercising. When he stopped for a moment, he heard the doorbell. He peered out the window and saw Sejer looming on the top step. He'd had a feeling they might come. He took a moment to gather his thoughts, smoothed down his clothes and his hair. He had already anticipated several questions. He felt prepared.

One thought was uppermost in Jensvoll's mind: had they found out about the rape? That had to be the reason why they were here. Once a criminal, always a criminal; that was a maxim he knew well. He assumed a strained expression, but then realised that this might make them suspicious; so he pulled himself together and tried a smile instead. Then he remembered that Annie was dead, and went back to the strained mask.

"Police. Can we come in?"

Jensvoll nodded. "I just have to close the door to

the laundry room." He waved them inside, disappeared for a moment, and returned at once. He cast a worried glance at Skarre, who was fishing a notebook out of his jacket. Jensvoll was older than they had expected, maybe even close to 50, and thickset. But his weight was well distributed; his body was firm and muscular, healthy and well-nourished, with good colour in his face, a thick mane of red hair, and an elegant, neatly trimmed moustache.

"I take it this has something to do with Annie?" he said.

Sejer nodded.

"I have never been so shocked in my life. I knew her well, so I think I have good reason to say that. But it's been a while since she left the team. That was a tragedy, by the way, because no one could replace her. Now we've got a real dunce out there who tends to duck when the ball comes towards her. But at least she fills up half the width of the goal."

He stopped his babbling and blushed a little.

"Yes, it's a real tragedy," Sejer said, somewhat more acidly than he had intended. "Has it been a long time since you last saw her?"

"As I said, she left the team. That was last autumn. In November, I think." He looked Sejer in the eye.

"Excuse me, but that sounds a little odd. She lived only a few hundred metres up the hill, didn't she?"

"Yes, no, well, I probably drove past her now and then. I thought you meant since I last had anything to do with her. In a proper sense, at practice. But I've seen her since then, of course. Downtown, maybe at the grocery shop."

"Then let me put the question this way: When did you last see Annie?"

Jensvoll had to think about it. "I don't know if I can remember. It must have been a while ago."

"We have plenty of time."

"Two or three weeks ago, maybe. At the post office, I think."

"Did you talk to her?"

"Just said hello. She wasn't particularly talkative of late."

"Why did Annie stop being a goalkeeper?"

"If only I knew." He shrugged. "I'm afraid I pressured her hard to change her mind, but it didn't do any good. She was fed up with it. Well, I don't really believe that, but that's what she said. Wanted to run instead, she said. And that's what she did, all right – day and night. I often drove past her on the plateau. Running full speed, long legs, expensive trainers. Holland spared no expense when it came to that girl."

He was still waiting for them to drag the skeleton out of the closet; he had no hope that it would be avoided.

"Do you live alone here?"

"I was divorced a while ago. My wife took the children and left, so now I'm on my own, and I like it this way. Don't have a lot of time to spare after I finish my job and sports practice. I coach a boys' team too, and I play on the Old Boys team. I'm in and out of the shower half the day."

"You didn't believe her when she said she was tired of it – so what do you think the real reason was?"

"I have no idea. But she had a boyfriend, and those kinds of things take up time. He wasn't especially athletic, by the way, a pipe-cleaner with skinny legs. Pale and slight, like a lima bean. He came to the matches once in a while, sat like a lump on the bench and never said a word. Just watched the ball going back and forth, back and forth. When they left, he wasn't even allowed to carry her bag. He wasn't the right type for her; she was a lot tougher than that."

"They were still together."

"Is that right? Well, each to his own."

Sejer nodded and kept his thoughts to himself. "I'm required to ask you this question. Where were you last Monday between 11 a.m. and 2 p.m.?"

"On Monday? You mean . . . on that day? At work, of course."

"And this can be confirmed by the warehouse?"

"I'm out driving a lot. We have home delivery, you see."

"So you were in your vehicle? Alone?"

"Part of the time I was in my truck. I delivered two wardrobes to a house on Rødtangen – that much, at least, they can confirm."

"When were you there?"

"Between 1 p.m. and 2 p.m., I think."

"Be a little more precise, Jensvoll."

"Hmmm . . . I suppose it was closer to 2 p.m."

Sejer did the calculation in his head. "And the hours before that?"

"Well, I was in and out. I overslept. And I grabbed a half hour at the tanning salon. We manage our own time, pretty much. Some days I have to put in overtime, which I don't get paid for. So I don't feel guilty. Even my boss has a tendency to . . ."

"Where were you, Jensvoll?"

"I got a late start that day," he said, clearing his throat. "A couple of us were out on the town on Sunday night. It's ridiculous, of course, to go out on the town on a Sunday when you know you have to get up and go to work, but that's how it was. I didn't get home until 1.30 a.m."

"Who were you with?"

"A friend. Erik Fritzner."

"Fritzner? Annie's neighbour?"

"Yes."

"So . . ." Sejer nodded to himself and stared at the coach, at his wavy shock of hair and his tanned face. "Do you think Annie was an attractive girl?"

Jensvoll knew what he was getting at. "What kind of question is that?"

"Answer it, please."

"Of course. You've seen her photo."

"Yes, I have," Sejer said. "She wasn't just nice to look at, she was quite grown up for her age. Mature, in a way, more than most teenage girls. Don't you agree?"

"Yes, I suppose so. Although I was more concerned with her expertise in the goal."

"Of course. That makes sense. Otherwise? Did you ever have any conflicts with the girls?"

"What type of conflicts?"

"Any kind," Sejer said deliberately, "regardless of type."

"Naturally I did. Teenage girls are quite volatile. But it was just the normal issues. No one wanted to replace Annie in goal, no one wanted to sit on the bench. Periods of unstoppable giggling. Boyfriends in the stands."

"What about Annie?"

"What about her?"

"Did you ever have a disagreement with Annie?"

He crossed his arms and nodded. "Well, yes, I did. On the day she called me and wanted to quit the team. I said a few desperate words that I should have held back. Maybe she took it as a compliment – who knows? She ended the conversation, hung up on me, and handed in her team uniform the next day. Done with it."

"And that's the only time the two of you had a falling out?"

"Yes, that's right. The only time."

Sejer nodded to Skarre. The conversation was over. They walked to the door, Jensvoll following. A good deal of suppressed frustration was about to get the better of him.

"Come on, be honest," he said, annoyed, as Sejer was opening the door. "Why are you pretending that you haven't looked at my record? Don't you think I have enough imagination to know that's the first thing you would do? That's why you're here, isn't it? I know what you're thinking."

Sejer turned around and stared at him.

"Do you have any idea what would happen to my team if that story got out around here? The girls would be locked in their rooms. The whole athletic programme would collapse like a house of cards, and years of work would come to nothing!"

His voice grew louder as he talked. "And if there's one thing this place needs, it's a good sports programme. The ones who aren't involved sit in pubs and buy dope. That's the only alternative. Just so you're aware what you'll be starting if you publicise what you know. And besides, it was eleven years ago!"

"I haven't said a word about it," Sejer said quietly. "And if you keep your voice down, maybe we can prevent it from getting out."

Jensvoll shut up at once and blushed bright red. He retreated back to the hall, and Skarre shut the door behind them. "Jesus," he said. "A landmine with hair and a moustache."

"If we had enough personnel," Sejer said, "I'd put a tail on him."

Skarre gave him an astonished look. "Why's that?"

"Probably just to be unpleasant."

Fritzner lay on his back in the dinghy, sipping a Hansa Premium. After each sip he took a drag on his cigarette. His concentration was completely absorbed by the book on his lap, propped against his knees. A steady stream of beer and nicotine seeped into his bloodstream. After a while he put down the beer and went to the living-room window. From there he could look down into

Annie's bedroom. The curtains were drawn, even though it was only early afternoon, as if it were no longer an ordinary room but almost a shrine into which no one must look. There was a faint glow from a single lamp, maybe the one on the desk.

He looked down the road and saw a police car by the letterboxes. There was the young officer with the curly hair. Probably going to the Holland house to give them the latest news. He didn't look particularly sombre; he walked with a light step, his face turned up to the sky, a slender, trim figure with lots of curls, surely on the borderline of what departmental regulations allowed. Suddenly he turned left and entered his own front yard. Fritzner frowned. Automatically he looked across the street to see if the visit had been noticed by anyone in the other houses. It had been. Isaksen was in his yard, raking leaves.

Skarre said hello and then went over to the window, just as Fritzner had done.

"You're looking down at Annie's bedroom," he said.

"Yes, I am."

Fritzner continued. "Actually, I'm a dirty old man, so I stood here often, gaping and drooling, hoping to catch a little peek. But she wasn't exactly the exhibitionist type. She would draw the curtains before she took off her jumper. I could see her silhouette, at least if she turned on the overhead light and there weren't too many folds in the curtains. Not a bad sight."

He had to smile when he saw Skarre's expression.

"If you want me to be honest," he said, "and I'm sure you do, I've never had any desire to get married. But I still would have liked to have one or two children to leave behind. And preferably with Annie. She was the kind of woman you wanted to impregnate, if you know what I mean."

Skarre still said nothing. He stood there, chewing on a sesame seed that had been stuck between two molars for a long while and had finally freed itself.

"Tall and slender, broad shoulders, long legs. Quick-witted. Beautiful as a wood nymph from Finnskogen. In other words, plenty of premium genes."

"She was only a teenager."

"They get older, you know. Although Annie won't."

"Frankly," he said, "I'm pushing 50 and I've got the same imagination as any other man. And I'm single. But as a bachelor I should have certain privileges, don't you think? There's no one out in the kitchen spluttering at me if I look at the ladies. If you lived here, right across the street from Annie, you would have cast an eye at her house now and then. That's not a crime, is it?"

"No, I don't believe it is."

Skarre studied the dinghy and the half-finished beer on the gunwale. He took his time, wondering whether it might be big enough to . . .

"Have you discovered anything?" Fritzner said.

"Of course. We have the silent witnesses. You know, the thousands of little things all around. Everyone leaves something behind."

Skarre watched Fritzner as he spoke. The man was standing with one hand in his pocket, and through the trouser material he could see the clenched fist.

"I see. By the way, did you know we have a crazy man here in the village?"

"Excuse me?"

"A guy with brain damage who lives with his father up on Kolleveien. Apparently he's very interested in girls."

"Raymond Låke. Yes, we know about him. But he doesn't have brain damage."

"He doesn't?"

"He has one too many chromosomes."

"Seems more like he has too few of something, if you ask me."

Skarre took another look at the Holland house, and at the window with the drawn curtains.

"Why do you think a snake would crawl into a sleeping bag?"

Fritzner opened his eyes wide. "Jesus, the things you know. I've asked myself the same thing. I'd actually forgotten about that; it was quite a little drama, I'll tell you. But it would make a perfect place to hibernate, wouldn't it? One of those bags from Ajungilak, with feather down and all that. I was sitting here in the dinghy with a whisky when that boyfriend of hers rang the bell. I guess they saw my light on. Annie was standing in a corner of her living room, white as a sheet. Normally she was pretty tough, but not that time. She was really frightened."

"How did you catch it?" asked Skarre with curiosity.

"My dear, it was nothing. I used my bucket. First I poked a hole in the bottom of it with an awl, about the size of a ten-øre coin. Then I crept inside the tent. It wasn't in the sleeping bag by then; it had crawled into a corner and coiled up. It was a big one. I slammed the bucket down over it and put my foot on the bottom. Then I sprayed Baygon into the hole."

"What's that?"

"Very powerful insect repellent. You can't buy it over the counter. The snake was knocked out at once."

"How do you have access to that kind of stuff?"

"I work at Anticimex. Pest control. Flies and cockroaches and all kinds of vermin."

"I see. Then what happened?"

"Then that skinny boyfriend of hers got a carving knife and I chopped the sucker in half, put it in a plastic bag, and tossed it into my rubbish bin. I really felt sorry for Annie. She hardly dared sleep in her own bed after that."

He shook his head at the thought.

"But you didn't come here to talk about my career as Superman, did you? In fact, why *are* you here?"

"Well . . ." Skarre pushed a curl back from his forehead. "The boss says we should always measure the pressure twice."

"Is that right? Well . . . my pressure is pretty stable. But I still can't comprehend that someone has taken Annie's life. A perfectly ordinary girl. Here, in this village, on this street. Her family can't understand it either. Now they'll leave her room untouched for years, exactly the way she had it. I've heard about this happening. Do you think it's because of a subconscious wish that she'll suddenly reappear?"

"Perhaps. Are you going to the funeral?"

"The whole village is going. That's what it's like when you live in a small place. No use having any secrets. People feel they have the right to know. It has its good and bad sides. Hard to keep anything secret."

"That could be an advantage for us," Skarre said. "If the killer is from here."

Fritzner went over to the dinghy, picked up the beer bottle, and emptied it. "Do you think he's from here?"

"Let's say that we hope so."

"I don't. But if he is, I hope you catch him fast, by God. I expect all 20 houses in the street have noted that you've come to see me. For the second time."

"Does that bother you?"

"Of course it does. I'd like to go on living here."

"Surely there's no reason for you not to."

"We'll see. As a bachelor, a man feels extra vulnerable."

"Why is that?"

"It's unnatural for a man not to have a woman. People expect a man to find a woman, at least by the time he turns 40. And if he doesn't, they think there must be some reason for it."

"Now I think you sound a little paranoid."

"You don't know what it's like, living so close to each other. There will be difficult times ahead for a lot of people."

"Are you thinking of anyone in particular?"

"As a matter of fact I am."

"Jensvoll, for example?"

Fritzner didn't reply, but stood there for a

moment, thinking. Looked at Skarre out of the corner of his eye and then seemed to make up his mind. He pulled his hand out of his pocket and held out something. "I wanted to show you this."

Skarre peered at it. It looked like a hair tie, covered with material, blue, with beads sewn on.

"It's Annie's," Fritzner said, staring at him. "I found it in the car. On the floor in front, stuck between the seat and the door. It was just a week ago that I gave her a lift into town. She dropped it in the car."

"Why are you giving this to me?"

He took a deep breath. "I could have kept it. Burned it in the fireplace, not said a word. It's to show you that I'm playing with a clean deck."

"I never thought otherwise," Skarre said.

Fritzner smiled. "Do you think I'm stupid?"

"Possibly," said Skarre, smiling back. "Maybe you're trying to trick me. Maybe you're such a conniving person that this whole sweet confession has been staged. I'll take the hair tie with me. And take you into consideration to a greater extent than before."

Fritzner turned pale. Skarre couldn't resist laughing at him.

"Where did you get the name for your boat?" he asked. "It's a strange name for a boat, isn't it? *Narco Traficante*?"

"It was just a whim."

He was trying to pull himself together after the incident. "But it sounds good, don't you think?"

He gave the young officer a worried look.

"Have you ever taken it out on the water?"

"Never," he said. "I get terribly seasick."

The district prosecutor had given his verdict. Annie Holland could be buried, and now Eddie saw by his watch that more than 24 hours had passed since the first shovelful of dry earth struck the top of the coffin. Earth on top of Annie. Full of twigs and stones and worms. In his pocket he had a crumpled piece of paper, a few words he had intended to read as they stood near the casket after the sermon. The fact that he merely stood there, gasping, without managing to utter a single word, would haunt him for the rest of his life.

"I wonder if Sølvi might have a little problem," he said, putting a plump finger to his forehead, then changing his mind and moving it to his temple. "Not something that would show up in a scan or anything, she's learned what she needs to learn here in the world, she's just a little slow. A little one-sided, perhaps. You mustn't talk to Ada about this," he said.

"Would she deny that Sølvi has a problem?" Sejer asked.

"She says that if they can't find anything, then it must not be there. People are just different, she says."

Sejer had called him to his office. Holland still seemed lost in a vast darkness.

"I have to ask you about a few things," Sejer said. "If Annie had met Axel Bjørk on the road, would she have got into his car?"

The question made Holland gape in surprise. "That's the most monstrous thing I've ever heard," he said.

"A monstrous crime has been committed here. Just answer my question. I don't know these people as well as you do, and I actually regard that as an advantage."

"Sølvi's father," he said. "Yes, I suppose so. They went to his place two or three times, so she knew him. She would probably have got into his car if he asked her to. Why wouldn't she?"

"What kind of relationship do you have with him?"

"We don't have a relationship."

"But you've talked to him?"

"Barely. Ada has always stopped him at the door. Claimed that he was trying to force his way in."

"What do you think about that?"

He shifted uncomfortably in his seat, as if his own weakness were obvious. "I thought it was pretty stupid. He didn't want to ruin things for us, he just wanted to see Sølvi once in a while. Now he's lost everything. Even his job."

"What about Sølvi? Did she want to see him?"

"I'm afraid Ada wrecked any desire she might have had. She can be very harsh. I think Bjørk has given up. But he was at the funeral, and at least then he had a chance to see her. You see, it's not easy to go against Ada," he said. "Not that I'm afraid of her, or anything," he gave a brief, ironic laugh. "But she gets so upset. It's not easy to explain. She gets very upset, and I can't deal with it."

He fell silent again, and Sejer sat, waiting, as he tried to imagine the interaction between these people. How thousands of threads became tangled up in each other over the years, forming a tough, finely woven net in which a person felt trapped. It fascinated him. And an individual's intense resistance to pulling out a knife and cutting himself loose, even though he was sick with longing for freedom. Holland would probably like to get out of Ada's net, but thousands of little ties held him back. He had made a choice; he would sit in those sticky threads for the rest of his life, and the decision had pushed him down a notch so that his whole, heavy body slumped and sagged.

"So you haven't got anything?" Holland asked after a while.

"Unfortunately, no," Sejer said. "All we have is a great many people who speak warmly and lovingly of Annie. There are very few forensic clues, and they haven't given us any leads, and there seems to be no apparent motive. Annie was not sexually assaulted or abused in any way. No one observed anything that might be of use to us in the vicinity of Kollen on that particular day, and everyone who travelled that stretch of road by car has been identified and checked out. There is one exception, but that car has been described in such vague terms that it hasn't led anywhere. The motorcyclist seen at Horgen's Shop seems to have vanished into thin air. Perhaps he was a tourist who was just passing through. No one saw his number plates. We've sent divers down to search for her bag, so far without success, so we have to assume that it's still in the killer's possession. We have no basis for an arrest, and so we can't search anyone. We don't even have a concrete theory to work with. We have so little to go on, in fact, that we're practically reduced to speculation. For instance, Annie might have come across some kind of sensitive information, perhaps quite by accident, and was murdered to ensure her silence. The information would have to have been extremely compromising, since it led to her death. She was naked but untouched, which might mean that the murderer wanted to steer us towards a sexual theory, possibly to divert attention from the real motive. That's why," he concluded, "we're interested in Annie's past."

He stopped and scratched the back of his hand, where he had a red, scaly patch as big as a 20-krone coin.

"You're one of the people who knew her best. And I'm sure you've had a thousand thoughts about this. I have to ask you again whether there was anything in Annie's past – experiences, acquaintances, opinions, impressions, anything at all – that surprised you. Don't limit yourself to a specific line of thought, just think about whether anything troubled you. Look for the smallest detail, even if it seems silly. A reaction you hadn't expected. Comments, hints, facts that have stayed with you. Annie had undergone a change in behaviour. I had the impression that it might have been due to something more than just puberty. Can you confirm that?"

"Ada says—"

"But what do *you* say?" Sejer held his gaze. "She rejected Halvor, quit the handball team, and then withdrew into herself. Did something happen at that time, something out of the ordinary?"

"Have you talked to Jensvoll?"

"Yes, we have."

"Well, I heard some rumours, but maybe they're

not true. Rumours spread fast around here," he said, a little embarrassed, his cheeks slightly flushed.

"What are you getting at?"

"Just something that Annie mentioned. That he was once in prison. A long time ago. I don't know why."

"Did Annie know?"

"So he *was* in prison?"

"That's correct, he was. But I didn't think anyone knew about it. We're checking everyone around Annie, to see whether they had an alibi. We've talked to more than 300 people, but unfortunately, no one is yet a suspect in the case."

"There's a man who lives up on Kolleveien," Holland said, "who's not all there. I've heard that he's tried things with girls around here."

"We've talked to him too," Sejer said patiently. "He was the one who found Annie."

"Yes, that's what I thought."

"He has an alibi."

"If it's reliable."

Sejer thought about Ragnhild and didn't tell Holland that his alibi was a six-year-old child.

"Why do you think she stopped baby-sitting?"

"I think she just grew out of it."

"But I understand that she really loved taking care of children. That's why I think it's a little strange."

"For years she did nothing else. First she'd do her homework and then she'd go outside to see if anyone on the block needed a ride in a pushchair. And if there was a fight going on, she'd calm everybody down. The poor child who threw the first stone would have to confess. Then he would be forgiven, and everything was fine again. She was good at mediating. She had authority, and everybody did what she said. Even the boys."

"A diplomatic personality, in other words?"

"Exactly. She liked to work things out. She couldn't stand unresolved conflicts. If there was something going on with Sølvi, for example, Annie would always find a solution for us. She was a kind of middleman. But in a way . . ." he said, "she seemed to lose interest in that too. She didn't get involved in things the way she used to."

"When was this?"

"Sometime last autumn."

"What happened last autumn?"

"I've already told you. She didn't want to be part of the team any more, didn't want to be with other people the way she used to do."

"But why!"

"I don't know," he said in despair. "I'm telling you that I don't understand it."

"Try to look beyond yourself and your immediate family. Beyond Halvor and the team and the problems with Axel Bjørk. Did anything else happen in the village at that time? Anything that might not have been directly related to you?"

Holland threw out his hands. "Well, yes. Although it doesn't have anything to do with this. One of the children she baby-sat for died in a tragic accident. That didn't help matters. Annie didn't want to take part in anything after that. The only thing she thought about was putting on her trainers and running away from home and the street."

Sejer could feel his heart take an extra beat.

"What did you just say?" He leaned his elbows on the table.

"One of the children she took care of died in an accident. His name was Eskil."

"Did it happen while Annie was baby-sitting for him?"

"No, no!" Holland gave him a frightened look. "No, are you crazy! Annie was extremely careful when she was caring for children. Didn't let them out of her sight for an instant."

"How did it happen?"

"At his house. He was only about two years old. Annie took it really badly. Well, we all did, of course, since we knew them."

"And when did this happen?"

"Last autumn, I told you. About the time that she

withdrew from everything. In fact, a lot was going on then, it wasn't a good period for us. Halvor kept calling and Jensvoll did too. Bjørk was putting on the pressure about Sølvi, and Ada was almost impossible to live with."

He fell silent, suddenly looking as if he were ashamed.

"When exactly did this death occur, Eddie?"

"I think it was in November. I don't remember the exact date."

"Did it happen before or after she left the team?"

"I don't remember."

"Then we'll keep going until you do. What kind of accident was it?"

"He got something caught in his throat and they couldn't get it out. He was in the kitchen alone, eating."

"Why didn't you tell me about this before?"

Holland gave him an unhappy look. "Because it's Annie's death you're supposed to solve," he whispered.

"And that's what I'm doing. It's important to eliminate certain things."

There was a long silence. There was sweat on Holland's high forehead, and he was constantly kneading his fingers, as if he had lost all sensation in them. Several idiotic pictures kept appearing in his mind, pictures of Annie wearing a red snowsuit and Russian cap, Annie wearing a wedding dress. Annie with an infant on her lap. Pictures that he would never take.

"Tell me about Annie, about how she reacted."

Holland straightened up in his chair and paused to think. "I don't remember the date, but I remember the day because we overslept. I had the day off. Annie was late for her bus, but she came home early from school because she wasn't feeling well. I didn't dare tell her right away. She went to her room to lie down, said she was going to have a sleep."

"She was sick?"

"Yes, well, no, she was never sick. It was just something temporary. She woke up later in the day, and I sat in the living room, dreading having to tell her. Finally I went to her room and sat down on the edge of her bed."

"Go on."

"She was stunned," he said thoughtfully. "Stunned and frightened. Turned away and pulled the covers over her head. I mean, what can you say to that? Afterwards she didn't show much of her feelings; she grieved in silence. Ada wanted her to take some flowers over to the house, but she refused. She didn't want to go to the funeral either."

"Did you and your wife go?"

"Yes, yes, we did. Ada was upset because Annie wouldn't go, but I tried to explain that's it's hard for a child to go to a funeral. Annie was only 14. They don't know what they're supposed to say, do they?"

"Did she visit his grave later?"

"Oh yes, she did. Several times. But she never went to their house again."

"But she must have talked to them, didn't she? Since she had baby-sat for the boy?"

"I'm sure she did. She had spent a lot of time with them. Mostly with the mother. She moved, by the way; they were separated after a while. Of course it's difficult to find each other again after a tragedy like that. You have to start over with a new relationship. And none of us will ever be the way we once were."

He seemed to have disengaged from the conversation and was sitting there talking to himself, as if the other man didn't exist. "Sølvi is the only one who's the same. I'm actually surprised that she can be the same after what's happened. But then she's not like other people. We have to take the children we've been given, though, don't we?"

"And . . . Annie?" Sejer said.

"Yes, Annie," he murmured. "Annie was never the same. I think she realised that we're all going to die. I remember the same feeling when I was a boy, when my mother died; that was the worst thing. Not that she was dead and gone. But that I was going to die too. And my father, and everyone I knew."

His gaze seemed fixed on something far away, and Sejer listened with both hands resting on his desk.

"We have more to talk about, Eddie," he said after a while. "But there's something you should know first."

"I don't know if I can stand to hear anything else."

"I can't keep it from you. Not with good conscience."

"What is it?"

"Can you remember if Annie ever complained of feeling pain?"

"No . . . I can't. Except from the time before she got shock-absorbent trainers. Her feet used to hurt."

"Did she ever mention having abdominal pain."

Holland gave him an uneasy look.

"I never heard her say anything like that. You should ask Ada."

"I'm asking you because it's my understanding that you were the person closest to her."

"Yes. But those kinds of girl's things . . . I never heard about anything like that."

"She had a tumour in her abdomen," Sejer said in a low voice.

"A tumour?"

"About as big as an egg. Malignant. It had spread to her liver."

Now Holland's whole body grew rigid.

"They must be mistaken," he said. "Nobody was healthier than Annie."

"She had a malignant tumour in her abdomen," Sejer repeated. "And in a short time she would have been very sick. There was a high chance that her illness would have led to death."

"Are you saying she would have died anyway?"

Holland's voice had an aggressive edge to it.

"That's what the pathologist says."

"Am I supposed to be happy that she didn't have to suffer?" he screamed, a drop of spit striking Sejer on the forehead. Holland hid his face in his hands. "No, no, I didn't mean that," he said, his voice choking, "but I don't understand what's happening. How could there be so many things I didn't know about?"

"Either she didn't know herself, or else she concealed the pain and purposely decided not to consult a doctor. There's no mention of it in her medical records."

"It probably doesn't say anything at all in them," Holland said. "There was never anything wrong with her. She had a couple of vaccinations over the years, but that was all."

"There's also one thing I want you to do," Sejer said. "I want you to talk to Ada and ask her to come down here to the station. We need to have her fingerprints."

Holland smiled wearily and leaned back in his chair. He hadn't slept much, and nothing seemed to be standing still any more. The chief inspector's face was flickering slightly, along with the curtain at the window, or maybe there was a draft, he wasn't quite sure.

"We found two fingerprints on Annie's belt buckle. One of them was Annie's. One of them might be your wife's. She told us that she often laid out Annie's clothes in the morning, so it might be her fingerprint on the buckle. If it's not hers, then it belongs to the killer. He undressed her. He must have touched the buckle."

At last Holland understood.

"Please ask your wife to come here as soon as possible. She should ask for Skarre."

"That eczema you have," Holland said suddenly, nodding at Sejer's hand. "I've heard that ash is supposed to help."

"Ash?"

"You smooth ash over the area. Ash is the purest substance that exists. It contains salts and minerals."

Sejer didn't reply. Holland's thoughts seemed to withdraw inward. Sejer left him in peace. It was so quiet in the room that they could almost feel Annie's presence.

CHAPTER 9

Halvor ate his pork sausage and boiled cabbage at the counter in the kitchen. Afterwards he cleaned up and put a blanket over his grandmother, who was dozing on the sofa. He went to his room, drew the curtains, and sat down in front of the monitor. This was how he spent most of his spare time now. He had tried out a lot of the music that he knew Annie liked, typing in titles and the names of musicians she had in her stack of CDs. Then movie titles, rather half-heartedly, because it wouldn't be like Annie to choose something like that. The task seemed insurmountable. She could have changed passwords several times, the way they did in the defence ministry to protect military secrets. They used passwords that changed automatically several times a second. He had read about it in a magazine from Ra Data. A password that kept changing was almost impossible to crack. He tried to remember when exactly he and Annie had created their own files and attached passwords to them. It was several months ago, sometime late in the autumn. He knew she wouldn't have chosen anything at random, she would have used something that had made an impression on her, or something that was familiar and dear to her. He knew quite a lot about things that were familiar and dear to Annie, and so he kept going. Until he heard his grandmother calling from the living room that she was done with her nap. Then he took a break to make coffee for her and butter a few pieces of *lefse* or some waffles, if they had any. To be polite, he watched TV for a while, keeping her company. But as soon as he felt able, he slipped back to his room. She didn't complain. He sat there until midnight, then dragged himself to bed and turned off the light. He always lay still for a while, listening, before sleep came. Often it didn't come at all, and then he would slip into his grandmother's room and steal a sleeping pill from her bottle. He didn't hear the footsteps outside going back and forth. As he waited to fall asleep, he thought about Annie. Blue was her favourite colour. The chocolate bar she liked best was a Dove with raisins. He made a mental note of several words and stored them away for later. The important thing was not to give up. When he finally found the right password, it would seem so obvious that she had chosen it, and he would say to himself: I should have thought of that before!

Outside, the courtyard was dark and quiet. The entrance to the empty kennel gaped like an open, toothless mouth, but it wasn't visible from the road, and a thief might still think there was a dog inside. Behind the kennel stood the shed with a modest woodpile, his bicycle, an old black-and-white TV, and a pile of newspapers. He always forgot when there was a paper drive, and he didn't read the local paper any more. In the far corner, behind a foam mattress, lay Annie's school bag.

He had run out to Bruvann and back, thirteen kilometres. Had tried to stay below the pain threshold, at least on the home stretch. Elise used to pour an ice-cold Farris and hand it to him when he came out of the shower. Often he would have only a towel wrapped around his waist. Now no one stood waiting for him, except for his dog, who lifted his head expectantly when Sejer opened the door and let the steam out. He got dressed in the bathroom and then found a bottle for himself. He snapped off the bottle cap against the counter edge and put the beer to his lips. The doorbell rang as he was half-done with the bottle. Sejer's doorbell didn't ring very often, so he was a little taken aback. He raised an admonishing finger at the dog and went to open the door. Outside stood Skarre, by the railing, with one foot on the stairs, as if to indicate that he would retreat quickly if he had come at a bad time.

"I was in the neighbourhood," he said.

He looked different. His curls were gone, sheared off close to his scalp. His hair had acquired a darker sheen, making him look older. And his ears actually stuck out a bit.

"Nice haircut," Sejer said. "Come on in."

Kollberg came leaping, as he always did.

"He's a little overzealous," Sejer said. "But he's good-natured."

"He ought to be, at that size. He's like a wolf."

"He's supposed to look like a lion. That's what the chap who mixed the breeds and created the first Leonberger intended. He was from the town of Leonberg in Germany and wanted to create a town mascot."

"A lion?" Skarre studied the big animal and smiled. "No, I'm not that gullible."

Skarre took off his jacket and hung it in the hall. "Did you have a talk with Holland today?"

"I did. What have you been doing?"

"I visited Halvor's grandmother."

"Did you?"

"She served me coffee and *lefse*, along with all the misery of her old age. I now know what it's like to get old."

"What's it like?"

"A gradual decline. An insidious, almost unnoticeable process that you only discover at sudden, shocking moments."

Skarre sighed like an old man and shook his head anxiously.

"The cell division process decreases, that's what it's all about. It slows down more and more, until the cells practically stop renewing themselves altogether, and everything starts to shrink. In fact, that's the first stage of the decomposition process, and it starts when you're about 25."

"That's tough, all right. That means you're well on your way. I think you're actually looking a little older already."

Sejer led the way into the living room.

"The blood starts to stagnate in the veins. Nothing smells or tastes the way it should. Malnutrition also becomes apparent. It's not so strange that we die when we get old."

This made Sejer chuckle. Then he thought about his mother in the hospital and stopped.

"How old is she?"

"She's 83. And she's obviously not all there." He pointed to his own close-cropped head. "I think it would be better if we died a little earlier. Maybe at about the age of 70."

"I don't think many 70-year-olds would agree with you," Sejer said. "Do you want a Farris?"

"OK, thanks."

Skarre ran his hand over his head, as if to check to see if the new haircut was real.

"You certainly have a lot of CDs, Konrad." He was staring at the shelf next to the stereo. "Have you counted them?"

"Approximately 500," Sejer shouted from the kitchen.

Skarre jumped up from his chair to study the titles. Like most people, he thought that musical taste said a lot about who a person was, deep inside.

"Laila Dalseth. Etta James. Billie Holiday. Edith Piaf. My God," he stared with astonishment, smiling. "They're all women!" he exclaimed.

"Is that right?"

Sejer poured the Farris.

"All women, Konrad! Eartha Kitt. Lill Lindfors. Monica Zetterlund – who's that?"

"One of the best. But you're too young to know that."

Skarre sat back down, drank his Farris, and wiped the bottom of his glass on his pants leg. "What did Holland say?"

Sejer pulled his tobacco pouch out from under the newspaper and opened it. He took out a paper and began to roll a cigarette.

"Jesus!" exclaimed Skarre in surprise. "You smoke!"

"Only one a day, in the evening. He told me that Annie knew that Jensvoll had been in prison. Maybe she knew why."

"Go on."

"And one of the children she often baby-sat for died in an accident."

Skarre fumbled for his own cigarettes.

"It happened in November, at about the same time everything got so difficult. Annie didn't want to go over there any more. She refused to take them flowers, she wouldn't go to the funeral, and she didn't want to baby-sit any more. Holland didn't think it was strange, since she was only 14, and wasn't old enough to handle death."

He looked at Skarre as he talked and noticed how his expression grew more alert. "After that she left the handball team, temporarily broke up with Halvor, and withdrew into herself. So it happened in that order. The child died. Annie withdrew from everyone around her."

Skarre lit a match and watched as Sejer licked the paper of the cigarette he had rolled.

"The child's death was apparently a tragic accident – the boy was only two – and I can understand why a teenager would be shaken by that kind of experience. She knew him well. And she knew his parents. But . . ."

He stopped to light up.

"So that's the reason for the change in her?"

"Possibly. But she also had cancer. Even though she may not have known about it herself, it could have changed her. But I was hoping to find something else. Something we could use."

"What about Jensvoll?"

"I have a hard time believing that a man would commit murder just to guarantee silence about a rape that took place eleven years ago, and which he's done time for. Unless it's a matter of his having tried it again. And the whole thing went wrong . . . Do you have time to take a drive?"

"Of course. Where are we going?"

"To Lundeby Church." He took a deep drag on his cigarette and held it for a long time.

"Why there?"

"I'm not sure. I like to snoop around; that's the only reason."

"Maybe you think better out of doors?" Skarre scraped at a patch of candle wax on the sand-blasted table.

"I've always thought that a person's surroundings affected how they think, that you understand more about something if you go to the actual scene. If you have a sort of awareness inside, an awareness of objects. For 'what objects have to say'."

"Fascinating theory," Skarre said. "Do you dare mention it out loud at headquarters?"

"We have a kind of silent agreement not to. The district prosecutor isn't interested in my beliefs. He knows they're there, of course, and he does take them into consideration, though he would never admit it. Another silent agreement."

Sejer exhaled the smoke reverently and looked up.

"What else did Halvor's grandmother give you? Aside from the *lefse* and a lecture on decay?"

"She told me a lot about Halvor's father. About how terribly nice he was as a boy. And how he was an unhappy man."

"I believe it. Since he was capable of beating his own children."

"And she says that Halvor has been holed up in his room. He apparently sits in front of his PC all evening and sometimes well into the night."

"What do you think he's doing?"

"I have no idea. Maybe he's writing a diary."

"In that case, I'd like to read it."

"Are you going to bring him in again?"

"Certainly."

They emptied their glasses and got to their feet. On their way out Skarre caught sight of a photo of Elise, with her dazzling smile.

"Your wife?" he said.

"The last one she had taken."

"She looks like Grace Kelly," Skarre said. "How

did an old grouch like you ever capture such a beauty?"

Sejer was so taken aback by this boundless impudence that he actually stuttered as he answered mildly, "I wasn't an old grouch back then."

The car crunched over the gravel road to Lundeby Church. It was floodlit now and stood in the pink-coloured light with solemn self-possession, as if it had stood there forever. In reality it was only 150 years old, a minuscule sigh in the crown of eternity. They shut the car doors without a sound, stood next to the vehicle, and listened for a moment. Skarre looked around, took a few steps towards the chapel, and headed for the rows of graves in the foreground. Ten white headstones, evenly spaced.

"What's this?"

They stopped to read the gravestones.

"Military graves," Sejer said. "British and Canadian soldiers. The Germans shot them here in the woods on the ninth of April 1940. Children put white anemones on the graves every May 17th. My daughter Ingrid told me about it."

"'Pilot Officer, Royal Air Force. A. F. Le Maistre of Canada. Age 26. God gave and God has taken.' A long way to come for such a brief heroic act."

Skarre looked around him. "All the way from

252

Canada, in his new uniform, to fight for those on the side of justice. And then gunfire and death."

They had laid Annie to rest at the edge of the cemetery, down near a large field of barley. The flowers had faded and were beginning to decay. The two officers stared at them, each lost in his own thoughts. Then they began to read the inscriptions on the other headstones. Two rows beyond Annie's grave, Sejer found what he was looking for. A small headstone, rounded on top, with a beautifully etched inscription. Skarre bent down and read what it said. "Our beloved Eskil?"

Sejer nodded. "Eskil Johnas. Born August 4, 1992, died November 17, 1994."

"Johnas? The carpet dealer?"

"The carpet dealer's son. He got something caught in his throat and choked to death. After he died the marriage fell apart. Which isn't so strange; indeed, apparently it's quite common. But Johnas has an older son who lives with his mother."

"He had pictures of the boys on the wall," Skarre said, sticking his hands in his pockets. "What's that little hollow on the top?"

"Someone must have stolen something from the headstone. Maybe there was a bird or an angel. There often is on children's graves."

"Strange that they haven't replaced it. It seems such a fragile little grave. Looks almost neglected. I thought it was only old people who were forgotten like this."

They turned and looked down at the fields surrounding the cemetery on all sides. Lights from the nearby rectory flickered piously in the blue dusk. "I suppose it's not easy to get out here. The mother moved to Oslo and it's a long way from there."

"It would only take Johnas two minutes."

Skarre looked in the other direction, towards Fagerlund Ridge, where the houses glittered below Kollen.

"He can see the church from his living-room window," Sejer said. "I remember seeing it when we were at his house. Maybe he thinks that's enough."

"His dog must have had her pups by now."

Sejer didn't answer.

"Where are we headed next?"

"I don't really know, but this little chap is dead." He glanced down at the grave again and frowned. "And Annie became a different person afterwards. Why would she take it so hard? She was a tough girl with lots of energy. Isn't it true that healthy, normal people get over these things? Isn't it in our nature to accept death and go on living, at least after a certain amount of time has passed?"

He fell silent. A little confused, he knelt down and once again examined the almost bare grave, distractedly rearranging the sparse foliage.

"So the fact that she reacted the way she did, in spite of her tough character, means something?" asked Skarre.

"I'm not sure. I don't know what I'm getting at."

"How could anyone steal from a grave?"

"The fact that you can't comprehend it is a good sign," Sejer said, getting to his feet.

They started back to the car.

"Do you believe in God?" Skarre asked.

Sejer pursed his lips into an odd little pout. "Well, no, I don't think I do. I believe more in . . . some kind of power," he said.

Skarre smiled.

"I've heard that sort of thing before. A *power* is more acceptable. Seems strange that it's so difficult for us to give it a name. But it's obvious that 'God' is an enormously loaded word. So where do you think this power is leading us?"

"I said power," Sejer said, "not will."

"So you believe in a power that has no will?"

"I didn't say that either. I simply call it a power; whether it's guided by a will or not is an open question."

"But a power with no will would be terribly depressing, don't you think?"

"You don't give up, do you! Is this a clumsy attempt at confessing your faith?"

"Yes," Skarre said.

"Jesus. The things a person doesn't know." Sejer pondered this unexpected revelation for a moment and then muttered, "I've never understood faith."

"What do you mean?"

"I don't understand what it takes to have it."

"It's just a matter of a certain attitude. You choose an attitude to life, which in time brings you benefits and joy. It gives you a sense of connection to the past and it lends a meaning to life and death that is intensely reassuring."

"Choose an attitude? Haven't you been saved?"

Skarre opened his mouth and let out a peal of laughter redolent of the coastland and skerries and salt water. "People make everything so complicated when it's actually very simple. You don't have to understand everything. The important thing is to feel. Understanding comes gradually."

"Then that's for me," Sejer said.

"I know what you're betting on," Skarre said, grinning. "You don't believe in God, but you can clearly imagine the Pearly Gates. And like most people, you hope that Saint Peter will be asleep over his books so that you can slip inside at an unguarded moment."

Sejer laughed heartily, from the very depths of

his soul, and did something he would never have thought possible. He put his arm around Skarre's shoulders and gave them a squeeze.

They had reached their car. Skarre plucked off a leafy twig that had caught on the windshield.

"I would have bought another bird," Skarre said, "and had it properly attached to the headstone. If it was my child."

Sejer started up the old Peugeot and let the engine run as he sat in silence for a moment.

"I would too."

Halvor was still at his computer. He hadn't thought it would be easy, because his life had never been easy. It might take months, but that didn't frighten him. He was going over everything he could remember about what she had read or listened to, selecting titles at random, or a character's name from a book, or specific words or phrases that had been part of her vocabulary. Often he simply sat and stared at the screen. He didn't care about anything else any more, not TV or his CD player. He sat alone in the silence, spending most of his time in the past. Finding the password had become an excuse for staying in the past and avoiding the future. There was nothing to look forward to anyway. Only loneliness.

What he had shared with Annie was of course

too good to last; he should have known that. He had often wondered where it was leading and how it would end.

His grandmother said nothing, although she did have her opinions; like that he should do something useful, such as mowing the little patch of lawn behind the house, raking the courtyard, and maybe cleaning up the shed. That was what most people did in the spring: threw out the rubbish from the winter. The flowerbed in front of the house needed weeding; she had been out there herself and noticed how the tulips were ailing, strangled by dandelions and weeds. Every time she mentioned it, he nodded distractedly, and then went back to what he was doing. Eventually she gave up, deciding that whatever he was working on must be terribly important. With much effort she managed to tie the laces on a pair of trainers and limp outside with a crutch under one arm. She didn't often go into the yard. Only on a few golden days could she make it as far as the grocery shop. She leaned heavily on the crutch, feeling a bit discouraged about the decay. Apparently it wasn't just happening to her. Everything seemed so grey and faded – the buildings, the yard – or maybe it was just that her eyesight was failing. She plodded across the courtyard and opened the door to the shed, succumbing to a sudden impulse to look inside. Maybe the old garden furniture was still usable, or at least could be put in front of the house as decoration. It would look cosy. Everyone else would have put out their outdoor furniture a long time ago. She fumbled for the switch on the wall and turned on the light.

CHAPTER 10

Astrid Johnas owned a wool shop on the west side of Oslo.

She was sitting at a knitting machine and working on something soft and angora-like, perhaps something for a new-born. He walked across the room and cleared his throat, stopping behind her to admire her work with a slightly awkward expression on his face.

"I'm making a blanket," she said, smiling. "To put in a baby's pram. I make them on commission."

He stared at her, at first with some surprise. She was a good deal older than her former husband. But more than that, she was astonishingly beautiful, and for a moment her beauty took his breath away. Hers was not the gentle, restrained beauty that Elise had possessed, but rather a dark beauty evident at first glance. Against his will he stood there staring at her. It was only then that he noticed her fragrance, perhaps because she gestured towards him. She smelled like a sweet shop, with the faint scent of vanilla.

"Konrad Sejer," he said. "From the police."

"I thought so." She gave him a smile. "Sometimes I wonder why it's always so easy to tell, even when you're not wearing a uniform."

He blushed and wondered whether he might have acquired a different posture or a way of dressing after so many years on the police force, or whether she was simply more astute than most people.

She stood up and turned off her work lamp.

"Come into the back room. I have a small office where I eat my lunch."

She moved in a very feminine way.

"This whole thing with Annie is so awful that I almost can't even think about it. And I feel so guilty for not going to the funeral, but to be honest, I just couldn't face it. I sent flowers."

She pointed to a chair. He stared at her, slowly overcome by an almost forgotten sensation. He was with a beautiful woman, and there was no one else in the room that he could hide behind. She smiled at him, as if the same thought had occurred to her. But she didn't lose her composure. After all, she had always been beautiful.

"I knew Annie well. She spent a lot of time at our house and took care of Eskil. We had a son who died last year," she said. "His name was Eskil."

"I know."

261

"You've talked to Henning, of course. Unfortunately, we lost contact with her afterwards; she didn't come to see us any more. Poor thing, I felt so sorry for her. She was only 14, and at that age it's not easy to know what to say."

Sejer nodded as he fumbled with the buttons on his jacket. It was suddenly very warm in the small office.

"Have you any idea who might have done it?" she asked.

"No," he said. "At the moment we're just gathering information. Then we'll see if we can move on to what we call the tactical phase."

"I'm afraid I won't be of much help." She looked down at her hands. "I knew her well; she was a lovely girl, much smarter and nicer than most girls her age. She was never silly. She trained hard and kept in shape and paid attention in school. She was pretty too. She had a boyfriend, a boy named Halvor. But maybe they weren't together any more?"

"Yes, they were," he said.

There was a pause. He waited to see what her reaction would be.

"What is it you want to know?"

He said nothing, studying her. She had a trim, slender figure and dark eyes. All of her clothes were knitted, like one big advertisement for her shop. An attractive suit with a straight skirt and fitted jacket, deep red with green and mustard-coloured borders. Black, low-heeled shoes. A simple, straight hair style. Lipstick that matched the red in her outfit. Bronze arrowhead earrings, partially hidden by her dark hair. Some years younger than Sejer, with the first hint of fine lines at her eyes and mouth. She was clearly much older than her former husband. Her son Eskil must have been born at the very end of her youth.

"I'm not looking for anything in particular," he said. So Annie came to your house to baby-sit Eskil?"

"Several times a week," she said. "No one else wanted to baby-sit for him; he wasn't easy to deal with. But you've probably heard this already."

"Yes, it was mentioned," he lied.

"He was so full of energy, almost bordering on the abnormal. Hyperactive, I guess it's called. You know, up and down, always restless."

She gave a rather helpless laugh. "I hope you understand that this isn't an easy thing to admit. But to be quite frank, he was a difficult child. Annie was one of the few who could handle him."

She paused and thought for a moment. "She came over a lot. Henning and I were always so worn out, and it was a blessing whenever she appeared in the doorway, smiling and offering to baby-sit. He would sit in the pushchair, and we usually gave them some money so they could go downtown and buy something. Sweets or ice cream or something like that. It would take them an hour or two; I think she deliberately took her time. Now and then they'd take the bus into the city and be gone the whole day. They would ride around in the little train at the marketplace. I was working the night shift at the hospital and often needed to sleep during the day, so it was a welcome break for me. We have another son, Magne. But he was too old to go out pushing a pram. At any rate, he didn't want to. So he wriggled out of it, as most boys do."

She smiled again and shifted her position on the chair. Every time she moved he noticed the scent of vanilla. She kept an eye on the shop door as she spoke, but no one came in. Talking about her son seemed to make her uneasy. Her eyes were on everything except Sejer's face, flitting around like a bird trapped in much too small a space, moving from the shelves of wool to the table to the front of the shop.

"How old was Eskil when he died?" Sejer asked.

"Only 27 months," she whispered, and seemed to flinch.

"Did it happen while Annie was baby-sitting him?"

She glanced up. "No, thank God. I kept on saying how lucky that was; it would have been unbearable. It was bad enough for poor Annie; she didn't need to have that on her conscience too."

Another pause. He breathed as quietly as he could and took a new approach.

"But . . . what kind of accident was it?"

"I thought you talked to Henning," she said.

"I did," he lied. "But he didn't go into detail."

"Eskil got some food caught in his throat," she said. "I was upstairs in bed. Henning was in the bathroom shaving and didn't hear a thing. But Eskil couldn't scream anyway, with the food caught in his throat. He was strapped to his chair with a harness, the kind children have at that age. They are meant for their protection. He was sitting there eating his breakfast."

"I know them. I have a daughter and a grand-child," he said.

She swallowed and then went on. "Henning found him hanging in the harness, blue in the face. It took the ambulance more than 20 minutes to arrive, and by then there was no hope."

"They came from the central hospital?"

"Yes."

Sejer looked at the front room of the shop and saw a woman at the window. She was admiring a jumper that Mrs Johnas had on display.

"So it happened in the morning?"

"Early in the morning," she said.

"And you were asleep the whole time, is that right?"

Suddenly she looked him straight in the eye. "I thought you wanted to talk about Annie."

"You're welcome to tell me something about Annie," he said, and he felt a twinge in his chest.

But she didn't say anything. She sat up and crossed her arms.

"I take it you've talked to everybody who lives in Krystallen?"

"Yes, we have."

"So you already know all about this?"

"Yes, that's true. But what concerns me is Annie's reaction to the accident," he said. "The fact that she reacted so strongly."

"That's not so strange, is it?" she said, her voice a little sharp. "When a two-year-old dies like that. A boy she knew well. They were very attached to each other, and Annie was proud of the fact that she was really the only one who could handle him."

"I suppose it's not so strange. I'm just trying to find out who she was. What she was like."

"But I told you. I'm not trying to be uncooperative, but it's not easy to talk about this." She looked directly at him again. "But . . . you're looking for a sex criminal, aren't you?"

"I'm not sure."

"You're not? Well, that's what I assumed straight

away, since it said that she was found naked. You know, after reading the papers, and they're always talking about sex." Now she was blushing as she fidgeted with her fingers. "What else could it be?"

"That's the question. As far as we know, she had no enemies. But if the motive wasn't sex, then the question is: what was it?"

"Those kinds of people probably aren't very logical. I mean, crazy people. They don't think like the rest of us."

"We have no idea how crazy he might be. How long were you married to your husband?"

She gave a start. "For 15 years. I was pregnant with Magne when we got married. Henning – he's a lot younger than I am," she said, as if to confirm something that she thought might have surprised him. "Eskil was actually the result of long discussions, but we were in total agreement, we really were."

"A kind of afterthought?"

"Yes." She stared at the ceiling, as if there were something of interest up there.

"So your older son is getting on for 17 now?"
She nodded.

"Does he have contact with his father?"

She gave him a look of dismay. "Of course he does! He often goes to Lundeby to visit old friends. But it's not always easy for us. After everything that has happened."

"Do you go out to Eskil's grave very often?"

"No," she said. "But Henning tends to it. It's difficult for me. As long as I know it's being looked after, I can bear it."

He thought about the neglected grave. Then the door opened and a young man came into the shop. Mrs Johnas glanced up.

"Magne! I'm in here!"

Sejer turned and studied her son. He bore a strong resemblance to his father, although he was much more heavily built. He paused in the doorway, apparently reluctant to talk. His expression was stony and remote; it suited his black hair and the bulging muscles of his upper arms.

"I must get going, Mrs Johnas," Sejer said, standing up. "You'll forgive me if I have to come back another time."

He nodded to mother and son, and was gone. Mrs Johnas stared after him for a long time and then gave her son an agonised look.

"He's investigating Annie's murder," she said. "But all he wanted to talk about was Eskil."

Outside the shop, Sejer paused for a moment. A motorcycle was parked next to the entrance; perhaps it belonged to Magne Johnas. A big Kawasaki. Leaning on the motorcycle, with her rear end against the seat, was a young woman. She didn't notice him because she was concentrating on her nails. Maybe she'd broken one of them and was now trying to save it by scraping at the break with another fingernail. She was wearing a short red leather jacket covered with studs, and she had a cloud of blonde hair that reminded him of angel-hair, the kind they used to put on the Christmas tree when he was a child. Then she looked up. He smiled and straightened his jacket.

"Hello, Sølvi," he said, and headed across the street.

He drove slowly, ordering his thoughts in neat rows. Eskil Johnas. A difficult child whom only Annie could handle. And who suddenly died, all alone, harnessed to his chair, with no one to help him. He thought of his own grandson and shivered as he took the Lundeby exit and headed for Halvor's house.

Halvor Muntz was standing in the kitchen, running cold water over some spaghetti. He kept forgetting to eat. Now he felt dizzy, and the sleeping pill he had taken in the night had left him feeling heavy and sluggish. He didn't hear the car pull up outside because the water was gushing out of the tap. But he heard his grandmother slam the door, mutter something to herself and shuffle across the floor in her Nike trainers with their black stripes. She looked comical. On the counter stood a bottle of ketchup and a bowl of grated cheese. He remembered that he had forgotten to add salt. His grandmother was groaning in the living room.

"Look what I found in the shed, Halvor!"

Something fell to the floor with a thud. He peeked into the room.

"An old school bag," she said. "With books inside. It's fun to look at old textbooks. I didn't know you were saving them."

Halvor took two steps forward and then stopped abruptly. From the buckle on the bag hung a bottle opener with an ad for Coke on it.

"That's Annie's," he whispered.

A pen had leaked blue ink through the leather and made little blotches along the bottom of the zippered compartment.

"Did she leave it here?"

"Yes," he said quickly. "I'll put it in my room for the time being and take it over to Eddie later."

His grandmother looked at him, and an anxious expression spread over her wrinkled face. Suddenly a familiar figure appeared in the dimly lit hallway. Halvor felt his heart sink; he stiffened and stood as if frozen to the spot, with the bag dangling from one strap.

"Halvor," Sejer said. "You'll have to come with me."

Halvor swayed and had to take a step sideways in

order not to fall. The ceiling was moving down towards him, soon he would be crushed against the floor.

"You can take the bag to Annie's house on the way," his grandmother said nervously, twisting her wedding ring, which was much too big, around and around. Halvor didn't reply. The room was starting to swirl around him, and sweat poured out of him as he stood there shaking, with the bag in his hand. It wasn't very heavy because Annie had removed most of its contents. Inside was Sigrid Undset's novel *The Wreath*, the new biography of the author, and a notebook – along with her wallet, which contained a picture of him from the previous summer when he looked tanned and handsome, with his hair bleached by the sun. Not as he looked now, with sweat on his forehead and his face chalk-white with fear.

The mood was tense. Normally he had no trouble staying the course and taking whatever came his way. But now he felt caught off guard.

"You realise that this was necessary?" Sejer said.

"Yes."

Halvor raised one leg and studied his trainer, the frayed laces and the sole, which was beginning to separate along the edges.

"Annie's school bag was found in the shed at

your house, which directly connects you with the murder. Do you understand what I'm saying?"

"Yes. But you're wrong."

"Since you were Annie's boyfriend, you were a suspect. The problem was that we couldn't charge you with anything. But now your grandmother has done the job for us. I'm sure you hadn't expected that, Halvor, since she isn't very mobile. All of a sudden she decides to clean out the shed. Who would have thought that would happen?"

"I have no idea where it came from! She found it in the shed, that's all I know."

"Behind a foam mattress?"

Halvor's face looked grimy and paler then ever. From time to time the taut corner of his mouth would twitch, as if finally, after a very long time, it wanted to tear itself away.

"Someone's trying to frame me."

"What do you mean by that?"

"Someone must have put the bag there. I heard someone sneaking around outside my window the other night."

Sejer smiled sadly.

"Go ahead and sneer," Halvor said, "but it's true. Somebody put it there, someone wants me to take the blame, someone who knew that Annie and I were together. So it has to be someone she knew, doesn't it?"

He gave the chief inspector a stubborn stare.

"I've always thought that the killer knew her," Sejer said. "I think he knew her well. Maybe as well as you did?"

"I didn't do it! Listen to me! I didn't do it!"

He wiped his brow and tried to calm down.

"Do you think there's someone we should talk to that we might have overlooked?"

"I have no idea."

"A new boyfriend, for instance?"

"There wasn't anyone else."

"How can you be so sure?"

"She would have told me."

"Do you think girls come running to confess the minute they fall for someone else? How many girlfriends have you had, Halvor?"

"She would have told me. You don't know Annie."

"No, I didn't. And I realise that she was unusal. But she must have had some things in common with other girls, don't you think, Halvor? A few things?"

"I don't know any other girls."

He huddled on his chair. Stuck a finger between the rubber sole and the canvas of his shoe and began prising them apart.

"Why don't you look for fingerprints on the bag?"

"We will, of course. But it's not hard to wipe them clean. I have a strong suspicion that we won't

273

find a single one, except for yours and your grand-mother's."

"I never touched it before. Not until today."

"We'll see. Finding the bag also gives us reason to do a closer check on your motorcycle and gear and helmet. And the house you live in. Is there anything you need before we continue?"

"No."

The gap in his shoe was now quite big. He pulled his hand away.

"Do I have to stay here tonight?"

"I'm afraid so. If you could look at the situation objectively, you'd understand that I have to hold you."

"For how long?"

"I don't know yet."

He looked at the boy's face across the table and changed tactics.

"What have you been writing on your PC, Halvor? You sit in front of the monitor for hours, from the minute you get home after work until close to midnight every day. Can you tell me what you've been doing?"

Halvor looked up. "Have you been spying on me?"

"In a way. We've been spying on a lot of people lately. Are you writing a diary?"

"I just play games. Chess, for example."

"With yourself?"

"With the Virgin Mary," he said.

Sejer blinked. "I would advise you to tell me what you know. You're keeping something from me, Halvor, I'm sure of that. Were there two of you? Are you covering up for someone?"

Halvor remained silent.

"If we end up charging you, we may have to confiscate your PC."

"Go ahead," he said, smiling suddenly. "But you won't be able to get in!"

"We won't get in? Why not?"

Halvor stopped talking and went back to working on his trainer.

"Because you've put a password on it?"

His mouth was dry, but he didn't want to beg for a Coke. In the refrigerator at home he had a Vørter beer; he sat there thinking about it.

"So I assume that it contains something important, since you've made sure that no one could find it."

"I just did it for fun."

"Could you give me more than one-line answers, Halvor?"

"There's nothing important. Just things I scribble when I'm bored."

Sejer stood up, and his chair slid back without a sound on the linoleum.

"You look thirsty. I'll get us a couple of Cokes."

Sejer left and the office closed in around Halvor. There was now a real hole in his trainer, and he peered at his filthy tennis sock. Far off in the distance he could hear a siren, but he couldn't tell what kind of emergency vehicle it came from. Otherwise there was a steady hum in the big building, like the sound in a movie theatre before the film starts. Sejer came back with two bottles and an opener.

"I'm going to open the window a little. OK?"

Halvor nodded. "I didn't do it."

Sejer found two plastic cups and poured the Coke. Foam spilled over the sides.

"There was no reason for me to do it."

"It's not immediately clear to me either why you would do it." He sighed and took a sip of the Coke. "But that doesn't mean that you didn't have a reason. Sometimes our feelings can run away with us – that's often the simple answer. Has that ever happened to you?"

Halvor didn't reply.

"Do you know Raymond on Kolleveien?"

"The guy with Downs syndrome? I see him in the street once in a while."

"Have you ever been to his house?"

"I've driven past. He has rabbits."

"Ever talk to him?"

"Never."

"Did you know that Knut Jensvoll, who was Annie's coach, once served time for rape?"

"Annie told me that."

"Did anyone else know?"

"I have no idea."

"Did you know the little boy she used to baby-sit for? Eskil Johnas?"

Now he looked up, startled. "Yes! He died."

"Tell me about him."

"Why?"

"Just do as I ask."

"Well, he was sweet . . . and funny."

"Sweet and funny?"

"Full of energy."

"Difficult?"

"A bit of a handful, maybe. Couldn't sit still. I think he took medication for it. Had to be strapped down all the time, to his chair, in the pushchair. I went along a few times when Annie took care of him. She was the only one who could handle him. But you know, Annie . . ."

He emptied his cup and wiped his mouth.

"Did you know his parents?"

"I know who they are."

"How about the older son?"

"Magne? I know what he looks like."

"Did he ever show any interest in Annie?"

"Just the usual. Long looks whenever she walked past."

"What did you think about that, Halvor? The fact that other boys were giving your girlfriend the once over?"

"First of all, I was used to it. Second, Annie let them know she wasn't interested."

"And yet she went off with someone. There's an exception here, Halvor."

"I realise that."

Halvor was tired. He closed his eyes. The scar at the corner of his mouth shone like a silver cord in the light from the lamp. "There was a lot about Annie that I didn't understand. Sometimes she'd get angry for no reason, or really irritated, and if I asked what was the matter, she'd get even worse and snap at me, saying that it's not always easy to understand everything in this world."

He gasped for breath.

"So you have a feeling that she knew something? That something was bothering her?"

"I don't know. I guess so. I told Annie a lot about myself. Almost everything. So she should have known that it wasn't dangerous to confide in someone."

"But your own confidences couldn't have been exactly earthshaking. Maybe hers were worse?"

Nothing could have been worse. Nothing in the world.

"Halvor?"

"There was something," he said in a low voice as he opened his eyes again, "that had locked Annie up tighter than a sealed drum."

CHAPTER 11

Something had locked Annie up tighter than a sealed drum.

The sentence was so delicately formulated that he realised he believed it. Or was it simply that he *wanted* to believe it? In any case . . . there was the school bag, hidden. The strong feeling that Halvor was keeping something concealed. Sejer stared at the pavement ahead of him and arranged several ideas in his mind. Annie liked to baby-sit for other people's children. The boy she preferred to take care of was particularly difficult, and he had died. She would never have had children of her own, and she didn't have long to live. She had a boyfriend at whom she occasionally snapped; she broke off with him and then took him back. As if she didn't really know what she wanted. He could see no clear connections between this set of facts.

He stuck his hands in his pockets and headed across the car park, got into his car and carefully manoeuvred it out to the street. Then he drove to the next county, the community where Halvor had spent his childhood, or rather non-existent child-hood. Back then the community police department was in an old villa, but now he found it located in a new shopping centre, squeezed in between a Rimi supermarket and the Inland Revenue office. He waited a short time in the reception area and was lost in thought when the community officer came into the room. A pale, freckled hand was extended. The man was in his late 40s, thin, with little pigmentation on his skin and scalp and barely concealed curiosity in his blue-green eyes. And entirely obliging. It wasn't every day that they were visited by a chief inspector from the city. Most of the time it felt as though the rest of the world had forgotten them.

"It's good of you to take the time," Sejer said, following the community officer down the corridor.

"You mentioned a homicide. Annie Holland?"

Sejer nodded.

"I've been following the case in the papers. And as you're here, I assume that you have someone in the spotlight whom you think I might know?"

He pointed to a chair.

"Well, yes, in a way. We do have someone in custody. He's just a boy, but what we found at his house gave us no choice but to arrest him."

"And you would have preferred to have a choice?"

"I don't think he did it." Sejer gave a little smile at his own words.

"I see. That happens sometimes."

The community officer's voice held no hint of irony. He folded his pale pink hands and waited.

"In December 1992 you had a suicide here in your district. Two brothers were subsequently sent to the Bjerkeli Children's Home, and the mother ended up in the psychiatric ward of the Central Hospital. I'm looking for information on Halvor Muntz, born 1976, the son of Torkel and Lilly Muntz."

The community officer recognised the name, and at once he looked anxious.

"You dealt with the case, didn't you?"

"Yes, unfortunately, I did. Along with a younger officer. Halvor, the older boy, called me at home. It happened at night. I remember the date, December 13, because my daughter had the role of Lucia at the school celebration that day. I didn't want to go out there alone, so I took along a new recruit. When it came to Halvor's family, we never knew what we might find. We drove out to the house and found the mother on the sofa in the living room, huddled under a quilt, and the two boys upstairs. Halvor didn't say a word. Next to him in bed was his little brother, who wouldn't even open his eyes. There was blood everywhere. We checked the boys, saw that they were still alive, and breathed a sigh of relief. Then we started searching. The father was lying inside an old, rotting sleeping bag. Half of his head was blown away."

He stopped, and Sejer could almost see the images like shadows in the community officer's pupils as they tumbled out.

"It wasn't easy to get anything out of the boys. They clung to each other and refused to say a word. But after a lot of coaxing, Halvor told us that his father had been drinking heavily since morning and had worked himself up into a terrible rage. He was ranting incoherently and had started smashing up the house. The boys had spent most of the day outside, but when night fell, they had to come in because it was cold. Halvor woke up to find his father bending over his bed with a bread knife in his hand. He stabbed Halvor once and then seemed to come to his senses. He rushed out and Halvor heard the door slam, and then they heard him struggling with the door to the shed and slamming it shut. They had one of those old-fashioned woodsheds behind the house. After a little while they heard a shot. Halvor didn't dare go out to investigate; he tiptoed down to the living room and called me. But he guessed what had happened. Told us he was afraid that something was wrong with his father. The Child Welfare Service had been trying to take custody of those kids for years, but Halvor had always refused. After that night, he didn't object."

"How did he take it?"

The community officer got up and paced the room. He seemed strained and uneasy. Sejer had no intention of filling the silence.

"It was hard to tell what he was feeling. Halvor was a very closed sort of child. But to be honest, it definitely wasn't despair. It was more a sort of determination, maybe because he could finally start a new life. His father's death was a turning point. It must have been a relief. The boys had lived in constant fear, and they never had the things they needed."

The community officer fell silent and stood with his back turned, waiting for Sejer's questions. He was the chief inspector, after all, who had come to him for assistance. But Sejer remained motionless. Finally he turned around.

"It wasn't until later that we started to think about things." He went back to his chair. "The father was lying inside a sleeping bag. He had taken off his jacket and boots, had even rolled up his sweater and stuck it under his head. I mean, he had really settled in for the night. Not . . ." he said, taking a breath, "not to die. So it occurred to us afterwards that someone might have helped him on his way to eternity."

Sejer shut his eyes. He rubbed hard at a spot on one eyebrow and felt a scrap of dried skin fall.

"You mean Halvor?"

"Yes," the community officer said sombrely, "I mean Halvor. Halvor could have followed him out, watched him fall asleep, stuck the shotgun inside the sleeping bag, into his father's hands, and pulled the trigger."

The information made Sejer freeze.

"What did you do?"

"Nothing."

The community officer threw out his hands in a helpless gesture. "We didn't do anything at all. We didn't find anything that could connect him to it, nothing concrete. The wound was typical for a suicide. A 16 calibre, fired at close range, with the entrance wound under the chin and the exit wound at the top of the skull. No other fingerprints on the shotgun. No suspicious footprints outside the shed. Unlike you, we had a choice. But you might call it something else, I suppose. Breach of duty or a serious misjudgement?"

"I could probably think of even worse things." Sejer smiled. "If I was so inclined. But you talked to him?"

"We brought them in for questioning, but we didn't get anywhere. The younger brother was only about six; he didn't know a thing and couldn't confirm or deny the timing. The mother was full of Valium, and none of the neighbours heard the shot. Their house was quite isolated, a hideous place that had originally been a grocer's shop. A brick building with steep stone staircase and two huge windows on either side of the door."

He wiped his nose, a nervous gesture.

"But fortunately there were a number of contra-indications."

"Such as?"

"If Halvor was the one who fired the shot, he would have had to lie down next to his father, with the shotgun pressed to his chest and the muzzle up under his chin. Would a 15-year-old be able to think that clearly, with his cheek sliced open?"

"It's not impossible. Someone who lives in a house with a psychopath year after year has to learn a lot of tricks. Halvor's a bright kid."

"Were they sweethearts? Halvor and the Holland girl?"

"Sort of sweethearts," Sejer said. "I'm not happy about your theory, but I'm going to have to take it into consideration."

"So you're going to make it public?"

"If you give me a copy of the case file, that would be great. But it's probably impossible now, after so much time, to prove anything. I don't think you need to worry. I've served on a district police force myself. I know how it is. You get too tied to the people."

The community officer stared sadly out the window.

"I've probably damaged Halvor's case by telling you this. He deserved better. He's the most considerate boy I've ever met. He took care of his mother and brother all those years, and I've heard that he's been living with old Mrs Muntz now, and taking care of her."

"That's right."

"So he finally found a girlfriend. And it ends up like this? How's he doing? Is he keeping his head above water?"

"Yes, he is. But perhaps he didn't expect anything from life other than repeated catastrophes."

"If he killed his father," the community officer said, looking Sejer straight in the eye, "then it was in self-defence. He saved the whole family. It was him or them. I have a hard time believing that he would kill for any other reason. So it would not be fair to use this as evidence against him, an incident that we've never properly solved. After I've solved the problem for myself by acquitting him, giving him the benefit of the doubt."

He rubbed his hand over his mouth. "Poor Lilly didn't know what she was doing when she said yes to Torkel Muntz. My father was the community officer here before me, and there were problems with Torkel even in his day. He was a trouble-maker, but he was a handsome guy. And Lilly was so pretty. Separately they might have made something of themselves in the world. But there are certain combinations that just can't work, don't you agree?"

Sejer nodded. "We have a departmental meeting later today, and we'll have to evaluate the charges. I'm afraid . . ."

"Yes?"

"I'm afraid I won't be able to convince the team to let him go free. Not after this."

Holthemann leafed through the report and gave them a stern look, as if he wanted to coerce the results through the sheer force of his eyes. The departmental head was not a man anyone would suspect of having a shrewd mind or a high-ranking position if they stood behind him in the check-out queue at a Rimi supermarket. He was as dry and grey as withered grass, with a shiny, sweaty bald pate and a wary gaze behind his bifocal lenses.

"What about that character up on Kolleveien?" he said. "How thoroughly have you investigated him?"

"Raymond Låke?"

"The jacket found on the body was his. And Karlsen says that there are rumours about him."

"There's a lot of that kind of thing," Sejer said. "Which rumours are you thinking of?"

"That he drives around drooling over girls. There are also rumours about his father. That there's nothing wrong with him, that he just lies in bed reading porn magazines and lets his poor son run around for him. Maybe Raymond has been reading the magazines on the sly and got inspired."

"I think we're definitely looking for a local man," Sejer said. "And I think he's trying to mislead us."

"You believe Halvor?"

"I do believe him. We also have an unidentified person who appeared in Raymond's yard, and convinced Raymond that the car he saw was red."

"A rather far-fetched story. Maybe it was just a hiker. Raymond doesn't have all his wits about him, does he?"

Sejer bit his lip. "I don't think Raymond's smart enough to make up a story like that. I think someone really did speak to him."

"And this is the man who allegedly sneaked past Halvor's window? And put Annie's bag in the shed?"

"It's possible, yes."

"It's not like you to be so gullible, Konrad. Have

you let a dimwit and a teenager win you over with their charm?"

Sejer felt extremely uncomfortable. He didn't like to be reproached, but perhaps he was letting his instincts overshadow the facts. Halvor was the closest person to the victim. He was her boyfriend.

"Did Halvor give you any details?" Holthemann asked. He got up from his chair and sat down on the desk, which meant that he could look down at Sejer.

"He heard a car starting up. Possibly an old car, possibly with one cylinder out. The sound came from the main road."

"There's a turning place there. Lots of cars stop."

"I realise that. Let's release him. He's not going to run away."

"After what you've told us, he might well be a killer. Someone who killed his own father in cold blood. It doesn't look good for him, Konrad."

"But he loved Annie, he really did, in his own strange way. Even though she never gave him much encouragement."

"He probably got impatient and lost control. And if he blew his father's head off, that shows there's plenty of explosive material inside that young man."

"If he really did kill his father – and we don't know that for sure – it must have been because he believed he had no choice. His whole family was being destroyed, after years of abuse and neglect. And he'd been stabbed in the face. I have no doubt that he would have been acquitted."

"Quite possibly. But the fact remains that he might be capable of murder. Not everyone is. What do you think, Skarre?"

Skarre was chewing on his pen and shaking his head.

"I picture an older murderer," he said.

"Why is that?"

"She was in extremely good physical shape. Annie weighed 65 kilos, and most of it was muscle. Halvor is only 63 kilos, so they were about the same weight. If Halvor really did shove her into the water, he would have encountered enough resistance so that Annie would have been marked by some outward signs of a struggle – such as cuts and scratches. But all indications are that the killer was bigger than she was and probably much heavier. From what I've seen, I believe that Annie was physically superior to Halvor. I don't mean that he couldn't have done it, but I think it would have been very difficult for him."

Sejer nodded silently.

"OK. That sounds reasonable enough. But then we're left with nothing. Have we found any other persons close to Annie who might have a motive?" Holthemann said.

"Halvor doesn't have any apparent motive either."

"He had the bag, along with a strong emotional attachment. I'm the one who has to take the responsibility here, even though I don't particularly like it, Konrad. What about Axel Bjørk? Bitter and alcoholic, with a dangerous temper? Did you find anything there?"

"We have no evidence that Bjørk was in Lundeby on the day in question."

"I see. From the report, you both seem more interested in the death of a two-year-old boy." Now he smiled, though not in an obviously scornful way.

"Not in the boy himself. More in Annie's reaction to the death. We've tried to work out the reason for the change in her personality; it might have something to do with the boy, or possibly the fact that she was ill. I was hoping to find something there."

"Such as what?"

"I don't know. That's what is so difficult about this case; we have no idea what kind of man we're looking for."

"An executioner, maybe. He held her head underwater until she died," Holthemann said harshly. "There wasn't a scratch on her."

"That's why I think they were sitting on the shore, side by side, talking. Completely at ease.

Maybe he had some kind of hold over her. Suddenly he puts his hand at the back of her neck and throws her down on her stomach in the water. All in the blink of an eye. But the idea may have occurred to him earlier, maybe while they were in the car, or on the motorcycle."

"He must have been wet and muddy," Skarre said.

"No one saw a motorcycle on Kolleveien?"

"Only a car, going fast. But the owner of Horgen's Shop saw a motorcycle. He didn't see Annie. Johnas didn't see her get on the motorcycle either. He let her out, saw the motorcycle, and thought that she seemed to be heading towards it."

"Do you have any other new leads?"

"Magne Johnas."

"What about him?"

"Not much, actually. He looks full of anabolic steroids, and he had his eye on Annie for a while. She wasn't interested. Maybe he's the type who won't stand for that. He also went to Lundeby occasionally, to visit old friends, and he drives a motorcycle. He seems to have taken up with Sølvi instead. We can't rule him out, at any rate."

Holthemann nodded. "What about Raymond and his father? Isn't it true that Raymond was away from home for a long time?"

"He went to the shop, and when he came back he

says he sat down for a while and watched Ragnhild sleeping."

"Rock-solid alibi, Konrad," Holthemann said. "It's my understanding that he's impulsive and muscle-bound in an adolescent way, with the mental age of a five-year-old."

"Exactly. And there aren't many five-year-old murderers."

Holthemann shook his head. "But he's interested in girls, isn't he?"

"Yes. But I don't think he would know what to do with them."

"There's no knowing whether you're right. On the other hand, you have good instincts. But there's one thing you do have to realise." He lifted an admonishing finger and pointed at Sejer. "You are *not* the hero of a detective novel. Try to keep an objective mind."

Sejer threw back his head and laughed so heartily that Holthemann jumped to his feet.

"Is there something I missed?" He stuck a finger under his glasses and rubbed his eye, then he blinked and continued.

"All right," he said. "If something doesn't happen soon, I'm going to have to charge Halvor. Why, for instance, would the murderer take Annie's school bag home with him?"

"If they arrived by car, they must have got out at

294

the turning place, and then the bag would have been left in the car," Sejer said. "Afterwards it may have been too awkward to go back and throw it in the water."

"Sounds reasonable."

"One question," Sejer said, catching his eye. "If the fingerprint on Annie's belt buckle doesn't belong to Halvor, shouldn't we let him go?"

"Let me think about that."

Sejer went over to the map on the wall, where the road from Krystallen was highlighted with red, traced via the roundabout, down to Horgen's Shop, and up Kolleveien to the lake. Several little green magnets marked the locations along the way where Annie had been seen. The magnets looked like the green man on the "walk" sign of a traffic light. One was placed outside her house in Krystallen, one at the intersection of Gneisveien, where she crossed the street and took a detour, one was at the roundabout where she was seen by a woman as she got into Johnas's car. One was at Horgen's Shop. Johnas's car and the motorcycle outside the shop were also indicated. Sejer plucked off one of the Annie magnets, the one near the grocery shop, and put it in his pocket.

"Who was really the closest to her?" he said. "Was Halvor? What are the chances that someone managed to pick her up in that short space of time, from the moment she walked from Johnas's car to the shop, until she was found? The motorcyclist has not come forward. No one saw her get on the motorcycle."

"But she was going to meet someone, wasn't she?"

"She was going to Anette's house."

"That's what she told Mrs Holland. Maybe she had another rendezvous," Holthemann said.

"Then she had to take the risk that Anette might call and ask where she was."

"Annie knew Anette wouldn't call."

"I suppose that's true. But what if she never got out of Johnas's car? What if it's that simple?" He stood up and took a few steps as his thoughts whirled. "All this time we've only had Johnas's word that she did."

"As far as I know, he's a respectable businessman with his own gallery and an impeccable reputation. Also he was grateful to Annie for regularly freeing him from a difficult child."

"Exactly. She knew him. And he had good feelings towards her."

He closed his eyes. "Maybe she was mistaken."

"What are you saying?" Holthemann leaned forward.

"I'm wondering whether she might have made a mistake," he repeated.

"Oh, sure. She went off all alone with a murderer to some desolate spot."

"Yes, that too. But before that. She underestimated him. Thought she was safe."

"I doubt he was wearing a warning sign round his neck," Holthemann said. "But even if she did know him, if she was as careful as you say, they must have been quite close."

"Maybe they shared a secret," Sejer said.

"A bed, for example?"

Sejer put the Annie magnet back in place and turned around with a doubtful look.

"It wouldn't be the first time," Holthemann said, smiling. "Some young girls have a thing for older men. Have you noticed it yourself, Konrad?"

"Halvor denies that there was another man," Sejer said.

"Of course he does. He can't bear the thought."

"A relationship that she might reveal, is that what you mean? Someone with a wife and children and a big salary?"

"I'm just thinking out loud. Snorrason says she wasn't a virgin."

Sejer nodded. "She and Halvor tried sex once or twice, in spite of everything. In my opinion every male in Krystallen should be a possible candidate. They saw her every day, summer and winter, whenever she set foot outside. Watched her grow up and get more and more attractive. They gave her a lift whenever she needed one, she took care of their children, went in and out of their houses; she trusted them. They're all grown men she knew well. There are 21 houses minus her own; that gives us 20 men. Fritzner, Irmak, Solberg, Johnas, it's a whole gang. Maybe one of them was lusting after her in secret."

"Lusting after her? I thought that there had been no sexual assault."

"Maybe he was interrupted."

Sejer studied the map on the wall. The possibilities were piling up, but how could anyone have killed the girl but left her otherwise untouched? Not assaulted the dead body, looked for jewellery or money, or left any visible sign of despair, rage, or perversion. Simply arranged her body nicely, thoughtfully, considerately, with her clothes next to her. He picked up the last Annie magnet. Pressed it hard between his fingers and then, almost reluctantly, put it back on the map.

Later, Sejer walked slowly up towards the lake.

He listened, trying to picture them as they plodded along the path. Annie wearing jeans and a blue sweater, with a man at her side. A vague outline in Sejer's mind, a dark shadow, almost certainly older and bigger than Annie. Perhaps they carried on a muted conversation as they walked through the woods, maybe about something important. He let himself imagine how it was. The man gestured and explained, Annie shook her head, he continued, trying to be persuasive, the temperature rose. They approached the water, which glittered through the trees. He sat down on a rock, had not yet touched her, and she sat down reluctantly at his side. The man was good with words, amiable, friendly, or perhaps pleading; Sejer wasn't sure. Then the man stood up abruptly and threw himself at her, a powerful splash as she hit the water with him on top of her. Now he was using both hands and the full weight of his body, birds rose up in fright, screeching, and Annie pressed her lips tight so as not to fill her lungs with water. She fought back, clawing at the mud with her hands as dizzying red seconds passed and the life ebbed out of her in the shimmering water.

Sejer stared down at the small patch of shore-line.

An eternity passed. Annie had stopped kicking and flailing. The man stood up, turned around, and stared up at the path. No one had seen them. Annie lay on her stomach in the muddy water. Perhaps it seemed wrong to leave her lying that way, so he pulled her out of the water. Thoughts slowly began to circle through his mind. The police would find her, comb the scene, draw a number of conclusions. A young girl, dead in the woods. A rapist, of course, who had gone too far. So he undressed her, but carefully, struggling with the buttons and zipper and belt, and placed her clothes neatly at her side. Decided he didn't like the indecent way she was lying, on her back with her legs spread out, but it was the only way he'd been able to remove her jeans. He turned her on to her side, drew her legs up, arranged her arms. Because this picture, the last, would be with him for the rest of his life, and the only way for him to bear it was to make it as peaceful as possible.

How did he dare to take so much time?

Sejer went all the way down to the tarn and stood with the tips of his shoes a few centimetres from the water. He stood like that for a long time. The recollection of how they had found her appeared to him, and the immediate sense wasn't of evil. It seemed more like a desperate, heart-wrenching act. He was struck by the image of a despairing wretch, floundering around in a vast darkness. It was cold inside and airless, he was smashing his head against a barrier, could hardly breathe, could not escape. And then he broke through. The barrier was Annie.

Sejer turned and slowly made his way back. The killer's car, or motorcycle perhaps, was probably parked where he had left his own Peugeot. The killer opened the car door and caught sight of the school bag. Hesitated a moment, but didn't remove it, and drove off with the incriminating object. Passed Raymond's house, saw them walking along, the strange man and a little girl with a doll's pram. They saw his car. Some children are good at remembering details, he thought. Felt the first stab of fear in his chest. He kept on driving, passed three farms, finally reached the main road. Sejer could no longer see him.

He got into his car and drove off. In his mirror he saw the cloud of dust from his car. Raymond's house was quiet, seeming almost abandoned. White and brown rabbits darted back and forth in their cages as he passed. The van with its dead battery was parked in the yard. An old car, maybe with one cylinder out? The chicken wire and all the movement behind it reminded him of his own childhood, years before they moved from Denmark to Norway. They had brown bantam chickens in a cage down by the vegetable garden. He had collected eggs each morning, tiny little eggs, wondrously round, hardly bigger than his largest marbles – the ones they called "twelvers". Sejer thought he saw the curtains fluttering at a window in his rear-view mirror. Raymond's father's bedroom window.

He turned right and passed Horgen's Shop,

where the motorcycle had stood. Now there was a blue Blazer parked in front of the store, and the yellow Inuit, a sure sign of spring. He rolled his window down and felt the warm breeze on his face. The motive could, of course, be sexual, even though she hadn't been assaulted. Maybe the act of undressing her had been enough, seeing her lie there like that, defenceless and naked and completely motionless, while he helped himself to a release he'd been waiting for, and imagined what he could have done to her if he wanted to. In the killer's imagination she might have endured almost anything. Of course that could be what happened. Again, Sejer felt uneasy at the range of possibilities. He continued along the main road and stopped at the turn-off to the church. Allowed a tractor pulling crates of cabbages to pass him and then turned in. The withered flowers on Annie's grave were gone now, and the wooden cross had been removed. A stone had been put in its place, an ordinary grey stone, round and shiny, as if washed and polished by the sea. Perhaps it came from the shores where she had windsurfed in the summer. He read the inscription.

Annie Sofie Holland. May God have mercy on you.

He was taken aback, tried to decide if he liked what it said, and found that he didn't. It implied that she had done something for which she needed to be forgiven. On his way out he passed the grave of Eskil Johnas. Someone, maybe some children, had put a bouquet of dandelions on the grave.

that she may steal something for which she
hoped to be forgiven. On his way out he found
in grave ... of rolled. Softer or more sente
children of the ... [illegible] ... of his ...
past

CHAPTER 12

Kollberg needed to pee. Sejer walked the dog
behind the apartment building, let him do his
business in the barberry bushes, and then took the
lift back upstairs. Padded out to the kitchen and
peered inside the freezer. A packet of sausages, hard
as cement, a pizza, and a little package marked
"bacon". He squeezed it with a smile, remembering
something. He decided on eggs instead, four fried
eggs with salt and pepper, and a sliced sausage for
the dog. Kollberg gulped down his food and then
stretched out under the table. Sejer ate his eggs and
drank some milk, his feet nestled under the dog's
chest. The meal took him ten minutes. He had the
newspaper spread out next to his plate. *"Boyfriend
Taken into Custody."* He sighed, feeling annoyed.
He didn't have much patience with the press and
the way they covered life's miseries. He cleared off
the table and plugged in the coffee maker. Maybe
Halvor had killed his father. Pulled on a pair of
gloves, stuck the shotgun inside the sleeping bag
and pressed it into his hands, pulled the trigger,

swept the ground in front of the shed door, and ran back to the bedroom to his brother. Who felt such an intractable loyalty to Halvor that he wouldn't have said so even if Halvor had been out of his bed when the shot was fired.

Sejer took his coffee to the living room. When he'd finished, he took a shower and then leafed through the catalogue of bathrooms and fixtures. They were having a sale on bathroom tiles, including some white ones adorned with blue dolphins. He lay down on the sofa, which wasn't very comfortable. It was too short for him, and he had to prop his feet up on the armrest. It kept him from falling asleep. He didn't want to ruin the chance of a good night's rest; sleeping was hard enough because of his eczema. He stared at the window and noticed that it needed cleaning. Being on the thirteenth floor meant that he could see nothing out the window but the blue sky, which was starting to deepen into twilight.

Suddenly he saw a fly crawling across the glass on the inside. A fat, black bluebottle. That too was a sign of spring, he thought, as one more appeared, crawling across the pane and circling near the first one. He didn't really have anything against flies, but there was something disgusting about the way they rubbed their legs. It seemed such a private gesture, something equivalent to a person scratching his private parts in front of others. The flies seemed to be looking for something. Another one appeared. Now he was staring at them intently; and an uneasy feeling came over him. Three flies on his window at the same time. Strange that they didn't fly away. There was another one now, and another; soon the window was swarming with big black flies. Finally they flew away and disappeared behind the chair near the window. There were so many now that he could hear them buzzing. Reluctantly he raised himself up from the sofa with a feeling of dread. There must be something behind the chair, something they were feasting on. He stood up, walked across the room, approaching cautiously, his heart in his throat. He pulled the chair aside. The flies flew in all directions, a whole swarm of them. The rest had congregated on the floor, eating something. He poked at it with his toe. An apple core. Rotten and soft.

He sat up, feeling a little dizzy, still on the sofa. His shirt was soaked with sweat. Confused, he rubbed his eyes and looked at the window. Nothing. He'd been dreaming. His head felt heavy and dazed; his neck was stiff, and so were his calves. He stood up and couldn't resist the impulse to look behind the chair. Nothing. He went to the kitchen to fetch his bottle of whisky and packet of tobacco. Kollberg stared at him expectantly. "OK," he said, changing his mind. "Let's go for a walk."

It took them an hour to walk from the block of flats to the church in the middle of town and back. He thought about his mother. He ought to visit her; it had been a long time since he'd seen her last. Someday, he thought dejectedly, his daughter Ingrid would glance at her calendar and think the same thing: I suppose I should pay the old man a visit. It's been a long time. With no delight; only a sense of duty. Perhaps Skarre was right after all, perhaps it was unreasonable to live to be as ancient as a spruce tree and then just lie in bed, nothing but a burden. He picked up the pace, a little over-whelmed by these thoughts. Kollberg leaped and bounded beside him. But it wasn't good just to let yourself go. He would fix up the bathroom. Elise would have liked those tiles, he was sure of it. If she knew that he still hadn't got around to it . . . no, he didn't even want to think about that. Eight years with imitation marble was shameful.

At last he poured himself a well-earned whisky. It was late enough now; he might be able to fall asleep. The doorbell rang as he was putting the top back on the bottle.

It was Skarre, not quite as shy as he'd been the previous time. He had come on foot, but frowned when Sejer offered him a whisky.

"Do you have any beer?"

"I don't, but I can ask Kollberg. He sometimes

has a small supply at the back of the fridge," Sejer said. He went out and then returned with a beer.

"Do you know how to put up bathroom tiles?" he asked.

"I certainly do. I took a course in it. The key is not to skimp with the preparation. Do you need help?"

"What do you think about these?" Sejer pointed to the blue dolphins in the brochure.

"Those are great. What do you have now?"

"Imitation marble."

Skarre nodded sympathetically and raised his beer. "Halvor's fingerprints don't match the ones on Annie's belt buckle," he said. "Holthemann has agreed to release him for the time being."

Sejer didn't reply. He felt a sense of relief, mixed with irritation. He was glad that it wasn't Halvor, but frustrated because they didn't have a suspect.

"I had a nasty dream," he said, a little surprised by his own candour. "I dreamed that there was a rotten apple behind that chair over there. Completely covered with big, black flies."

"Did you check?" Skarre said with a grin.

Sejer took a sip of his whisky. "Just some dust. Do you think the dream means anything?"

"Maybe there's a piece of furniture that we've forgotten to look behind. Something that's been standing there the whole time, and we've forgotten all about it. It's definitely a warning. Now it's just a matter of identifying the chair."

"So we should go into the furniture business?" Sejer chuckled at his joke, a rare phenomenon.

"I was hoping you still had a few cards up your sleeve," Skarre said. "I can't believe that we haven't made any progress. The weeks keep passing. Annie's file is getting older. And you're the one who's supposed to be giving advice."

"What do you mean by that?"

"Your name," Skarre said. "Konrad means: 'The one who gives advice'."

Sejer raised one eyebrow in an impressive arc without moving the other. "How do you know that?"

"I have a book at home. I look up a name whenever I meet someone new."

"What does Annie mean?" Sejer asked at once.

"Beautiful."

"Good God. Well, at the moment I'm not living up to my name. But don't let that discourage you, Jacob. What does Halvor mean, by the way?" he asked with curiosity.

"Halvor means 'the guard'."

He called me "Jacob", Skarre thought with astonishment. For the very first time he used my Christian name.

*

The sun was low in the sky, slanting across the pleasant balcony and making a warm corner so they could take off their jackets. They were waiting for the grill to heat up. It smelled of charcoal and lighter fluid, along with lemon balm from Ingrid's planter-box which she had just watered.

Sejer was sitting with his grandson on his lap, bouncing him up and down until his thigh muscles began to ache. Something inside him would disappear with the boy's youth. In a few years he would be taller than his grandfather and his voice would change. Sejer always felt a sort of wistfulness when he held Matteus on his lap, but at the same time he felt a shiver run down his back from sheer physical well-being.

Ingrid picked up her clogs from the floor of the balcony and banged them together three times. Then she stuck her feet into them.

"Why do you do that?"

"An old habit," she said, smiling. "From Somalia."

"But we don't have snakes or scorpions here."

"I can't help myself. And we do have wasps and garter snakes."

"Do you think a garter snake would crawl into your shoe?"

"I have no idea."

He hugged his grandson and snuggled his nose in the hollow of his neck.

"Bounce more," Matteus said.

"My legs are tired. Why don't you find a book and I'll read to you instead?"

The boy hopped down and raced into the apartment.

"So how are things going otherwise, Papa?" Ingrid said, her voice as light as a child's.

Otherwise . . . he thought. What she means is *in reality*; how are things going *in reality*? How was he feeling deep inside, in the depths of his soul? Or it could be a camouflaged way of asking whether anything had happened? Whether, for instance, he had found a girlfriend, or was having a long-distance romance with someone. Which he wasn't. He couldn't imagine anything like that.

"Fine, but what do you mean?" he said, trying to sound sufficiently guileless.

"I was wondering if perhaps the days don't seem so long any more."

She was being terribly circumspect. It occurred to him that she had something on her mind.

"I've been very busy at work," he said. "And besides, I have all of you."

This last comment prompted her to start fidgeting with the salad servers. She tossed the tomatoes and cucumbers energetically. "Yes, but you see, we're thinking of going south again. For another term. The last one," she said quickly, giving him a glance and looking more and more guilty.

"South?" He hung on to the word. "To Somalia?"

"Erik has an offer. We haven't given them our answer yet," she said quickly. "But we're giving it serious consideration. Partly because of Matteus. We'd like him to see some of the country and learn the language. If we leave in August, we'll be there in time for the start of the school year."

Three years, he thought. Three years without Ingrid and Matteus. In Norway only at Christmas. Letters and postcards, and his grandson taller each visit, and a year older, such abrupt changes.

"I have no doubt that you're needed down there," he said, making an effort to keep his voice steady. "You're not thinking that my welfare should stop you from going, are you? I'm not 90, Ingrid."

She blushed a little.

"I'm thinking about Grandmother too."

"I'll take care of my mother. You're going to crush that salad to bits," he said.

"I don't like it that you're all alone," she said.

"I have Kollberg, you know."

"But he's just a dog!"

"You should be glad he doesn't understand what you're saying." Sejer cast a glance at Kollberg who was sleeping peacefully under the table. "We do pretty well. I think you should go if that's what you really want to do. Is Erik tired of treating appendicitis and swollen tonsils?"

"Things are different there," she said. "We can be so much more useful."

"What about Matteus? What will you do with him?"

"He'll go to the American kindergarten, along with a whole bunch of other children. And besides," she said, "he actually has relatives there that he's never met. I don't like that. I want him to know everything."

"American?" he said. "What do you mean by 'know everything'?"

He thought about Matteus's real parents and their fate.

"We won't tell him about his mother until he's older."

"You should go!" he said.

She looked at him and smiled. "What do you think Mama would have said?"

"She would have said the same thing. And then she would have had a good cry in bed later on."

"But you won't?"

Matteus came running over with a picture book in one hand and an apple in the other. "'It was a dark and stormy night.' Doesn't that sound a little scary?" Sejer said.

"Ha!" his grandson snorted, climbing up on to his lap.

"The coals are hot," Ingrid said. "I'm going to put on the steaks."

"Put them on," he said.

She placed the meat on the grill, four pieces in all, and went inside to get the drinks.

"I have a green rubber python in my room," Matteus whispered. "Should we put it in her shoe?"

Sejer hesitated. "I don't know. Do you think that's a good idea?"

"Don't you?"

"As a matter of fact, I don't."

"Old people are such chickens," he said. "I'm the one she'll blame."

"OK," he said. "I'll look the other way."

Matteus hopped down, ran to get his snake, and then carefully stuffed it inside his mother's clog.

"You can keep reading now."

Sejer cringed at the thought of the awful rubber snake and how it would feel against her toes. "'It was a dark and stormy night. There were robbers in the mountains, and wolves as well.' Are you sure this isn't too scary?"

"Mama has read it to me lots of times." He bit into his apple and chewed contentedly.

"Don't take such big bites," Sejer said. "You might get it caught in your throat."

"Read, Grandpa!"

I must be getting old, he thought. Old and anxious.

"'It was a dark and stormy night,'" he began again, and just at that moment Ingrid came back, carrying three bottles of beer and a Coke. He stopped and gave her a long look. Matteus did too.

"Why are you staring at me like that? What's wrong with you?"

"Nothing," they said in unison, bending over their book. She set the bottles on the table, opened them, and looked around for her shoes. Picked them up, turned them upside down, and knocked them together three times. Nothing happened. It's stuck in the toe, they thought gleefully. Then everything happened at once. Sejer's son-in-law Erik appeared in the doorway, Matteus jumped down from his lap and rushed across the room. Kollberg leaped up from under the table and wagged his tail so hard that the bottles fell to the floor, and Ingrid stuck her feet inside her shoes.

Sølvi stood in her room, taking things out of a box. For a moment she straightened up and peered outside. Directly across the street, Fritzner was standing at his window, watching her. He had a glass in his hand. Now he raised it, as if offering a toast.

Sølvi turned her back on him at once. True, she didn't mind men looking at her, but Fritzner was bald. Imagining life with a bald man was as unthinkable as imagining life with a man who was fat. They had no place in her dreams. That her stepfather was both bald and fat didn't trouble her. Other men could be bald, but not the one she went out with. She looked up again. He was gone. He was probably sitting in his boat again, the weirdo.

She heard the doorbell ringing and went out to open the door, wearing a light-blue trouser suit with a silver belt around her waist and ballet slippers on her feet.

"Oh!" she said. "It's you! I'm cleaning up Annie's room. Come on in. Mama and Papa will be home in a minute."

Sejer followed her through the living room to her own room, which was next to Annie's. It was quite a bit bigger, decorated in pastels. A photograph of her sister stood on her bedside table.

"I have inherited a few things from her," she said with an apologetic smile. "Some knick-knacks and clothes and things like that. And if I can persuade Papa, I want to knock down the wall to Annie's room so I'll have one big room."

"That will be very nice," Sejer said. But at the same time he felt a little ashamed at the emotions that crept over him. He had no right to judge anyone. They were struggling to go on with their lives and had every right to do it in their own way. No one could tell anyone else how to grieve. He gave himself this little reprimand and then looked around. He had never seen a room with so many knick-knacks.

"And I'm going to get my own TV," she said. "With an extra antenna so I can get TV-Norway." She bent down to a cardboard box on the floor and began pulling more things out of it. "It's mostly books. Annie didn't have any make-up or jewellery or anything like that. Plus a bunch of CDs and cassettes."

"Do you like to read?"

"Not really. But the bookshelves look nice when they're full."

He nodded in agreement.

"Has something happened?"

"Yes, actually. But we don't know yet what it means."

She took one more thing out of the box. It was wrapped in newspaper.

"So you know Magne Johnas, Sølvi?"

"Yes," she said. He thought she blushed, but she had such rosy cheeks, he couldn't be sure. "He's living in Oslo now. Works for Gym & Greier."

"Did you know that he and Annie once had something going?"

"Had something going?" She gave him a look of pure incomprehension.

"That they might have had a romance, or that

317

Magne might have been in love with her, or might have tried something? Before your time?"

"Annie just laughed at him," she said, her tone almost plaintive. "Not that Halvor was anything to boast about. At least Magne looks like a guy should. I mean, he has muscles and everything."

She pulled away the newspaper wrapping, avoiding his eye.

"Do you think he might have been offended?" he asked carefully as something shiny appeared in the newspaper.

"He could have been. It wasn't enough for Annie to say no. She could be really snide sometimes, and she wasn't impressed by muscles. Everybody keeps on talking about how wonderful and nice she was, and I don't mean to say anything bad about my half-sister. She was often snide, but nobody dares talk about it. Because she's dead. I can't understand how Halvor could bear it. Annie was the one who decided on everything."

"Is that right?"

"But she was nice to me. She was always nice." For a moment she looked stricken at the memory of her sister and everything that had happened.

"How long have you and Magne been together?" he asked.

"Only a few weeks. We go to the movies and stuff like that."

Her reply was a little too quick.

"He's younger than you, isn't he?"

"Four years," she said reluctantly. "But he's very mature for his age."

"I see."

She held something up to the light and squinted at it. A bronze bird sitting on a perch. A chubby little feathered creature with its head tilted.

"It's broken," she said uncertainly.

Sejer stared in astonishment. The sight of the bronze bird struck him like an arrow at his temple. It was the sort of thing that was placed on the gravestones of small children.

"I could roll up a lump of clay and make a stand for it," Sølvi said. "Or Papa might help me. It's really pretty."

A picture of a new Annie was slowly taking shape, a more complex Annie than the one Halvor and her parents had presented to him.

"What do you think it's for?" he said.

Sølvi shrugged. "No idea. Just some kind of decoration that's broken, I suppose."

"You've never seen it before?"

"No. I wasn't allowed in Annie's room when she wasn't home."

She put the bird on her desk, and bent down to the box again.

"Has it been a long time since you saw your

father?" he asked as he continued to stare at the bird. His brain was working in high gear.

"My father?" She straightened up and looked at him in confusion. "You mean . . . my father who lives in Adamstuen?"

He nodded.

"He was at Annie's funeral."

"You must miss him, don't you?"

She didn't answer. It was as if he had touched on something that she rarely examined properly. Something unpleasant that she tried to forget, a trace of guilty conscience perhaps, about not visiting her father. Sejer felt a little too aggressive at that moment. He had to remember to be respectful, to approach people on their own terms.

"What do you call Eddie?" he asked.

"I call him Papa," she said.

"And your real father?"

"I call him Father," she said simply. "That's what I've always called him. It's what he wanted, he was always so old-fashioned."

Was. As if he no longer existed.

"I hear a car!" she said, sounding relieved.

Holland's green Toyota pulled up in front of the house. Sejer saw Ada Holland set one foot on the gravel and cast a glance at the window.

"That bird, Sølvi, could I have it?" he said quickly.

"The broken bird? Sure, take it."

She handed it to him with an inquisitive look.

"Thanks. I won't disturb you any longer," he said, and left the room. He tucked the bird into an inside pocket and went back to the living room. He leaned against the wall and waited.

The bird. Torn from Eskil's headstone. In Annie's room. Why?

Holland came in first. He nodded and held out his hand, with his face turned away. There was something resigned about him that hadn't been there before. Mrs Holland went to the kitchen to make coffee.

"Sølvi's going to have Annie's room," Holland said. "So it won't stand there empty. And we'll have something to keep us busy. We're going to take out the dividing wall and put up new wallpaper. It'll be a lot of work."

Sejer nodded.

"I have to get something off my chest," Holland said. "I read in the paper that an 18-year-old boy was taken into custody. Surely Halvor couldn't be the one who did this? We've known him for two years. It's true that he's not an easy person to get to know, but I have good instincts about people. Not to insinuate that you don't know what you're doing, but we just can't imagine Halvor as a murderer, we just can't, none of us can."

Sejer could. Murderers were like most people. Maybe he'd blown his father's head off, killed him in cold blood as he slept.

"Is Halvor the one in custody?"

"We've released him," Sejer said.

"Yes, but why was he taken into custody?"

"We had no choice. I can't tell you any more than that."

"So as not to prejudice the investigation?"

"That's right."

Mrs Holland came in with four cups and some cookies in a bowl.

"But has something else come up?"

"Yes." Sejer stared out the window, searching for something that would divert their attention. "For the time being I can't say much."

Holland gave him a bitter smile. "Of course not. I imagine we'll be the last people to find out. The newspapers will know long before we do, when you finally catch the killer."

"That's not true at all." Sejer looked into his eyes, which were big and grey like Annie's. They were brimming with pain. "But the press is everywhere, and they have contacts. Just because you read something in the paper doesn't mean that we've given them the information. When we make an arrest, you will be told, I promise you that."

"No one told us about Halvor," Holland said in a low voice.

"That's because, quite simply, we don't think he was the right person."

"Now that I think about it, I'm not sure that I even want to know who did it."

"What are you saying?"

Ada Holland was staring at him in dismay.

"It doesn't matter any more. It's like the whole thing was an accident. Something unavoidable."

"Why do you say that?" she asked in despair.

"Because she was going to die anyway. So it doesn't matter any more."

He stared down at his empty cup, picked it up and began swirling it, as if trying to cool off the hot coffee that wasn't there.

"It *does* matter," Sejer said, stifling his anger. "You have the right to know what happened. It may take time, but I'll find out who did it, even it turns out to be a very long process."

"A very long process?" Holland smiled, another bitter smile. "Annie is slowly disintegrating," he said.

"Eddie!" Mrs Holland said in anguish. "We still have Sølvi!"

"*You* have Sølvi."

He stood up and left the room, disappearing somewhere in the house. Neither of them went after him. Mrs Holland shrugged her shoulders dejectedly.

"Annie was a daddy's girl," she said.

"I know."

"I'm afraid that he'll never be the same again."

"He won't. Right now he's getting used to being a different Eddie. He needs time. Perhaps it will be easier when we do discover the truth."

"I don't know whether I dare find out."

"Are you afraid of something?"

"I'm afraid of everything. I imagine all kinds of things up there at the lake."

"Can you tell me about it?"

She shook her head and reached for her cup. "No, I can't. It's just things that I imagine. If I say them out loud they might come true."

"It looks as if Sølvi is managing all right," he said, to change the subject.

"Sølvi is strong," she said, suddenly sounding confident.

Strong, he thought. Yes, maybe that *is* the proper term. Perhaps Annie was the weak one. Things began whirling through his mind in a disquieting way. Mrs Holland went out to get cream and sugar. Sølvi came in.

"Where's Papa?"

"He'll be right back!" Mrs Holland called from the kitchen in a firm voice, perhaps in the hope that

Eddie would hear her and reappear. It's bad enough that Annie is dead and gone, Sejer thought. But now her family is falling apart, the welded seams are failing, there are big holes in the hull, and the water is gushing in, and she's stuffing old phrases and commands into the cracks to keep the ship afloat.

She poured the coffee. Sejer's fingers were too big for the handle and he had to hold the cup in both hands.

"You keep talking about why," she said wearily, "as if he must have had a good reason for doing it."

"Not a good reason. But the killer had a reason, which at that moment seemed to him to be the only choice."

"So evidently you understand them – these people that you lock up for murder and other appalling crimes."

"I couldn't stay in the job otherwise." He drank some more coffee and thought about Halvor.

"But surely there must be some exceptions."

"They're rare."

She sighed and glanced at her daughter. "What do you think, Sølvi?" she said. Softly, using a different tone than he'd heard her use before, as if for once she wanted to penetrate that carefree blonde head of her daughter's and find an answer, maybe even one that would make sense of it all. As if the only daughter she had left might be a different person than she had initially thought, maybe more like Annie than she knew.

"Me?" Sølvi stared at her mother in surprise. "For my part I've never liked Fritzner across the street. I've heard that he sits in his dinghy in his living room and reads all night long, with the rowlocks full of beer."

CHAPTER 13

Skarre had turned off most of the lights in his office. Only the desk lamp was on, 60 watts in a white spotlight on his papers. A gentle, steady hum came from the printer as it spewed out page after page, covered with perfect text, set in Palatino, the typeface he liked best. In the background, as if from far away, he heard a door open and someone come in. He was about to look up to see who it was but just at that moment the pages tumbled off the printer. He bent down to get them, straightened up, and discovered that something was sliding into his field of vision, across an empty page. A bronze bird sitting on a perch.

"Where?!" he said at once.

Sejer sat down. "At Annie's house. Sølvi has inherited her sister's things, and this was among them, wrapped in newspaper. I went out to the cemetery. It fits like a glove." He looked at Skarre. "Someone could have given it to her."

"Who?"

"I don't know. But if she went there and took it herself, really went there, under cover of darkness, and used some kind of tool to break it off the headstone, then that's quite an unscrupulous thing to do."

"But Annie wasn't unscrupulous, was she?"

"I'm not entirely sure. I'm not sure about anything any more."

Skarre turned the lamp away from the desk so that it made a perfect half-moon on the wall. They sat and stared at it. On impulse, Skarre picked up the bird, gripping it by its perch, and held it up to the lamp with a swaying motion. The shadow it made in the white moon was like a giant drunken duck on its way home from a party.

"Jensvoll has resigned from his job as coach of the girls' team," Skarre said.

"What did you say?"

"The rumours are starting to circulate. The rape conviction has come out, and it's hovering over the waters. The girls stopped showing up."

"I thought that would happen. One thing leads to another."

"And Fritzner was right. Things are going to be tough for a lot of people now, until the murderer is caught. But that will happen soon, because by now you've worked it all out, haven't you?"

Sejer shook his head. "It has something to do

with Annie and Johnas. Something happened between the two of them."

"Maybe she just wanted a keepsake to remind her of Eskil."

"If that was it, she could have knocked on the door and asked for a teddy-bear or something."

"Do you think he did something to her?"

"Either to her or maybe to someone else she had a relationship with. Someone she loved."

"Now I don't follow you – do you mean Halvor?"

"I mean his son, Eskil. He died because Johnas was in the bathroom shaving."

"But she couldn't very well blame him because of that."

"Not unless there's something unresolved about the way Eskil died."

Skarre whistled. "No one else was there to see what happened. All we have to go on is what Johnas said."

Sejer picked up the bird again and gently poked at its sharp beak. "So what do you think, Jacob? What really happened on that November morning."

Memories flooded over him as he opened the double glass doors and took a few steps inside. The hospital smell, a mixture of antiseptic and soap, combined with the sweet scent of chocolate from

329

the gift shop and the spicy fragrance of carnations from the flower stand.

Instead of thinking about his wife's death, Sejer tried to think about his daughter Ingrid on the day she was born. This enormous building held memories of both the greatest sorrow and the greatest joy of his life. Back then he had stepped through these same doors and noticed the same smells. Involuntarily he had compared his own new-born daughter to the other infants. He thought they were redder and fatter and had more wrinkles, and that their hair was more rumpled. Or they were born prematurely and looked like undernourished miniature old men. Only Ingrid was utterly perfect. The recollection helped him to relax at last.

He was not arriving unannounced. It had taken him exactly eight minutes on the phone to locate the pathologist who had overseen the autopsy of Eskil Johnas. He made it clear in advance what he was interested in, so they could find the files and reports and get them out for him. One of the things he liked about the bureaucracy, that unwieldy, cumbersome, difficult system that governed all departments, was the principle that everything had to be recorded and archived. Dates, times, names, diagnoses, routines, irregularities, everything had to be on the file. Every facet of a case could be taken out and re-examined, by other people with different motives, with fresh eyes.

That's what he was thinking as he got out of the lift. He noticed the hospital smell grow stronger as he walked along the corridor of the eighth floor. The pathologist, who had sounded staid and middle-aged on the phone, turned out to be a young man. A stout fellow with thick glasses and soft, plump hands. On his desk stood a card file, a phone, a stack of papers, and a big red book with Chinese characters on it.

"I have to confess that I took a quick glance at the case file," the doctor said. His glasses made him look as if he were in a constant state of fear. "I was curious. You're a chief inspector, isn't that what you said?"

Sejer nodded.

"So I'm assuming that there must be something unusual about this death?"

"I have no opinion about that."

"But isn't that why you're here?"

Sejer looked at him and blinked twice, and that was all the answer he gave. When he remained silent, the doctor started talking again – a phenomenon that never ceased to amaze Sejer, one that had produced numerous confessions over the years.

"A tragic case," the pathologist said, looking down at the papers. "A two-year-old boy. An accident at home. Left without supervision for a few minutes. Dead on arrival. We opened him up and found a total obstruction of his windpipe, in the form of food."

"What type of food?"

"Waffles. We were actually able to unfold them, they were practically whole. Two whole, heart-shaped dessert waffles, folded together into one lump. That's an awful lot of food for such a small mouth, even though he was a sturdy boy. It turned out that he was quite a greedy little fellow, and hyperactive too."

Sejer tried to picture the waffle-iron that Elise used to have, with five heart shapes in a circle. Ingrid's iron was a more modern kind with only four hearts that weren't properly round.

"I remember the autopsy clearly. You always remember the very sad cases; they stay in your mind. Most of the people we see, after all, are between 80 and 90 years old. And I remember the waffle hearts lying in the bowl. Children and dessert waffles go together. It seemed especially tragic that they should have caused his death. He was sitting there having such a good time."

"You said 'we'. Were there others working with you?"

"Arnesen, the head pathologist, was with me. I had just been hired back then, and he liked to keep an eye on the new people. He's retired now. The new departmental head is a woman." The thought made him glance down at his hands.

"Two whole waffles shaped like hearts. Had he chewed them?"

"No, apparently not. They were both nearly whole."

"Do you have children?"

"I have four," he said happily.

"Did you think about them when you were doing the autopsy?"

The doctor gave Sejer a look of uncertainty, as if he didn't quite understand the question.

"Well, yes, I suppose I did. Or I might have been thinking more about children in general, and how they behave."

"Yes?"

"At that time my son had just turned three," the doctor went on. "And he loves dessert waffles. I'm forever scolding him, the way parents do, about stuffing too much food into his mouth at one time."

"But in this case no one was there to scold the boy," Sejer said.

"No. Because then, of course, it wouldn't have happened."

Sejer didn't reply. Then he said, "Can you picture your own son when he was about the same age with a plate of waffles in front of him? Do you think he would have picked up two of them, folded them in half, and stuffed both into his mouth at the same time?"

Now there was a long silence.

"Well . . . this was a special kind of child."

"Where exactly did you get that information from? I mean, the fact that he was special?"

"From his father. He was here at the hospital all day. The mother arrived later, together with his half-brother. By the way, all of this is included in the file. I've made copies for you, as requested."

He tapped the pile in front of him and pushed the Chinese book aside. Sejer recognised the first character on the cover, the symbol for "man".

"From what I've been told, the father was in the bathroom when the accident occurred, is that right?"

"That's right. He was shaving. The boy was strapped to his chair; that's why he couldn't get loose and run for help. When the father came back to the kitchen the boy was lying across the table. He had knocked his plate to the floor so it broke. The worst thing was that the father actually heard the plate fall."

"Why didn't he come running?"

"Apparently the boy broke things all the time."

"Who else was home when it happened?"

"Only the mother, from what I understood. The older son had just left to catch a school bus or something, and the mother was asleep upstairs."

"And didn't hear anything?"

"I suppose there was nothing to hear. He didn't manage to scream."

"Not with two heart-shaped waffles in his mouth. But she was awakened eventually – by her husband, of course?"

"It's possible that he shouted or screamed for her. People react very differently in those kinds of situations. Some can't stop screaming, while others are completely paralysed."

"But she didn't come with the ambulance?"

"She arrived later. First she went to get the older brother from school."

"How much later did they arrive?"

"Let's see . . . about half an hour, according to what it says here."

"Can you tell me a little about how the father acted?"

Now the doctor fell silent, closing his eyes as if he were conjuring up that morning, exactly the way it was.

"He was in shock. He didn't say much."

"That's understandable. But the little he did say – can you remember what it was? Can you remember any specific words?"

The doctor gave him an inquisitive look and shook his head. "It was a long time ago. Almost eight months."

"Give it a try."

"I think it was something like: 'Oh God, no! Oh God, no!'"

"Was it the father who called the ambulance?"

"Yes, that's what it says here."

"Does it really take 20 minutes from here to Lundeby?"

"Yes, unfortunately, it does. And 20 minutes back. They didn't have personnel with them who could perform a tracheotomy. If they had, he might have been saved."

"What are you talking about now?"

"About going in between two cartilages and opening up the windpipe from the outside."

"You mean cutting open his throat?"

"Yes. It's actually quite simple. And it might have saved his life, although we don't know how long he sat in that chair before his father found him."

"About as long as it takes to shave?"

"Well, yes, I suppose so." The doctor leafed through the papers and shoved his glasses up. "Do you suspect something . . . criminal?"

He had been holding back this question for a long time. Now he felt that he finally had the right to ask it.

"I can't imagine what that might be. What do you mean?"

"How could I have any opinion about that?"

"But you opened up the boy afterwards and examined him. Did you find anything unnatural about his death?"

"Unnatural? That's the way children are. They stuff things in their mouth."

"But if he had a plate full of waffles in front of him and was sitting there alone and didn't need to worry that anyone was going to come and take them away from him – why would he stuff two pieces in his mouth at once?"

"Tell me something: where are you going with these questions?"

"I have no idea."

The doctor sat there, lost in thought; he was thinking back again, to the morning when little Eskil lay naked on the porcelain table, sliced open from his throat down. To the moment when he caught sight of the lump in his windpipe and realised that it was two waffles. Two whole hearts. One big sticky lump of egg and flour and butter and milk.

"I remember the autopsy," he said. "I remember it in great detail. Maybe by that I mean that I was actually surprised. No, I can't really say that. But," he added suddenly, "how did you come up with the idea that there might be something irregular about his death?"

Irregular. A vague word that could cover so many different possibilities.

"Well," said Sejer, looking closely at the doctor, "he had a baby-sitter. Let me put it this way: some of the signals she sent out in connection with the death have made me wonder."

"Signals? You can just ask her, can't you?"

"No, I can't ask her." Sejer shook his head. "It's too late."

Dessert waffles for breakfast, he thought. They must have been left over from the day before. It was unlikely that Johnas had got up and bustled around so early in the morning. Dessert waffles from the day before, tough and cold. He buttoned his jacket and got into his car. No one would wonder about it. Children were always putting things down their throats. As the pathologist had said: they stuff things in. He started the car, crossed Rosenkrantzgaten, and drove down to the river, where he turned left. He wasn't hungry, but he drove to the courthouse, parked, and took the lift up to the cafeteria, where they sold waffles. He bought a plate of them, with some jam and coffee and sat down by the window. Carefully he tore loose two of the hearts. They were freshly made and crisp. He folded them in half and then again in half and sat there staring at them. With a little effort he could put two of them in his mouth and still have room to chew. He did so, feeling the way they slid down his oesophagus without any trouble. Newly made dessert waffles were slippery and greasy. He drank some coffee and shook his head. Against his will he allowed the flickering pictures to force their way into his mind, pictures of the little boy with his throat full. The way he must have flailed and waved his hands, breaking the plate and fighting for his life without anyone hearing him. His father had heard the plate smash. Why hadn't he come running? Because the boy was always breaking things, said the doctor. But still – a little boy and a smashed plate. Even I would have come running at once, he thought. I would have imagined the chair toppling over, that he might have been hurt. But his father had finished shaving. What if the mother had been awake after all? Would she have heard the plate fall? He drank more coffee and spread jam on the rest of the waffles. Then he began reading through the report. After a while he stood up and went out to his car. He thought about Astrid Johnas, who had been lying in bed alone upstairs, with no idea what was going on.

Halvor picked up a sandwich from the plate and turned on his computer. He liked the fanfare sounds and the stream of blue light in the room when the programme started up. Each fanfare was a solemn moment. He thought of it as welcoming him like a VIP, as if he were expected. Today he decided on a special strategy. He was in a reckless mood, the way Annie often was. That's why he started off with "Leave me alone", "Private", and "Hands off". It was the sort of thing she would say whenever he put his arm around her shoulder, very tentatively and in a purely affectionate way. But she always said it kindly. And when he dared to ask her for a kiss she would threaten to bite off his sullen grin. Her voice said something different from her words. Of course that didn't mean he could ignore what she said, but at least it made it a little easier to bear. Basically he was never allowed to touch her. But she still wanted him around. They used to lie close together, stealing warmth from each other. That alone wasn't half bad, lying like that in the dark, close to Annie, listening to the silence outside, free from the terror and nightmares of his father. The bad dreams could no longer come rushing in to tear off the covers; they could no longer reach him. Safety. He was used to having someone lying next to him, the way his brother had for so many years. Used to hearing someone else breathing and feel their warmth against his face.

Why had she written anything down in the first

place? What was it about? And would he even understand it if he did find it? He chewed on the bread and liverwurst, listening to the roar of the TV in the living room. He felt a little guilty because his grandmother was sitting in there all alone in the evenings, and she would continue to do so until he came up with the password and found his way into Annie's secret. It must be something dark, he thought, since it's so inaccessible. Something dark and dangerous that couldn't be said out loud, could only be written down and then locked away. As if it were a matter of life and death. He typed that in. "Life and death". Nothing happened.

Mrs Johnas was having her lunch break. She peered at him from the back room, a piece of crispbread in one hand, wearing the same red suit as the time before. She looked uneasy. She put the food down on the paper it had been wrapped in, as if it would be inappropriate to sit there and chew while they were talking about Annie. She concentrated on her coffee instead.

"Has something happened?" she asked, taking a sip from her thermos cup.

"Today I don't want to talk about Annie."

She lifted her cup and looked at him, her eyes wide.

"Today I want to talk about Eskil."

"Excuse me?" Her full lips became smaller and narrower. "I'm done with all that; I've put it behind me. And if you don't mind my saying so, the effort has cost me a great deal."

"I'm sorry I can't be more considerate. There are a few details about the boy's death that interest me."

"Why is that?"

"That's not something I have to tell you, Mrs Johnas," Sejer said gently. "Just answer my questions."

"And if I refuse? What if I just can't bear to talk about it?"

"Then I'll leave," he said. "And give you time to think. And I'll come back another day with the same questions."

She pushed her cup aside, put her hands in her lap, and straightened her back. As if this was exactly what she had expected and needed to steel herself.

"I don't like it," she said. "When you came here before, wanting to talk about Annie, it never occurred to me to refuse to co-operate. But if this has to do with Eskil, tell me what you want to know and then you'd better leave."

She fumbled with her hands and then clasped them tight. As if there were something frightening her.

"Just before he died," Sejer said, looking at her,

"he knocked his plate to the floor and it smashed. Did you hear it?"

The question surprised her. She stared at him with astonishment, as if she had expected something else, perhaps something worse. "Yes," she said.

"You heard it? So you were awake?" He studied her face, noted the little shadow that flitted over it, and then went on. "You weren't asleep after all? Did you hear the electric shaver?"

She bowed her head. "I heard him go into the bathroom and the door slam."

"How did you know he was going into the bathroom?"

"I just knew. We lived in that house for a long time. Each door had its own sound."

"And before that? Before he went there?"

She hesitated a little, searching her memory.

"Their voices, in the kitchen. They were having breakfast."

"Eskil was eating dessert waffles," he said cautiously. "Was that usual in your house? Dessert waffles for breakfast?" He added a warm smile to his question.

"He must have begged for them," she said wearily. "And he always got what he wanted. It wasn't easy to say no to Eskil because it would set off an avalanche inside him. He couldn't stand any

343

kind of resistance. It was like blowing on hot embers. And Henning wasn't especially patient; he hated to hear him screaming.

"So you heard him screaming?"

She tore her hands apart and reached for her cup.

"He was always making a great deal of noise," she said, staring at the steam rising from her coffee.

"Were they having a fight, Mrs Johnas?"

She smiled faintly. "They fought all the time. Eskil was begging for waffles. Henning had buttered some toast and he wanted him to eat it. You know how it is – we do all we can to get our kids to eat, so he must have got out the waffles, or maybe Eskil had caught sight of them. They were on the counter covered with plastic from the night before."

"Could you hear any words? Anything they said to each other?"

"What are you driving at with all these questions?" she blurted out. Her eyes had darkened. "You should talk to Henning about it. I wasn't there. I was upstairs."

"Do you think he has anything to tell me?"

Silence. She folded her arms, as if to lock him out. Her fear was growing.

"I can't speak for Henning. He's not my husband any more."

"Was it the loss of your child that made your marriage difficult?"

"Not really. We would have split up anyway. We argued too much."

"Were you the one who wanted to leave?"

"What does this have to do with anything?" she said.

"Most likely nothing. I'm just asking." He placed his hands on the table, turning them palm up. "When Henning found Eskil at the table, what did he do? Did he call out to you?"

"He just opened the door to the bedroom and stood there staring. It struck me how quiet it was, there wasn't a sound from the kitchen. I sat up in bed and screamed."

"Is there anything about your son's death that seems unclear to you?"

"What?"

"Have you and your husband gone over what happened? Did you ask him about it?"

Again Sejer saw a trace of fear in her eyes.

"He told me everything," she said carefully. "He was inconsolable. Blamed himself for what happened, thought he hadn't paid enough attention. And that's not an easy thing to live with. He couldn't bear it. I couldn't bear it. We had to go our separate ways."

"But there's nothing about the death itself

that you didn't understand, or that hasn't been resolved?"

Sejer had big, slate-grey eyes that at the moment were very gentle because she was on the edge of something, and maybe, if he was lucky, she would take the next step.

Her shoulders began to shake. He sat still for a moment, waiting patiently, knowing that he mustn't move, mustn't break the silence. She was getting close to a confession. He recognised it; it was in the air. Something was bothering her, something she didn't dare think about.

"I heard them screaming at each other," she whispered. "Henning was furious; he had a fierce temper. I was lying in bed with a pillow over my head. I couldn't stand listening to them."

"Go on."

"I heard Eskil making a lot of noise, he might have been banging his cup against the table, and Henning was shouting and slamming drawers and cupboard doors.

"Could you make out any words they said?"

Her lower lip began trembling. "Only one sentence. The last thing I heard before he rushed off to the bathroom. He screamed so loud that I was afraid the neighbours would hear him, afraid of what they might think of us. But we didn't have it easy. We had a child who didn't behave the way we had

346

expected. We had an older boy, as you know. Magne was always so quiet; he still is. There were never any problems, he did what we told him to do, he . . ."

"What did you hear? What did he say?"

The bell suddenly rang in the shop, and the door opened. Two women swept in and looked around at all the wool, their eyes alight. Mrs Johnas jumped up, about to head into the shop. Sejer stopped her by putting his hand on her shoulder.

"Tell me!"

She bowed her head, as if she were ashamed.

"It just about destroyed Henning. He could never forgive himself. And I couldn't live with him any more."

"Tell me what he said!"

"I don't want anyone to know. And it doesn't matter any more. Eskil is dead."

"But he's no longer your husband, is he?"

"He's Magne's father. He told me how he stood there in the bathroom, shaking with despair because he couldn't act the way he should. He stood there until he calmed down; then he was going to go back and apologise for being angry. He couldn't bear to go to work without clearing the air. Finally he went back to the kitchen. You know the rest."

"Tell me what he said."

"Never. I'll never tell a living soul."

*

The ugly thought that had taken root in his mind was beginning to sprout and grow. He had seen so much that it was rare for him to be surprised. Maybe it would have been convenient to be rid of a child like Eskil Johnas.

He collected Skarre from his office and took him down the corridor.

"Let's go and look at some Oriental carpets," he said.

"Why?"

"I just came from Astrid Johnas's shop. I think she's tormented by some terrible suspicion, the same one that has occurred to me. That Johnas is partially to blame for the boy's death. I think that's why she left him."

"But how was he to blame?"

"I don't know. But she's terrified by the idea. Something else has occurred to me. Johnas didn't say a single word about the boy's death when we talked to him."

"That's not so strange, is it? We were there to talk about Annie, after all."

"I think it's strange that he didn't mention it. He said there weren't any children to baby-sit any more because his wife had left him. He didn't mention that the boy Annie took care of had died. Not even when you commented on the picture of him that was hanging on the wall."

"He probably couldn't stand to talk about it. You have to forgive me for mentioning this," Skarre said, lowering his voice, "but you've also lost someone close to you. How easy is it for you to talk about it?"

Sejer was so surprised that he stopped in his tracks. He felt his face grow pale, as if someone had drained it of colour. "Of course I can talk about it . . . If it's a situation where I felt it was appropriate or absolutely necessary. If other considerations were stronger than my own feelings."

The smell of her, the smell of her hair and skin, a mixture of chemicals and sweat, her forehead had an almost metallic gleam. The enamel of her teeth was destroyed by all the pills, bluish, like skimmed milk. The whites of her eyes slowly turned yellow.

In front of him stood Skarre, with his head held high, not in the least self-conscious. Sejer had expected this; hadn't he babbled too much, crossed the line in getting too friendly with Skarre? Shouldn't he apologise?

"But you've never felt it was necessary?"

Now he was staring at the young man standing in front of him. He seemed to be holding out a fist.

"No," he said firmly, shaking his head.

He started walking again.

"I see," Skarre said, unperturbed. "What did Mrs Johnas say?"

"They had a fight. She heard them screaming at each other. The bathroom door slammed, the plate smashed. Johnas had a bad temper. She says he blames himself."

"I would too," Skarre said.

"Do you have anything at all encouraging to say?"

"In a way. Annie's school bag."

"What about it?"

"Remember that it had some kind of grease on it? Most likely to wipe away any fingerprints?"

"So?"

"We've identified what it is. A kind of cream that contains tar, among other things."

"I have cream like that," Sejer said, surprised. "For my eczema."

"No. It's a special cream for dogs. For injured paws."

Sejer nodded. "Johnas has a dog."

"And Axel Bjørk has a German shepherd. And you have a lion. I'm just mentioning it," Skarre said quickly, holding the door open. The chief inspector led the way, feeling rather confused.

CHAPTER 14

Axel Bjørk put the leash on his dog and let him out of the car.

He cast a swift glance in both directions, saw no one, and headed across the square, fishing a master key out of his uniform. He turned again and looked back at his car, which was parked in full view in front of the main entrance, a leaden-grey Peugeot with a ski-box on the roof and the security company's logo on the door and bonnet. The dog waited, unsuspecting, while he fumbled with the lock; they had done this so many times before, in and out of the car, in and out of doors and lifts, thousands of different smells. The dog followed faithfully. He had a good life for a dog, with plenty of exercise, an abundance of changes of scene and good food.

The factory building was quiet and empty, no longer in operation, used only as a warehouse. Crates, boxes and sacks were piled up from floor to ceiling; the place smelled of cardboard and dust and mouldy wood. Bjørk didn't turn on the lights.

Hanging from his belt was a torch, which he switched on as they walked through the dark hall. His boots rang hollowly on the stone floor. Each step echoed, unique, in his mind. His own footsteps, one after another, alone in the silence. He didn't believe in God, the dog was the only one who heard them. Achilles walked along on a slack leash, taking measured steps, meticulously trained. The dog anticipated calm, not danger, and he loved his master.

They approached the machinery, a huge rolling machine. Bjørk squeezed himself in behind the iron and metal, pulling the dog with him. He fastened the leash to a steel lever and gave the command to sit. The dog sat down but stayed alert. A smell was starting to spread through the room. A smell that was no longer unfamiliar, that was becoming a bigger and bigger part of their daily life. But there was something else too. The rank smell of fear. Bjørk slid down to the floor; a rustling noise from his nylon coveralls and the panting of the dog the only audible sounds. He took a bottle out of his hip pocket, unscrewed the top, and began drinking.

The dog waited, his eyes shining, his ears alert. He knew he wouldn't be getting any biscuits just then, but he sat there all the same, waiting and listening. Bjørk stared into the dog's eyes, not a word passed his lips. The tension in the dark hall grew. He could feel the dog watching him, as he watched the dog. In his pocket he had a revolver.

Halvor grunted with displeasure. Not a living soul is going to get into this file, he thought despondently. The hum of the monitor had started to annoy him. It was no longer a gentle sighing but an endless din, as if coming from some vast machine far away. It stayed with him all day long; he felt almost naked each time he shut off the computer and silence took over for a few seconds, until the sound reappeared inside his own head. Spit it out, Annie, he thought. Talk to me!

The movie theatre was showing a travelogue. She bought Smarties and lemon drops at the kiosk while he waited at the entrance with the tickets in his hand. "Do you want anything to drink?" she asked. He shook his head, too preoccupied with looking at her, comparing her to all the others crowded together in front of the theatre. The attendant appeared in the doorway, dressed in a black uniform and holding a punch in his hand, and as he clipped everyone's tickets, he studied the faces before him. Most of the kids kept their eyes lowered because they were under the age restriction for this movie. A Bond film. The very first one they had seen together, their first date, practically like a real couple. He swelled with pride. And the movie was a good one, at least according to

Annie. He hadn't actually followed much of it; he was much too preoccupied with staring at her out of the corner of his eye and listening to the sounds she made in the dark. But he did remember the title: For Your Eyes Only.

He typed the title into the field and waited for a moment, but nothing happened. Got up impatiently, took a couple of steps, and tore the lid off a jar standing on the windowsill where he kept a packet of King of Denmark tobacco. This was hopeless. He shoved any trace of guilt to the far corner of his mind. It was a secret part of his mind, and it contained something from his past. There was no stopping Halvor now; he walked through the kitchen to the living room and over to the bookshelf where the phone was. He looked up the listing for computer equipment, found the number he wanted, and punched it in.

"Ra Data. Solveig speaking."

"Hi. I'm calling about a locked file," he stammered. His courage disintegrated; he felt small, like a thief or a voyeur. But it was too late for that now.

"You can't get in?"

"Er, no. I can't remember the password."

"I'm afraid the technician has left for the day. But wait just a minute and I'll ask somebody."

He was pressing the receiver to his head so hard

that his ear went numb. On the other end of the line he could hear the hum of voices and telephones. He glanced over at his grandmother, who was reading the paper with a magnifying glass, and he thought, "Annie should have known you could do this."

"Are you still there?"

"Yes."

"Do you live far away?"

"On Lundebysvingen."

"You're in luck. He can drop by on his way home. What's your address?"

He sat in his room and waited, his heart pounding in his throat and the curtains open so he could see the car when it pulled into the courtyard. It took exactly 30 minutes before the technician appeared in a white Kadett Combi with the Ra Data logo on the door. A surprisingly young man got out of the car and glanced uncertainly at the house.

Halvor ran to open the door. The systems specialist turned out to be a nice guy, plump as a dumpling, with deep dimples. Halvor thanked him for taking the trouble. Together they went to his room.

The technician opened his briefcase and took out a stack of charts. "Is it a numerical or alphabet password?" he asked.

Halvor turned bright red.

"Can't you even remember that much?" he asked in surprise.

"I've used so many different ones," Halvor muttered. "I change them regularly."

"Which file is it?"

"That one."

"'Annie'?"

He didn't ask any more questions. A certain etiquette went with the job, after all, and he had big ambitions. Halvor went over to the window and stood there, his cheeks burning with a mixture of shame and nervousness, and his heart was hammering so hard that it might have been a drumroll. Behind him he heard the keys clacking rapidly, like distant castanets. Otherwise there wasn't a sound, just the drumroll and the castanets. After what seemed like an eternity, the technician got up from the chair.

"OK, man, there it is!"

Halvor slowly turned around and stared at the screen. He took the invoice that was handed to him for signature.

"What? 750 kroner?" he gasped.

"Per hour and any fraction thereof," said the young man with a smile.

His hands trembling, Halvor signed the dotted line at the bottom of the page and asked to have the bill posted to him.

"It was a numeric password," said the expert, smiling again. "One seven one one nine four. Date and year, right?"

His dimples got even deeper. "But obviously not your birth-date. In that case you wouldn't be more than eight months old!"

Halvor escorted him out and thanked him, then ran back and sat down in front of the monitor. A new command had appeared on the screen: "Please proceed".

He had to press his hand to his heart because it was beating so hard. The words scrolled into view and he started reading. He had to lean on the desk and blink several times as he scrolled through the document. Something had happened, Annie had written it down, and finally he had found it. He read with his eyes wide, and a terrible suspicion slowly began to develop.

Bjørk had worked up a high blood-alcohol content.

The dog was still sitting with his tongue hanging out, panting and impatient, his eyes shifting anxiously. After a while, Bjørk got laboriously to his feet, set the bottle on the ice-cold floor, hiccuped a few times, and straightened up. He immediately fell against the wall, his legs splayed out. The dog got up too, staring at him with yellow eyes. He wagged his tail tentatively two or three times. Bjørk fumbled for the revolver, which was stuck tight in his pocket. He got it out and cocked it, staring at the dog the whole time, as he listened to the sound of his own molars grinding against each other. He swayed, his hand shaking, but fought off the dizziness, raised his arm, and pulled. The violent explosion ricocheted off the walls. The skull split open, and the contents splashed across the walls, and some struck the dog on the snout. The shot continued to reverberate. Gradually it faded to what sounded like distant thunder. The dog lunged to break free, but the leash held. After repeated attempts, the animal was exhausted. He gave up and stood there, whimpering.

The gallery was located on a quiet street, not far from the Catholic church. Outside stood a Citroën, an older model, the kind with slanted headlights. Rather like Chinese eyes, Sejer thought. The car was covered with dust. Skarre went over and looked at it. The roof was cleaner than the rest of the car, as if something had been on top, protecting the surface. It was blue-green.

"No ski-box," Sejer said.

"No, it's been removed. There are marks from the fastenings."

They opened the gallery door and went in. It smelled quite similar to Mrs Johnas's shop, of wool and starch, with a faint hint of tar from the beams in the ceiling. A camera was aimed at them from a corner. Sejer stopped and peered into the lens. Everywhere lay great piles of carpets. A broad stone staircase led up to the floors above. Several carpets were spread out on the floor and some hung from poles on the walls. Johnas was coming down the stairs, dressed in flannel and velvet, red and green and pink and black. With his dark curls he seemed to fit his passion for carpets perfectly. There was something soft and gentle about him. His fierce temper, if it existed, was well concealed. His eyes were dark, almost black, and his whole manner was unmistakably that of a salesman. Friendly, slick, accommodating.

"Well, hello!" he said. "Come on in. So you want to buy a carpet, is that right?"

He gave a wave of his arm, as if they were close friends he hadn't seen for a long time, or perhaps potential customers with a weakness for this particular kind of handwork. The knots. The colours. The patterns with the religious symbols. Birth and life and death, pain, victories, pride. To put under the dining-room table or in front of the TV. Indestructible, unique.

"You have a lot of space here," Sejer said, looking around.

"Two whole floors, plus an attic. Believe me, this

has been a big investment. I've practically skinned myself alive on this place, and it didn't look like this when I took over. Mouldy and grey. But I gave it a proper cleaning and whitewashed the walls, and that's really all it needed. Originally it was an old villa. Follow me, please."

He pointed up the stairs and led them to what he called his office, but it was actually a spacious kitchen, with a stainless steel counter and stove, a coffee maker, and a small refrigerator. There were tiles above the counter with lovely, chastely attired Dutch girls, windmills, and thick waving grass. Old copper kettles with decorative dents hung from a beam in the ceiling. The kitchen table had brass edges and corners, as though it was from an old ship.

They sat down around the table, and without asking them Johnas went over to the refrigerator and poured grape juice into wine glasses.

"How did it go with the puppies?" Skarre asked him.

"Hera will get to keep one of them, and the other two are already spoken for. So it's too late for you to change your mind. Now what can I do for you?" He smiled and took a sip.

Sejer knew that his friendliness would quickly evaporate.

"Just a few questions about Annie. I'm afraid we

need to go over the same ground again and again." He wiped his mouth discreetly. "You picked her up at the roundabout – is that right?"

Sejer's choice of words, his intonation, and the tiniest hint of doubt about his previous statement sharpened Johnas's attention.

"That's what I said before, and that's exactly what I did."

"But she actually preferred to walk, didn't she?"

"Excuse me?"

"It took a little persuasion for you to get her into the car, is that correct?"

Johnas's eyes narrowed but he remained silent.

"She preferred to walk," Sejer said. "She declined your offer of a ride. Am I right?"

Johnas nodded suddenly and smiled. "She always did that; she was so unassuming. But I thought it was too far to walk to Horgen's Shop. It's quite a way."

"So you persuaded her?"

"No, no . . ." He shook his head hard and shifted position in his chair. "I coaxed her a little. Some people have a tiresome habit of needing to be coaxed all the time."

"So it wasn't that she didn't want to get into your car?"

Johnas heard quite clearly the extra stress on the words "your car".

"That's the way Annie was. A little aloof, maybe. Who have you been talking to?"

"Several hundred people," Sejer said. "And one of them saw her get into your car after a long discussion. You're actually the last person to see her alive, and we've got to focus on that, don't you agree?"

Johnas smiled back, a conspiratorial smile, as if they were playing a game and he was more than willing to participate.

"I wasn't the last person," he said. "Whoever killed her was the last person."

"It's proving rather difficult to get hold of him," Sejer said with deliberate irony. "And we have nothing to corroborate that the man on the motorcycle was waiting for Annie. The only thing we have is you."

"I'm sorry? What are you getting at?"

"Well," Sejer said, throwing out his hands, "I'm trying to get to the bottom of this case. It's the nature of my job to doubt what people say."

"Are you accusing me of lying?"

"I'm afraid that's what I have to think," Sejer said. "I hope you'll forgive me. Why didn't she want to get in?"

Johnas was visibly uneasy. "Of course she wanted to get in!" He had shown the first sign of anger, and now controlled himself. "She got in and I drove her to Horgen's."

"No further than that?"

"No, as I told you, she got out at the shop. I thought she was going there to buy something. I didn't even drive up to the door; I stopped on the road, and let her out. And after that," he stood up to get a pack of cigarettes from the counter, "I never saw her again."

Sejer steered his interrogation on to a new track.

"You lost a child, Johnas. You know what it feels like. Have you talked to Eddie Holland about it?"

For a moment Johnas looked surprised. "No, no, he's such a private person, I didn't want to bother him. Besides, it's not an easy thing for me to talk about either."

"How long ago was it?"

"You've talked to Astrid, haven't you? Almost eight months. But it's not the sort of thing you forget or get over."

He slipped a cigarette out of the pack. Lit up and smoked in an almost feminine way. Merits, filter-tipped.

"People often try to imagine what it's like." He stared at Sejer with weary eyes. "They do it with the best of intentions. Try to picture the empty bed and imagine themselves standing there and staring at it. And I did do that often. But the empty bed is only

363

part of it. I got up every morning and went out to the bathroom, and there was his toothbrush under the mirror. The kind that changes colours when it gets warm. The rubber duck on the edge of the bath. His slippers under the bed. I caught myself setting too many places at the table for dinner, I did it for days. There were stuffed animals that he had left in the car. Months later I found a Band-Aid under the sofa."

Johnas was speaking through clenched teeth, as if with great reluctance he was revealing things to them that they had no right to know.

"I threw things out, a little at a time, and it felt as if I was committing a crime. It was painful to look at his things day after day, it was horrible to pack them away. It haunted me every second of the day, and it haunts me still. Do you know how long a person's smell stays in a pair of cotton pyjamas?"

He fell silent, and his tanned face had turned grey. Sejer didn't say a word. He suddenly thought about Elise's wooden clogs, which always stood outside the door so that she could stick her feet into them if she had to take out the rubbish or go downstairs to get the post. Opening the door, picking up the shoes, and bringing them inside was something that he remembered with great pain.

"Not long ago we went over to the cemetery," Sejer said. "Has it been a while since you were there?"

"What kind of question is that?" Johnas asked, his voice hoarse.

"I just want to know if you realise that something has been removed from the grave."

"You mean the little bird. Yes, it disappeared just after the funeral."

"Did you consider getting another one?"

"There certainly are a lot of things you want to know. Yes, of course I considered it. But I couldn't stand going through the same thing again, so I decided to leave it the way it was."

"Do you know who took it?"

"Of course not!" he said, his voice sharp. "If I did, I would have reported it at once, and if I had the chance, I would have beaten the culprit within an inch of his life."

"You mean a verbal beating?"

He smiled acidly. "No, I do *not* mean a verbal beating."

"Annie took it," Sejer said lightly.

Johnas opened his eyes wide.

"We found it among her things. Is this it?"

He stuck his hand in his pocket and pulled out the bird. Johnas took it with trembling fingers. "It looks like it. It looks like the one. But why . . ."

"We don't know. We thought you might be able to help us discover why."

"Me? Dear God, I have no clue. I don't understand it. Why on earth would she take it? She wasn't exactly the type to steal things. Not the Annie I knew."

"That's why she must have had a reason for doing it. A reason far more important than merely wanting to steal things. Was she angry with you for something?"

Johnas sat and stared at the bird, struck dumb with surprise.

He didn't know about this, thought Sejer, casting a scowl at Skarre, who sat beside him with glass-blue eyes, studying the man's slightest movement.

"Do her parents know that she had this?" Johnas said at last.

"We don't think so."

"And it wasn't Sølvi? Sølvi is a little different, you know. Just like a magpie, grabbing anything that glitters."

"It wasn't Sølvi."

Sejer raised his glass by the stem and drank the grape juice. It tasted like a light wine.

"Well, I guess she had her secrets. We all do," Johnas said. "She was a bit secretive. Especially as she got older."

"She took it hard – Eskil's death?"

"She couldn't make herself come to see us any more. I can understand it; I couldn't be around people either for a long time. Astrid and Magne left me, and so much happened all at once. An indescribable chapter," he muttered, wincing at the memory.

"You must have talked to each other, though?"

"Just brief nods when we met on the street. We were practically neighbours, after all."

"Did she try to avoid you?"

"She seemed embarrassed, in a way. It was difficult for all of us."

"And what's more," Sejer said, as if he had only just thought of it, "you had a fight with Eskil right before he died. That must have made it even harder."

"You keep Eskil out of this!" he said bitterly.

"Do you know Raymond Låke?"

"You mean that strange fellow up near Kollen?"

"I asked you whether you know him."

"Everybody knows Raymond."

"Just give me a yes or no answer."

"I do *not* know him."

"But you know where he lives?"

"Yes, I do. In that old shack of a house, though he must think it's just fine, since he looks so idiotically happy."

"Idiotically happy?" Sejer stood up, pushing his

glass aside. "I think idiots are just as dependent on other people's good will to feel happy as the rest of us are. And here's something you should never forget: even though he can't interpret his surroundings in the same way you can, there's nothing wrong with his vision."

Johnas's face stiffened slightly. He escorted them out. As they went down the stairs to the first floor, Sejer felt the camera lens like a laser beam on the back of his neck.

They went to Sejer's apartment to collect Kollberg, and let him stretch out on the back seat of the car. The dog is alone too much, Sejer thought, tossing him an extra piece of dried fish. That must be why he's so impossible.

"Do you think he smells bad?"

Skarre nodded. "You should give him a Fisherman's Friend lozenge."

They drove towards Lundeby, turned off at the roundabout, and parked next to the letterboxes. Sejer walked along the street, fully aware that everyone could see him, all 21 houses. Everyone would think he was going to see Holland. But at the end of the road he stopped and looked back, towards the house belonging to Johnas. It looked semi-vacant. The curtains were drawn in many of the windows. Slowly he walked back.

"The school bus leaves the roundabout at 7.10

a.m. every morning," he said. "All the kids in Krystallen going to school take it. So they leave home at about 7 a.m. in order to catch the bus."

A slight breeze was blowing, but not a hair on his head moved.

"Magne Johnas had just left for school when Eskil got the food caught in his throat."

Skarre waited. A prayer for patience flitted through his mind.

"And Annie left a little later than the others. Holland remembered that they had overslept. She walked past his house, maybe while Eskil was sitting there eating breakfast."

"Yes. What about it?" Skarre looked at Johnas's house. "Only the windows to the living room and bedroom face the street. And they were in the kitchen."

"I know, I know," he said irritably. They kept on walking, approached the house, and tried to imagine that day, that very November day, at 7 a.m. It's dark at that time in November, Sejer thought.

"Do you think she might have gone inside?"

"I don't know."

They stopped and stared at the house for a moment. The kitchen window was on the side, facing the neighbours' house.

"Who lives in the red house?" asked Skarre.

"Irmak. With his wife and child. But isn't that a pathway between the houses?"

Skarre looked. "Yes, it is. And someone's coming."

A boy appeared between the two houses. He was walking with his head bowed and had not yet noticed the two men in the road.

"It's Thorbjørn Haugen, the boy who helped search for Ragnhild."

Sejer stood and waited for him as he strode briskly along the path. Over his shoulder he was carrying a black bag, around his forehead was the same patterned bandanna that he'd worn before. They watched him carefully as he passed Johnas's house. Thorbjørn was tall, and he reached to the middle of the kitchen window.

"Taking a short cut?" Sejer asked.

"What?" Thorbjørn stopped. "This path goes straight down to Gneisveien."

"Do most people take this route?"

"Sure, it saves you five minutes."

Sejer took a few steps along the path and stopped outside the window. He was taller than Thorbjørn and had no trouble peering into the kitchen. There was no high chair there now, just two ordinary kitchen chairs, and on the table an ashtray and a coffee cup on the table. Otherwise the house seemed practically uninhabited. The seventh of November, he thought. Pitch black outside and brightly lit indoors. Anyone outside could look in, but those inside wouldn't be able to see out.

"Johnas gets a little cranky when we go this way," Thorbjørn said. "Says he's sick of this short cut past his house. But he's moving."

"So all the young people use this short cut to catch the school bus?"

"Everyone who goes to the junior high and high school."

Sejer nodded to Thorbjørn and turned back to Skarre. "I remember something Holland said when we talked in my office. On the day Eskil died, Annie came home from school earlier than usual because she was sick. She went straight to bed. He had to go to her room to tell her about the accident."

"Sick in what way?" Skarre wanted to know. "I thought she was never sick."

"He said that she wasn't feeling well."

"You think she saw something, don't you? Through the window?"

"I don't know. Maybe."

"But why didn't she say anything?"

"Maybe she didn't dare. Or maybe she didn't fully understand what she had seen. Maybe she confided in Halvor. I've always had the feeling that he knows more than he's telling us."

"Konrad," Skarre said, "don't you think he would have told us?"

"I'm not so sure he would. He's an odd character. Let's go and have a talk with him."

At that moment his beeper went off, so he went over to the car to ring the number. Holthemann answered.

"Axel Bjørk has shot himself in the head with an old Enfield revolver."

Sejer had to lean on the car for support. The news tasted like bitter medicine, leaving an uncomfortable dryness in his throat.

"Did you find a suicide note?"

"Not on the body. They're searching his apartment. But the man obviously had a guilty conscience about something, don't you think?"

"I don't know. He had lots of problems."

"He was an irresponsible alcoholic. And he had a grudge against Ada Holland that was as sharp as a shark's tooth," Holthemann said.

"He was mostly just unhappy."

"Hatred and despair often look alike. People show whatever suits them best."

"I think you're wrong. He had finally given up. And that must be why he put an end to it all."

"Maybe he wanted to take Ada with him?"

Sejer shook his head and glanced down the street, towards the Holland house.

"He wouldn't have done that to Sølvi and Eddie."

"Do you want to find the killer or not?"

"I just want the right one."

He hung up and looked at Skarre. "Axel Bjørk is dead. I wonder what Ada Holland will think now. Maybe the same as Halvor did when his father died. That it was a relief."

CHAPTER 15

Halvor sprang to his feet. His chair fell over and he turned abruptly towards the window, staring out at the deserted courtyard. He stood like that for a long time. Out of the corner of his eye he could see the toppled chair and Annie's photograph on the bedside table. So that's what happened. That's what Annie saw. He sat down again in front of the monitor and read it through from beginning to end. Within Annie's text was his own story, what he had confided to her, in deepest secrecy. The raging father, the shot in the shed, December 13th. It had nothing to do with Annie's death. He took a deep breath, highlighted the section, and erased it from the document for all eternity. Then he inserted a floppy disk and copied the text. When he'd finished, he slipped quietly out of his room and went through the kitchen.

"What is it, Halvor?" his grandmother called as he came through the living room, pulling on his denim jacket. "Are you going out?"

He didn't answer. He heard her voice, but the words made no impression on him.

"Where are you going? Are you going to the movies?"

He started buttoning his jacket, thinking about his motorcycle and whether it would start. If it didn't he'd have to take the bus, and that would take him an hour to reach his destination. He didn't have an hour; he had to get there fast.

"When are you coming back? Will you be home for supper?"

He stopped and looked at her, as if he had just noticed that she was standing there, right in front of him, and nagging at him.

"Supper?"

"Where are you going, Halvor? It's almost suppertime!"

"I'm going out to see someone."

"Who is it? You look so pale, I wonder if you're getting anaemic. When was the last time you went to see the doctor? You probably don't even remember. What did you say his name was?"

"I didn't say. His name's Johnas."

Halvor's voice sounded unusually determined. The door slammed, and when she peeked out the window she could see him bending over his motorcycle, angrily trying to make it start.

*

The camera on the first floor was not very well placed. There was too much glare on the lens, reducing the customers to vague outlines, almost like ghosts. He liked to see who his customers were before he went out to greet them. Upstairs, where the light was better, he could distinguish faces and clothing, and if they were regular customers, he could prepare himself before leaving the office, assuming an attitude appropriate for each one. He took another look at the screen. A lone figure was standing in the room. As far as he could see, it was a man, or maybe a teenager, wearing a short jacket. It didn't look important, but he had to put in an appearance, correct and service-oriented, as always, to maintain the fast-growing gallery's reputation. Besides, it was impossible to tell from someone's appearance whether they had money. Not these days. For all he knew, this person could be filthy rich. He walked quietly down the stairs. His footsteps were almost inaudible; he had a light, discreet tread, and it wasn't his style to dash around as if he worked in a toy shop. This was a gallery, where people talked in muted tones. There were no price tags or cash registers. As a rule, he sent a bill; or occasionally people paid by credit card. He had almost reached the bottom when he stopped.

"Good afternoon," he said.

The young man was standing with his back

turned, but now he turned around. In his eyes was suspicion, mixed with astonishment. He didn't say anything, simply stared, as if he were searching for something. A secret perhaps, or the solution to a puzzle.

Johnas recognised him. For a second or two he considered acknowledging the fact. "Can I help you?"

Halvor didn't reply. He was scrutinising him. He knew that he had been recognised. Johnas had seen him many times. He had come over with Annie and they had met on the street. Now Johnas was on the defensive. Everything soft and dark about the man, the flannel and velvet and the brown curls, had hardened into a stiff shell.

"I'm sure you can," Halvor said, taking a few more steps into the room, crossing the floor and approaching Johnas, who was still on the stairs with one hand on the banister.

"You sell carpets." He looked around.

"That's right, I do."

"I want to buy a carpet."

"Well!" he said with a smile. "I assumed as much. What are you looking for? Anything in particular?"

He's not looking to buy a carpet, Johnas thought. And besides, he can't afford one; he's after something else. Maybe he's here out of sheer curiosity, a young man's sudden whim. He probably has no idea what carpets cost. But he'll find out soon enough, yes he will.

"Big or small?" he said, coming down the last steps. The youth was more than a head shorter that he was and as slender as a piece of kindling.

"I want a carpet that's big enough to cover the whole floor, so none of the chairs are on bare floor. It's such a bother to clean."

Johnas nodded. "Come upstairs. That's where we have the biggest carpets." He started walking up the stairs.

Halvor followed. It didn't occur to him to use the opportunity to ask questions; he felt as if he were being driven by unknown forces, as if he were gliding up a track into a dark mountain.

Johnas switched on the six chandeliers which had been sent from a glass-blowing studio in Venice. They hung from the tarred beams in the ceiling, casting a warm but powerful light over the large room.

"What colour were you thinking of?"

Halvor stopped at the head of the stairs and looked at the room. "All of them are red," he murmured.

Johnas gave him an indulgent smile. "I don't mean to sound arrogant," he said in a friendly voice, "but do you realise what they cost?"

Halvor looked at him with narrowed eyes. Something from the past rose up in his mind, something he hadn't felt for a long time. "I suppose I don't look awfully rich," he said tonelessly. "Maybe you'd like to see a bank statement?"

Johnas hesitated. "Please forgive me. But a lot of people wander in here and end up feeling embarrassed. I just wanted to do you a favour and spare you the awkwardness."

"That was considerate," Halvor said.

He stepped into the room, strode past Johnas, and headed straight for a large carpet that hung on the wall. He stretched out his hand and played with the fringe. In the patterns he could make out men and horses and weapons.

"Two and a half by three metres," Johnas said. "An excellent choice, if I may say so. The pattern depicts a war between two nomad groups. It's very heavy."

"You can have it delivered, can't you?" Halvor said.

"Certainly. I have a delivery truck. I was thinking more in terms of keeping it clean. It takes several men just to shake it out."

"I'll take it."

"Excuse me?" Johnas took a few steps closer and stared at him uncertainly. This young man was strange.

"It's almost the most expensive carpet I have – 70,000 kroner."

He watched the boy closely as he said the price. Halvor didn't blink an eye.

"I'm sure it's worth it."

Johnas didn't like it. A nagging suspicion was creeping up his spine like a cold snake. He couldn't tell what this kid wanted or why he was acting so strangely. He couldn't possibly have that much money, and if he did, he wouldn't spend it on a carpet.

"Please wrap it for me," Halvor said, crossing his arms. He leaned against a mahogany drop-leaf table that creaked alarmingly under his weight.

"Wrap it?" Johnas curled his lips into a smile. "I roll them up and put plastic and tape around the outside."

"OK, that's fine."

Halvor waited.

"It takes a little work to get it down from the wall. I suggest that I bring it out to you this evening. Then I can help you put it in place."

"No, no," Halvor said. "I want to take it now."

Johnas hesitated. "You want to take it now. And – forgive my rudeness – how will you pay for it?"

"Cash, if that's all right."

He patted his back pocket. He was wearing faded jeans with frayed cuffs. Johnas stood in front of him, still dubious.

"Is there something wrong?" Halvor said.

"I don't know. Perhaps."

"And what would that be?"

"I know who you are," Johnas said, deciding to take a firm stance. It was a relief to stop pretending.

"Do we know each other?"

Johnas nodded, standing there rocking back and forth with his hands on his hips.

"Yes, we do, Halvor. Of course we know each other. I think you'd better go now."

"Why? Is something wrong?"

"Let's cut the crap, right now!" Johnas said, tight-lipped.

"I agree!" snarled Halvor. "Take down that carpet, and do it fast!"

"On reflection, I don't think I want to sell it. I'm moving and I want to keep it for myself. Besides, it's much too expensive for you. Be honest now, we both know that you can't afford it."

"So you want to keep it for yourself?" Halvor turned on his heel. "Well, I can understand that. I'll take a different one."

He looked at the wall again and pointed at once to a carpet in pinks and greens. "I'll take that one instead," he said simply. "Please get it down for me, and give me a receipt."

"It costs 44,000."

"That's fine."

"Is that so?"

He was still waiting with his arms crossed and his pupils as hard as buckshot. "Would it be too presumptuous of me to ask to see that you actually do have the money?"

Halvor shook his head. "Of course not. I realise that it's impossible to know just from looking at people whether they have money these days."

He stuck his hand in his hip pocket and took out an old wallet made of nylon with Velcro, flat as a pancake. He poked his fingers inside and jingled some coins. Took out a few and put them on the drop-leaf table.

Johnas stared at him sceptically as the five-, ten-, and one-krone coins formed a little heap. "All right, that's enough," he said harshly. "You've already taken up enough of my time. Now get out of here!"

Halvor stopped and glanced up at him, looking almost offended.

"I'm not done yet. I have more." He dug further into his wallet.

"No, you don't! You live in an old shack with your grandmother, and you deliver ice cream! It costs 44,000," he said sharply. "You'd better cough up the money right now . . ."

"So you know where I live?" Halvor looked at him. Things were starting to get dangerous, but he wasn't scared; for some reason he wasn't scared at all.

"I do have this," he said suddenly, pulling something out of the slot for banknotes in his wallet. Johnas stared at him suspiciously, casting a dubious eye at what he was holding between two fingers.

"It's a disk," Halvor said.

"I don't want a disk; I want 40,000 kroner," Johnas snapped, feeling fear begin to hack at his chest.

"Annie's diary," Halvor said, waving the disk. "She started keeping a diary a while ago. In November, as a matter of fact. We've been looking for it, several of us. You know how girls are: always having to confide things."

Johnas was breathing hard. His gaze was aimed at Halvor like a stapling machine.

"I've read it," Halvor said. "It's about you."

"Give it to me!"

"Not until hell freezes over!"

Johnas gave a start. Halvor's voice had changed tone and was suddenly deeper. It was like listening to an evil spirit speaking through the mouth of a child.

"I've made copies of it," he said. "So I can buy as many carpets as I want. Every time I feel like having a new carpet, I'll just make another copy. Do you understand what I'm saying?"

"You hysterical little brat! What kind of institution did you escape from?"

383

Johnas steeled himself, and in a fraction of a second Halvor saw his torso swell up as he prepared to spring. He weighed about 20 kilos more than Halvor, and he was furious. Halvor dove to the side and saw the man miss his target and slide along the stone floor, slamming headfirst into the drop-leaf table. The coins scattered in all directions, jangling as they struck the floor. Johnas began to spew out the ugliest curses Halvor had ever heard, even taking into account his father's extensive vocabulary. In two seconds he was back on his feet. A single glance at his dark face made Halvor realise that the battle was lost. He was much bigger. Halvor made for the stairs, but Johnas was after him at once, taking three or four steps, and then lunging forward. He rammed into Halvor's back at shoulder level. Instinctively the boy kept his head up, but his body struck the stone floor with great force.

"Take your fucking hands off me!"

Johnas spun him around. Halvor felt the man's breath on his face and his fists tightening around his throat.

"You're out of your mind!" he said. "You're done for! I don't care what you do to me, but you're done for!"

Johnas was deaf and blind. He raised his clenched fist and took aim at the lean face. Halvor had been beaten before and knew what was in store for him. The knuckles struck him under the chin, and his fragile jaw snapped like dry tinder. His lower teeth struck with powerful force against his upper teeth, and tiny bits of crushed porcelain mixed with the blood that came gushing out of his mouth. Johnas kept on pounding at him, no longer taking aim, merely striking out at random as Halvor flung his body from side to side. Finally Johnas smashed his fist against the stone floor and howled, lurched to his feet and stared at his hand, panting. There was a great deal of blood. He stared at what was lying on the floor and took a long, deep breath. After a few minutes his heartbeat returned to normal and his mind cleared.

"He's not here," said the grandmother surprised, when Sejer and Skarre appeared at her door. "He was going out to visit somebody. I think his name was Johnas. He was all upset too, and he hadn't eaten anything. I don't know what's going on any more, and I'm too old to keep up with everything."

The news made Sejer pound his fist twice against the door frame.

"Did he get a phone call or anything like that?"

"Nobody calls us. Annie was the only one who called every once in a while. He's been sitting in his room all afternoon, playing with his computer. Suddenly he stormed out and disappeared."

"I'm sure we'll find him. You have to excuse us, but we're in a hurry."

"Of all things," he said to Skarre as he slammed the car door, "this was the worst he could have done."

"We'll soon see what's happened," Skarre said, tight-lipped, and spun the car around in the yard.

"I don't see Halvor's motorcycle."

Skarre jumped out. Sejer turned to Kollberg, who was still lying on the back seat, and took a dog biscuit from his pocket.

They pulled on the door, which swung slowly open, as they found themselves glaring defiantly at the video camera in the ceiling. Johnas saw them from the kitchen. For a moment he remained sitting at the ship's table, breathing calmly, as he blew on his injured knuckles. There was no rush. One thing at a time. True, a lot was happening all at once; even so, he was used to being able to take care of everything. He was a very capable man. Took each problem one at a time, as they cropped up. It was one of his special skills. Very calmly he stood up and proceeded to walk down the stairs.

"You're certainly getting around," he said. "It's beginning to border on harassment."

"Do you really think so?"

Sejer loomed in front of him like a giant pillar. Everything looked presentable; there were no other customers in the gallery.

"We're looking for someone. We thought we might find him here."

Johnas gave them an enquiring look, turned to look around the room, and threw out his hands. "I'm the only one here. And I was just about to close up. It's late."

"We'd like to take a look. We'll be quick, of course."

"Frankly . . ."

"Maybe he slipped inside when you weren't looking and is hiding somewhere. You never know."

Sejer was trembling, and Skarre thought that he looked as though a great storm were gathering force under his shirt.

"I'm closing up now!" Johnas said.

They walked past him and up the stairs. Took a good look around. Went into the office, opened the door to the toilet, continued on up to the attic. No one in sight.

"Who did you expect to find here?"

Johnas was leaning against the banister, studying them with one eyebrow raised. His chest was rising and falling visibly.

"Halvor Muntz."

"And who is that?"

"Annie's boyfriend."

"Why would he come here?"

"I'm not sure."

Unperturbed, Sejer wandered round the gallery. "But he hinted that he was coming here. He's been playing detective on his own, and I think we ought to put a stop to it."

"I agree wholeheartedly," Johnas said, with a condescending smile. "But there hasn't been anyone playing Hardy Boys here."

Sejer kicked at the rolled-up carpets with the tip of his shoe. "Does this building have a basement?"

"No."

"What do you do with the carpets at night? Do you leave them out?"

"Most of them, yes. But I put the most expensive ones in the vault."

"I see."

Suddenly he caught sight of the small mahogany table, beneath which a handful of coins lay scattered.

"Are you always so careless with your small change?" he said.

Johnas shrugged. Sejer didn't like the fact that it was so quiet. He didn't like the expression on the carpet dealer's face. In a corner of the room he noticed a pink bucket with a scrubbing brush next to it. The floor was damp. "Have you been washing the floor?" he asked.

"It's the last thing I do before I close up the shop. I save a lot of money by doing it myself. As you can see," he said after a moment, "there's nobody here."

Sejer looked at him. "Show us the vault."

For a moment Johnas looked as if he might refuse, but then he changed his mind and started heading down the stairs.

"It's on the first floor. You can see it of course, though naturally it's locked, and it would be impossible to hide inside."

They followed him down to the first floor to a corner under the stairs, where they saw a steel door, quite low but much wider than a normal door. Johnas went over and twisted the dial of a combination lock back and forth. With every twist a tiny click was audible. He was using his left hand, a little clumsily, because he was right-handed.

"Is this boy so valuable that you think I would hide him in here?"

"Possibly," said Sejer, staring at the clumsy left hand. Johnas gripped the handle of the heavy door and pulled with all his might.

"I'm sure it'd be easier if you used both hands," Sejer said.

Johnas raised an eyebrow, as if he didn't understand. Sejer peered into the cramped space, which contained a small safe, two or three paintings leaning against the wall, and a number of rolled carpets stacked up on the floor like logs.

"That's all there is." He gave them a belligerent look. The vault was brightly lit with two long fluorescent tubes in the ceiling. The walls were bare.

Sejer smiled. "But he was here, wasn't he? What did he want?"

"Nobody's been here, except for you two."

Sejer nodded and walked out of the vault. Skarre cast him an uneasy glance, but followed him out.

"If he happens to turn up, would you contact us immediately?" Sejer said. "He's been going through a difficult time lately after all that's happened. He needs help."

"Of course."

The vault door slammed shut.

Out in the car park Sejer signalled for Skarre to drive.

"Drive up the hill and pull into that driveway at the top. Do you see it?"

Skarre nodded.

"Park there. We'll wait until he leaves and then follow him. I want to see where he's going."

They didn't have long to wait. No more than five minutes passed before Johnas suddenly appeared in the doorway. He locked up, activated the burglar alarm, walked past the grey Citroën, and disappeared down the driveway to a back courtyard. He was out of sight for a few minutes, then reappeared in an old Transit truck. He stopped at the street and signalled left. Sejer could clearly hear the roaring of the engine.

"Ah, yes, he would have a delivery truck," Skarre said.

"With one cylinder gone. It's roaring like an old fishing boat. Let's get going, but be careful. He's making for the intersection down there; don't get too close."

"Can you see if he's looking in his rear-view mirror?" Skarre said.

"He's not. Let that Volvo get ahead of you, Skarre, that green one!"

The Volvo braked but Skarre waved it on ahead of them. The driver saluted in thanks.

"He's signalling right. Get over in the right lane! Where do you think he's going?"

"Possibly to Oscarsgaten. The man's in the middle of moving, isn't he? Careful now, he's slowing down. Watch out for that beer truck; if it gets in front of you, we'll lose him!"

"Easy for you to say. When are you going to get yourself a more powerful car?"

"He's slowing down again. I bet he's heading for Børresensgaten. Let's hope the Volvo is going the same way."

Johnas drove the big vehicle gently and smoothly through town, as if not wanting to attract attention. He signalled and changed gear as he approached Oscarsgaten, and now they could clearly see him looking in his rear-view mirror several times.

"He's stopping at the yellow building. It's number 15. Pull over, Skarre!"

"Right here?"

"Turn off the engine. He's getting out now."

Johnas jumped out of the truck, looked around, and crossed the street with long strides. Sejer and Skarre stared at the door where he stood, fumbling with a key. He was carrying a toolbox.

"He's going up to his apartment. We'll wait here for the time being. As soon as he's inside, slip out and run over to his truck. I want you to peek in through the back window."

"What do you think he has in there?"

"I don't even dare guess what it might be. OK, now. Hurry, Skarre!"

Skarre ran along the footpath, bent double like an old man, ducking behind a row of parked cars. He appeared again at the back of the truck, and put a hand on either side of his face to see better. Within seconds he turned and came sprinting back, threw himself into the driver's seat and slammed the door.

"A pile of carpets. And what looks like Halvor's Suzuki. It's in the back of the truck with the helmet on the handlebars. Shall we go up?"

"Absolutely not. We're just going to sit here. If I'm right, he won't be long."

"And then we'll keep following him?"

"That depends."

"Is there a light on anywhere?"

"Not that I can see. There he is now!"

They ducked down and peered at Johnas, who had paused on the footpath. Now he looked up and down the street and at the long row of cars parked on the left-hand side. He didn't see anyone in any of them. He went over to the Transit truck, got in, started the engine, and began backing up. Skarre stuck his head up over the dashboard.

"What's he doing?" asked Sejer.

"He's backing up. Now he's moving forward. He's backing across the street and parking right in front of the entrance. He's getting out. He's at the back door of the truck. Now he's opening it. Taking out a rolled-up carpet. Crouching down and putting it over his shoulder. He's swaying under the weight. It looks like it's god-awful heavy!"

"Christ, he's going to fall over!"

Johnas teetered under the weight of the carpet. His knees seemed about to give way under him.

Sejer put his hand on the door handle. "He's going back inside. He's probably trying to put it in the lift. Keep your eye on the front of the building, Skarre. See if he turns on a light!"

Kollberg started to whine.

"Be quiet, boy!" Sejer turned and patted the dog. They waited, peering at the façade of the building and the dark windows.

"There's a light on the fourth floor now. His apartment is there, right below that protrusion – can you see it?"

Sejer stared up at the wall. The yellow window had no curtains.

"Shouldn't we go up?" Skarre asked.

"Don't be too hasty. Johnas is clever. We should wait a bit."

"Wait for what?"

"The light has gone off again. Maybe he's coming out. Get down, Skarre!"

They ducked down. Kollberg began to whine again.

"If you start barking, you won't get any food for a whole week!" Sejer whispered between clenched teeth.

Johnas came back outside. He looked exhausted.

This time he didn't look to the right or left but just got into the truck, slammed the door, and started the engine.

Sejer cracked open the door.

"Follow him. Keep a good distance. I'm going up to his flat."

"How are you going to get inside?"

"I've taken a course in picking locks. Haven't you?"

"Of course, of course."

"Just don't lose him! Don't move until you see him turn the corner, then follow him. Most likely he'll wait until it's dark. When you see that he's headed for home, go to headquarters and get some back-up. Arrest him at his house. Don't give him a chance to change his clothes or put anything away, and don't say a word about this flat! If he stops along the way to dump the motorcycle, don't arrest him. Do you understand?"

"Yes, but why not?" Skarre asked.

"Because he's twice your size!"

Sejer grabbed Kollberg's leash, and got out of the car, pulling the dog after him. He ducked down behind the car as Johnas put the truck in gear and drove off down the street. Skarre waited a few seconds and then drove after him. He wasn't feeling terribly confident.

Sejer walked across the street, pushed a doorbell

at random, and growled "Police" into the inter-com. The door buzzed and he stepped inside. Ignoring the lift, he dashed up the stairs to the fourth floor. There were two doors, but he automatically turned to the door facing the street, where they'd seen the lights. There was no nameplate. He peered at the lock; a simple latch. He opened his wallet in search of a credit card. He was reluctant to use his bank card, but next to it was a library card with his name and number on it. On the back it said: "Books open all doors". He stuck the card into the crack, and the door slid open. The lock was useless, but maybe it was going to be changed. For the time being, the apartment was virtually empty. He turned on the light. Caught sight of the toolbox in the middle of the floor and two stools over by the window. There was a little pyramid of paint cans and a five-litre bottle of turpentine under the sink in the kitchen. Johnas was redecorating. Sejer tiptoed inside and listened. The flat was bright and open, with big bay windows and a good view of the street, and high enough to escape the worst traffic noise. It was an old block from the turn of the century, with a handsome façade and plaster rosettes in the ceiling. He could see all the way to the Brewery, which was reflected in the river some distance below.

He walked quietly from room to room, looking

around. The phone hadn't been installed, and there was no furniture. A few cardboard boxes stood along the walls, labelled with a black marker: Bedroom, Kitchen, Living Room, Hall. A couple of paintings. A half-empty bottle of Cardinal on the kitchen counter. Several carpets, rolled up, lay beneath the living-room window. Kollberg sniffed at the air. He recognised the smell of paint and wallpaper paste and turpentine. Sejer made another round, stopping at the window to look out. Kollberg was restless. The dog padded around on his own; Sejer followed, opening a cupboard here and there. The heavy carpet was nowhere in sight. The dog started whimpering and disappeared further into the apartment. Sejer followed.

Finally the dog stopped in front of a door. His fur stood on end.

"What is it, boy?"

Kollberg sniffed vigorously at the door, scraping at it with his claws. Sejer cast a glance over his shoulder, not exactly sure why, but he was suddenly gripped with a strange feeling. Someone was close by. He put his hand on the door handle and pressed down. Then he pulled the door open. Someone struck him in the chest with great force. The next second was a chaos of sound and pain: snarling, growling, and hysterical barking as the big animal dug its claws into his chest. Kollberg sprang and snapped his jaws just as Sejer recognised Johnas's Dobermann. Then he hit the floor with both dogs on top of him. Instinctively he rolled on to his stomach with his hands over his head. The animals tumbled on to the floor while he looked around for something to use as a weapon but found nothing. He dashed into the bathroom, caught sight of a broom, picked it up, and ran back to where the dogs were standing a couple of metres apart, growling and baring their teeth.

"Kollberg!" Sejer shouted. "It's a bitch, goddamn it!" Hera's eyes shone like yellow lanterns in her black face. Kollberg put his ears back; the other dog stood there like a panther, ready to attack. Sejer raised the broom and took several steps forward while he felt sweat and blood running down his back under his shirt. Kollberg looked at him, paused, and for an instant forgot to keep an eye on the enemy, who rushed forward like a black missile, her jaws open. Sejer closed his eyes and struck. He hit Hera on the back of her neck and blinked in despair as the dog collapsed. She lay on the floor, whimpering. Sejer lunged forward, grabbed the dog's collar, and dragged the animal over to the bedroom. He opened the door, gave the dog a violent shove inside, and slammed the door. Then he fell against the wall and slid down to the floor, staring at Kollberg, who was still in a defensive position in the middle of the room.

"Goddamn it, Kollberg. It's a bitch!" He wiped his forehead. Kollberg came over and licked his face. On the other side of the door they could hear Hera whining. For a moment Sejer sat with his face buried in his hands, trying to recover from the shock. He looked down at himself; his clothes were covered with dog fur and blood, and Kollberg was bleeding from one ear.

He got to his feet, and trudged into the bathroom. On a blanket in the shower stall he caught sight of something black and silky soft that was crying pitifully.

"No wonder she tried to attack us," he whispered. "She was just trying to protect her puppies."

The rolled-up carpet lay along one wall. He crouched down and stared at it. It was tightly rolled, covered with plastic, and taped up with carpet tape, the black kind that Sejer knew was nearly impossible to remove. He began tugging and pulling, the sweat pouring down under his shirt. Kollberg scratched and clawed and tried to help, but Sejer pushed him away. Finally he managed to get the tape off and began tearing at the plastic. He stood up and dragged the carpet into the living room. They could hear Hera whimpering in the bedroom. He bent down and gave the carpet a mighty shove. It unrolled, slow and heavy. Inside lay a compressed body. The face was destroyed. The mouth was taped shut, as was the nose, or what was left of it. Sejer swayed slightly as he stood there staring down at Halvor. He had to turn away and lean against the wall for a moment. Then he took the phone from his belt. He stood at the window as he punched in the number, fixing his eyes on a barge moving along the river. *Hexagon*. Sailing from Bremen. He heard the beep and a prolonged, melancholy ringing. Here I come, it was saying. Here I come, but there's no hurry.

"Konrad Sejer, 15 Oscarsgaten," he said into the phone. "I need back-up."

CHAPTER 16

"Henning Johnas?"

Sejer twirled a pen between two fingers and stared at him.

"Do you know why you're here?"

"What kind of a question is that?" he said hoarsely. "Let me say one thing: there's a limit to what I'll stand for. But if this has anything to do with Annie, then I have nothing more to say."

"We're not going to talk about Annie," Sejer said.

"I see."

He rocked his chair back and forth slightly, and Sejer thought he registered a hint of relief flit across the man's face.

"Halvor Muntz seems to have disappeared from the face of the earth. Are you still certain that you haven't seen him?"

Johnas pressed his lips together. "Absolutely positive. I don't know him."

"You're sure about that?"

"You may not believe it, but I'm still quite clear-headed, in spite of repeated harassment from the police."

"We were wondering what his motorcycle was doing in your garage. In the back of your truck."

Johnas uttered a snorting sound of fear.

"Excuse me? What did you say?"

"Halvor's motorcycle."

"It's Magne's motorcycle," he said. "I'm helping him repair it."

He spoke quickly, without looking at Sejer.

"Magne has a Kawasaki. Besides, you don't know anything about motorcycles – you're in a different field, to put it mildly. Try again, Johnas."

"All right, all right!" His temper flared and he lost his self-control, gripping the table with both hands. "He came trotting into the gallery and started pestering me. God, how he pestered me! Acting like he was on drugs, claiming that he wanted to buy a carpet. Of course he didn't have any money. So many strange people wander in and out of my shop, and I lost my temper. I gave him a slap. He ran off like the little brat he is, leaving behind his motorcycle and everything. I lugged it out to my truck and took it home with me. As punishment, he's going to have to come and get it himself. Beg me to give it back to him."

"For just a slap, your hand certainly took a beating, didn't it?" Sejer stared at the flayed knuckles. "The thing is that nobody knows where he is."

"Then he must have taken off with his tail between his legs. He probably had a guilty conscience about something."

"Do you have any suggestions?"

"You're investigating his girlfriend's murder. Maybe you should start there."

"I don't think you should forget, Johnas, that you live in a very small place. Rumours spread fast."

Johnas was sweating so heavily that his shirt stuck to his chest.

"So what? I'm going to move," he said.

"You mentioned that. Into town, is that right? So you taught Halvor a lesson. Maybe we should let him be for a while?"

Sejer wasn't happy. It just seemed like it.

"Could it be that you lose your temper rather easily, Johnas? Let's talk a little about that." He twirled the pen some more. "Let's start with Eskil."

Johnas was lucky. He had just bent down to take his cigarettes out of his jacket pocket. He took his time straightening up.

"No," he groaned, "I don't have the strength to talk about Eskil."

"We can take all the time we need," Sejer said. "Start with that day, that day in November, from the moment you got up, you and your son."

Johnas shook his head and nervously licked his lips. The only thing he could think about was the disk, which he hadn't managed to read. Maybe Sejer had taken it and read through everything that Annie had written. The thought was enough to make him feel faint.

"It's hard to talk about it. I've tried to put it behind me. Why are you so interested in an old tragedy? Don't you have more pressing matters to occupy your time?"

"I realise that it's hard. But try anyway. I know that you were having a difficult time and that you really should have had professional help. Tell me about him."

"But why do you want to talk about Eskil!"

"The boy was an important part of Annie's life. And everything about Annie needs to be brought to light."

"I realise that, I realise that. I'm just confused. For a moment I thought you might have suspected me of . . . you know. Of having something to do with Annie's death."

Sejer smiled, a rare open smile. Then he gave Johnas a look of surprise and shook his head.

"Would *you* have a motive for killing Annie?"

"Of course not," he said. "But to be honest, it took a lot for me to call you and say that she had been in my car. I knew I was sticking my neck out."

"We would have found out anyway. Someone saw you."

"That's what I thought. That's why I called."

"Tell me about Eskil," Sejer said, unperturbed.

Johnas slumped forward and took a drag on his cigarette. He looked confused. His lips were moving, but not a sound came out.

In his mind everything was clear, but now the room was closing in around him, and all he could hear was the breathing of the man on the other side of the table. He glanced at the clock on the wall in order to organise his thoughts. It was early evening, 6 p.m.

Eskil woke up with a gleeful shout at 6 a.m. Tumbled around in our bed, hurling himself this way and that. Wanted to get up at once. Astrid needed to sleep some more, she hadn't slept well, and so I had to get up. He followed me out of the room and into the bathroom, hanging on to my pyjama legs. His arms and legs were everywhere, and he talked non-stop, an endless stream of sounds and shouts. He wriggled around like an eel when I tried desperately to put his clothes on him. He didn't want to wear nappies. Didn't want to wear the outfit I found for him, kept on reaching for anything that wasn't nailed down, and finally climbed up on the toilet lid and began pulling things down from the shelf under the mirror. Astrid's jars and bottles crashed to the floor. I lifted him down and was immediately swept up in the same old patterns. I scolded him, kindly at first, and shoved a Ritalin pill in his mouth, which he promptly spat out as he grabbed the shower curtain and managed to pull it down. I tried to get dressed, tried to make sure he didn't damage anything, didn't break anything. Finally we were both dressed. I lifted him up and carried him into the kitchen to put him in his chair. On the way across the room he suddenly threw his head back and hit me in the mouth. My lip split open and began to bleed. I strapped him in and buttered a piece of bread, but he didn't want the food I fixed for him; he shook his head and threw the plate across the table while he screamed that he wanted sausage instead.

"Johnas?" Sejer said. "Tell me about Eskil."

Johnas shook himself and looked at the inspector. At last he made a decision.

"All right, if that's what you want. November 7th. A day like any other day, which means an indescribable day. He was a torpedo, he was destroying the whole family in his wake. Magne was getting worse and worse grades in school and couldn't stand to be home any more. He would go off with his friends every afternoon and evening. Astrid never got enough sleep; I couldn't keep regular hours at the shop. Every meal was a trial.

Annie," he said all of a sudden, smiling sadly, "Annie was the only bright spot. She would come and get him whenever she had time. Then silence would descend on the house like a hurricane. We would collapse wherever we were sitting or lying and completely pass out. We were exhausted and desperate, and no one gave us any help. We were told quite clearly that he would never grow out of it. He would always have trouble concentrating, and he would be hyperactive the rest of his life. The whole family would have to put up with him for years to come. For years. Can you even imagine that?"

"And that day, you had a fight with him?"

Johnas laughed wildly. "We were always fighting. It was a neurosis in our family. No doubt we did our part to make things worse for him; we had no idea how to tackle him. We screamed and shouted, and his whole life consisted of swear words and unpleasantness."

"Tell me what happened."

"Magne stuck his head in the kitchen and shouted goodbye. He went off to catch his bus with his bag over his shoulder. It was still dark outside. I buttered a new piece of bread and put some sausage on it. Then I cut it up in little pieces, even though he could easily have eaten the crust. The whole time he was banging his cup on the oilcloth-covered table, shouting and screaming, not with laughter or anger, just an endless stream of sounds. Suddenly he caught sight of the dessert waffles on the counter from the day before, and started nagging me for them, and even though I knew he would win, I said no. That word was like a red flag for him, so he refused to give up, banging his cup and rocking back and forth in his chair, which threatened to fall over. I stood at the counter with my back turned, shaking. Finally I stepped over and grabbed the plate, pulled off the plastic, and lifted up a ring of waffles. Threw the sausage bits in the trash and put the waffles in front of him. Tore off a couple of the hearts. I knew he wasn't going to eat them quietly. There was a lot more in store for me; I knew how he was. Eskil wanted jam on them. Furious, my hands shaking, I spread raspberry jam on two of the hearts. That's when he smiled. I remember it so well, that last smile. He was pleased with himself. I couldn't stand the fact that he was so happy, while I was on the edge of a nervous breakdown. He picked up his plate and started slamming it against the table. He didn't want the waffles after all, he didn't really like them, the only thing he wanted in all the world was to have his own way. The waffles slid off the plate and on to the floor, so I had to find a cloth. I looked everywhere, but couldn't find one, so I picked up the waffles and spread them out. He watched me with interest as I made a big lump. His little face didn't have a trace of fear for what was to come. I was boiling inside, and some of the steam had to be let out, I didn't know how. Suddenly I bent over the table and stuffed the waffles in his mouth, pushing them in as far as they would go. I still remember his surprised look and the tears that sprang to his eyes.

"'Right now!' I shrieked at him in fury. 'Right now you're going to eat your goddamn waffles!'"

Johnas collapsed like a broken stick.

"I didn't mean to do it!"

His cigarette was smouldering in the ashtray. Sejer swallowed and let his eyes slide towards the window, but he found nothing that could erase the image from his retina: the little boy with his mouth full of dessert waffles and his big, terrified eyes.

He looked at Johnas. "We have to accept the children we're given, don't you agree?"

"That's what they all said. Everyone who didn't know any better, and nobody knew. And now I'm going to be charged with abuse, resulting in death. I've charged and condemned myself long ago, and you can't make things any worse."

Sejer looked at him. "What exactly was the charge?"

"Eskil's death was entirely my fault. I was

responsible for him. Nothing can be excused or explained away. The only thing is that I didn't mean for him to die. It was an accident."

"It must have been terrible for you," Sejer said. "You didn't have anyone to go to with your despair. At the same time you probably feel that you've never been properly punished for what happened. Is that how it is?"

Johnas was silent. His eyes flitted around the room.

"First you lost your youngest son, and then your wife left you, taking your older son with her. You were left all alone, with no one."

Now Johnas began to cry. It sounded as if he had porridge in his throat that he was trying to regurgitate.

"And yet you've carried on. You have your dog to keep you company. You expanded your business, which is thriving. It takes a lot of energy to start afresh the way you have."

Johnas nodded. The words felt like warm water.

Sejer had taken aim; now he fired his shot.

"And then, after you had finally got a grip on things and your life was getting back to normal – then Annie popped up, didn't she?"

Johnas gave a start.

"Maybe she looked at you with accusing eyes when you met on the street. You must have wondered about that, about why she seemed so unfriendly. So when you caught sight of her running along with her schoolbag on her back, you had to find out what it was all about, once and for all, didn't you?"

A girl came running down the hill. She recognised me at once and pulled up short. Her face froze and she gave me a cold look. Her whole posture rebuffed me, a stubborn, almost aggressive attitude that was alarming.

She started walking again, taking swift strides, without looking back. Then I called out to her. I refused to give up, I had to find out what it was about! Finally she relented and got in, sitting with her arms wrapped around the bag that she held on her lap. I drove slowly, wanting to speak but not knowing exactly how to begin or whether I was about to do something that could be dangerous for both of us. So I kept on driving, and out of the corner of my eye I was aware of her tense figure, like one big trembling accusation.

"I need someone to talk to," I started off, hesitantly, clutching the steering wheel hard in my hands. "Things haven't been easy for me."

"I know that," she replied, staring out of the window, but suddenly she turned and looked at me for a brief moment. It felt like a small opening, and I tried to relax. There was still time to retreat and leave

it alone, but now she was sitting there, listening to me. Maybe she was grown-up enough to understand everything, and maybe that's all she wanted, some sort of confession or plea for forgiveness. Annie and all her talk about justice.

"Can we drive somewhere and talk a little, Annie? It's hard to do in the car. If you have some time, just a few minutes, and then I'll drive you to wherever you're going afterwards."

My voice was thin and pleading; I saw that it touched her. She nodded slowly and seemed to relax a bit, settling back in the seat and staring out the window again. After a while we passed Horgen's Shop, and I saw a motorcycle parked next to it. The driver was bending over the handlebars, studying something, maybe a map. I drove slowly and carefully up the bad road to Kollen and parked at the turning place. Annie suddenly looked worried. She left her bag on the floor of my car. I try to remember what I was thinking at that moment, but I can't. I remember only that we trudged up the overgrown path. Annie was tall and straight-backed, walking beside me, young and steadfast, yet not unimpressionable. She went with me down to the water and sat hesitantly on a rock. Plucked at her fingers for a while. I remember her short fingernails and the little ring on her left hand.

"I saw you," she said quietly. "I saw you through

412

the window. Right when you bent over the table. I ran away. Later Papa told me that Eskil was dead."

"I knew you were accusing me," I told her sombrely, "because of the way you've been acting. Every day when we met on the street or at the letterboxes or by the garage. You were accusing me."

I started to cry. I leaned forward and sobbed into my lap while Annie sat motionless at my side. She didn't say anything, but when I was done, I glanced up and saw that she had been crying too. I felt better than I had for a long time, I really did. A warm breeze was stroking my back, and there was still hope.

"What should I do?" I whispered then. "What should I do in order to put this behind me?"

She looked at me with her grey eyes, almost in surprise. "Turn yourself in to the police, of course. And tell them the truth. Otherwise you'll never find peace!"

At that moment she looked at me. My heart turned to stone in my chest. I put my hands in my pockets, tried hard to keep them there. "Have you told this to anyone?" I asked her.

"No," she said. "Not yet."

"You should mind your own business, Annie!" I shrieked in desperation. Suddenly I felt as if I were rising up from the bottom, out of the darkness and into the light. A single paralysing thought occurred to me. That Annie was the only person in the whole *world who knew about this. It was as if the wind had turned and was now roaring in my ears. Everything was lost. Her face wore the same astonished expression Eskil's face had. Afterwards I walked swiftly through the woods. I didn't turn around even once to look back at her.*

Johnas studied the curtains and the fluorescent light on the ceiling as he kept on shaping his lips to form words that wouldn't come. Sejer looked at him. "We've searched your house and secured the forensic evidence. You will be charged with the negligent homicide of your own son, Eskil Johnas, and the premeditated murder of Annie Sofie Holland. Do you understand what I'm saying?"

"You're wrong!"

His voice was a fragile peep. Several burst blood vessels had given his eyes a reddish sheen.

"I'm not the one who will assess your guilt."

Johnas stuck his fingers in his shirt pocket, searching for something. He was shaking so violently that he looked like an old man. Finally he pulled out a flat little metal box.

"My mouth is so dry," he said.

Sejer stared at the box. "But you didn't have to kill her, you know."

"What are you talking about?" he said faintly.

"You didn't have to kill Annie. She would have died on her own if you'd just waited a little longer."

"Are you joking?"

"No," Sejer said. "I would never joke about cancer of the liver."

"You must be mistaken. Nobody was healthier than Annie. She was standing by the water when I stood up and left, and the last thing I heard was the sound of a stone that she threw into the water. I didn't dare tell you the first time, that she actually went all the way up to the lake with me. But that's what happened! She didn't want to drive back with me; she wanted to walk instead. Don't you see that someone must have turned up while she was standing there at the lake? A young girl, alone in the woods. It's crawling with tourists up at Kollen. Does it ever occur to you that you might be mistaken?"

"It does occur to me on rare occasions. But you have to understand that you've lost the battle. We found Halvor."

Johnas grimaced, as if someone had stuck a needle in his ear.

"Sad, isn't it?"

Sejer sat motionless, his hands in his lap. He caught himself rubbing the spot above his wedding ring a few times. There wasn't much else to do. Besides, it was so quiet and practically dark in the small room.

Once in a while he glanced up and looked at Halvor's ruined face, which had been washed and tended to, but was still almost beyond recognition. His lips were slightly parted. Several of his teeth had been smashed, and the old scar at the corner of his mouth was no longer visible. His face had split open like an overripe fruit. But his forehead was still whole, and someone had combed back his hair so that the smooth flesh was visible, a small indication of how handsome he had been. Sejer bowed his head and placed his hands carefully on the sheet. They could be clearly seen in the circle of light from the lamp standing on a table. He heard only his own breathing and in the distance a lift creaking faintly. A sudden movement under his hands made him start. Halvor opened one eye and looked at him. The other was covered with a big liquid lump of bandages, rather like a jellyfish. He wanted to speak. Sejer put a finger to his lips and shook his head. "It's nice to see that smile of yours, but you mustn't say anything. The stitches will burst out."

"Tanks," Halvor said indistinctly.

They looked at each other for a long time. Sejer nodded a few times, Halvor kept on blinking his green eye.

"The disk that we found at Johnas's place," Sejer said. "Is it an exact copy of Annie's diary?"

"Mm."

"Nothing was erased?"

He shook his head.

"Nothing was changed or corrected?"

More shaking of his head.

"All right then," Sejer said.

"Tanks."

Halvor's eye filled with tears. He began sniffling.

"Don't fret!" Sejer said. "The stitches will come out. And your nose is running. I'll find some tissues."

He stood up and found some tissues by the sink. Tried to wipe away the snot and blood running from the boy's nose.

"I expect you found Annie difficult once in a while. But now you probably understand that she had her reasons. As a rule, we all do. "And this was a huge burden for her to carry all alone. I know this may be a stupid thing to say," he said, trying to comfort the boy because he felt such pity for him as he lay in bed, his face pulverised. "But you're still young. Right now you've lost so much. Right now you feel as if Annie is the only one you would like to have near. But time will pass, and things change. Someday you'll think differently."

Jesus, what a speech, he thought.

Halvor didn't reply. He stared at Sejer's hands lying on the covers, at the broad gold wedding band on his right hand. His expression seemed to be accusatory.

"I know what you're thinking," Sejer said. "That it's easy for me to talk, sitting here wearing a big wedding band. A real gaudy, ten-millimetre ring. But you see," he said with a sad smile, "it's actually two five-millimetre rings welded together."

He twisted the ring around.

"She's dead," he said. "Do you understand?"

Halvor closed his eye and a little more blood and tears ran down his face. He opened his mouth, and Sejer could see the broken remains of his teeth.

"Mm solly."

Finally the sun was shining full force and Sejer and Skarre strolled down the street with the dog between them. Kollberg plodded along happily, with his tail held high like a banner.

Sejer had a bouquet of flowers hanging from a string around his wrist, red and blue anemones wrapped in tissue paper. His jacket was slung over his shoulders, and his eczema was better than it had been in a long time. He strode along with his easy, supple gait while Skarre hopped and leaped beside him. The dog walked at a surprisingly brisk pace. Not too fast; they were wearing newly pressed shirts and didn't want to sweat too much before they reached their destination.

Matteus was scurrying around, full of anticipation, a killer whale in his arms, made of black and white felt. His name was Free Willy, and he was almost as big as he was. Sejer's first impulse was to rush forward and lift him up, roaring out his great joy in a jubilant voice. That's the way all children ought to be greeted, with genuine, exuberant joy. But Sejer wasn't made that way. He took the boy carefully on his lap and looked at Ingrid, who was wearing a new dress, a butter-yellow summer dress with red raspberries. He wished her happy birthday and squeezed her hand. Before long they would be leaving for the other side of the globe, to heat and war, and they would be gone an eternity. He shook hands with his son-in-law while he held Matteus tight. They sat quietly and waited for the food.

Matteus never nagged. He was a well-mannered boy, blessedly free of defiant or contrary behaviour. The only thing Sejer didn't recognise from his own family was a tiny tendency for mischief. Matteus's daily life was all smiles and love, and his origins, about which they knew very little, seemed not to have given him genes that would manifest themselves in abnormal behaviour, drive family members out of their wits, or make them cross disastrous boundaries. Sejer's thoughts wandered. Back to Gamle Möllevej outside Roskilde when he himself was a child. For a long time he sat lost in memory. Finally he was listening. "What did you say, Ingrid?"

He looked in surprise at his daughter and saw that she was brushing a lock of blonde hair away from her forehead as she smiled in that special way she had, reserved just for him.

"Coke, Papa? Do you want a Coke?"

At the same time, somewhere else, an ugly van bumped along the road in low gear, and a big man, his hair sticking up, was hunched over the steering wheel. At the bottom of the hill he stopped to let a little girl, who had just taken two steps forward, cross the road. She stopped abruptly.

"Hi, Ragnhild!" he cried out.

She was holding a skipping rope in one hand, so she waved with the other.

"Are you out taking a walk?"

"I'm on my way home," she said firmly.

"Listen to this!" Raymond said in a loud, shrill voice to be heard over the roar of the engine. "Caesar is dead. But Påsan had babies!"

"But he's a boy," she said.

"It's not easy to tell whether a rabbit is a boy or a girl. They have so much fur. But at any rate he had babies. Five of them. You can come and see them if you want."

"They won't let me," she said, disappointed, staring down the road and hoping vaguely that someone would appear to rescue her from such a spellbinding temptation. *Baby bunnies.*

"Do they have fur?"

"They have fur and their eyes are open. I'll drive you back home afterwards, Ragnhild. Come on, they're growing up so fast!"

She glanced down the road one more time, shut her eyes tight and opened them again. Then she dashed across and climbed in. Ragnhild was wearing a white blouse with a lace collar and tiny little red shorts. No-one saw her get in. Everyone was in their backyards, preoccupied with planting and weeding, tying up their roses and the clematis. Raymond felt so fine in Sejer's old windbreaker. He put the van in gear. The little girl was sitting excitedly on the seat beside him. He whistled happily and looked around. Nobody had noticed them.